Dear Reader,

Silhouette has spring fever! To celebrate this
extraspecial season for lovers, we're proud to
present *Spring Fancy '94*—a brand-new collection of
short fiction by three of your favorite authors:
Dixie Browning, Cait London and Pepper Adams.

The title of this collection was inspired by an
often-quoted line from ''Locksley Hall'' by
Alfred, Lord Tennyson: ''In the Spring, a young
man's fancy lightly turns to thoughts of love.'' Well,
whether we are young or not so young, man or
woman, spring fancy blossoms in all our hearts. And
boy, does it bloom for the three pairs of lovers in
Spring Fancy '94!

So succumb to spring fever—it'll catch you anyway.

The Editors
Silhouette Books

SPRING
fancy
'94

DIXIE BROWNING
CAIT LONDON
PEPPER ADAMS

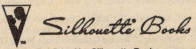

Silhouette Books

Published by Silhouette Books

America's Publisher of Contemporary Romance

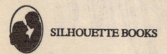 SILHOUETTE BOOKS

SPRING FANCY '94
Copyright © 1994 Harlequin Enterprises B.V.

ISBN 0-373-48266-3

The publisher acknowledges the copyright holders of the individual works as follows:

GRACE AND THE LAW
Copyright © 1994 by Dixie Browning

LIGHTFOOT AND LOVING
Copyright © 1994 by Lois Kleinsasser

OUT OF THE DARK
Copyright © 1994 by Debrah Morris & Pat Shaver

This edition published by arrangement with Harlequin Enterprises B.V.

® and TM are trademarks of Harlequin Enterprises B.V., used under license. Trademarks indicated with ® are registered in the United States Patent and Trademark Office, the Canadian Trade Marks Office and in other countries.

Printed in U.S.A.

CONTENTS

CONTENTS

GRACE AND THE LAW

Dixie Browning

Chapter One

She had come to the funeral to get her nephew. She should've had him from the beginning. *Would've* had him but for...

Grace's mind wandered. The preacher was young, and no doubt highly qualified, but he had that singsong style of delivery that always lulled her to sleep. The words "dear departed" alone had covered an octave.

Where are you, darn it? Where are you!

A little guilty for allowing her mind to wander at such a time, she concentrated on concentrating on the dear departed.

"Thomas Chancellor was a fi-*i-ine*—" the minister intoned. Grace had barely known Tom, her brother-in-law. As for her sister, whatever could have been between them had ended abruptly when their mother had left home, taking five-year-old Coral with her and leaving nine-year-old Grace behind. Grace could count on her fingers the number of times she had seen either Coral or their mother, Irene, since then.

Where was Chad?

Her nephew—Tom and Coral's only child— would be eight years old now. Grace had seen him exactly three times. Once when he was six weeks old, once when he was about three, and again when he was five. For seven wonderful days she'd had him all to herself when Coral and Tom, who had moved from Virginia Beach to Palm Springs shortly after they were married, had called her just before leaving for New York on their way to Paris. It seemed their son's nanny had come down with appendicitis at the last minute, their trip simply couldn't be put off, and they couldn't find another baby-sitter at such short notice.

Grace had agreed to meet them in Norfolk at the airport, some three hours away, take Chad home with her and keep him until they picked him up on the way home. She'd been nervous, but Coral had easily overridden her doubts. "It's about time you got to know your nephew, sweetie," her sister had said gaily. "Besides, you probably need something to cheer you up, stuck down there all by yourself."

Their father, Bartram O'Donald, had died only a few months earlier. Coral, for reasons Grace had never fully understood, had been unable to fly east for the funeral. But she'd been right about one thing—Grace had needed something to cheer her up.

Seven whole days. Grace had loved it. She knew practically nothing about children, but Chad had been quiet and obedient—almost too quiet and obedient at first. They'd got along just fine, walking on the beach, watching gulls, fishermen, tourists and weather fronts, and talking about the grandfather he had seen only once, when he'd been too young to remember.

Chad had been fascinated by the idea of commercial fishing. He'd wanted to know all there was to know about it, and Grace had described pound netting, drop netting, gill netting and crab potting. In the short time he was with her he had gone from a pale, solemn child, far too polite and afraid of the dark, to a tanned, boisterous little boy who raced along the shore after sea gulls and wanted to keep a soft crab as a pet.

By the time Tom and Coral had returned to collect their son for the flight home, Chad had his whole life planned. He was going to hurry up and finish kindergarten and then move back east to live in his grandfather's house and fish with his Aunt Grace.

Coral had been horrified when he'd announced his plans. Tom had simply lifted one thin blond eyebrow and laughed. "You're regressing, Chadwick. Last week it was a fireman. The week before that, it was a cowboy. I suspect we'd better see about sending you off to school next year before you go getting any more fanciful notions. Now make your manners to Miss O'Donald and thank her for looking after you. I'm sure she had better things to do with her time."

It was at that point that Tom had tried to hand Grace a roll of bills. He had actually tried to *pay* her for looking after her own nephew! Grace could have murdered him on the spot.

But she certainly hadn't wished him dead.

Oh, Lord, would this nightmare ever end so that she could take that poor baby home with her and get on with their lives?

The bass notes of the enormous pipe organ rolled over the congregation, stirring Grace to attention. Where was he, anyway? She had come in late, having driven all over Chesapeake before she'd finally located the right church. When the usher had taken one look at her and seated her in the very back, she hadn't argued. How could he have known she was family? She wasn't swathed in furs and jewels. She wasn't even wearing black.

Did anyone wear mourning these days? Black made her look sallow. According to her mother, she'd been born sallow. Even so, there was certainly nothing disrespectful about her camel tan coat and her taupe pumps, which was all anyone could see.

There must be a wing off to one side where the families were seated, she thought restlessly. Although, as far as she knew, she was the only one except for Chad who qualified as family. Coral had mentioned at the time of the wedding that Tom had no family. Grace herself had been only a spectator at the wedding, Coral's bridesmaids having been chosen from among her best friends, all pretty, if not quite in the same league with Coral. "You understand, don't you, sweetie?'' she'd pleaded when Grace had gone upstairs in her mother's Norfolk house to watch the bride get dressed.

And, of course, Grace had. Looks meant a lot to Coral and Irene. Irene O'Donald, beautiful in crushed pink silk with tons of crystal beads, had been her daughter's matron of honor. Bartram O'Donald, looking miserable in a rented tuxedo, had given his daughter away. Irene had wanted her current lover to do the job, but Grace had put her foot down, and Coral, for once, had sided with her sister instead of her mother.

Thoughts of her sister's wedding inevitably brought on thoughts of the man who had been Tom's best man. Grace hadn't been able to take her eyes off him during the entire ceremony. Neither had any other woman there, including Irene, but then, no woman with eyes in her head and a viable hormone in her body could ignore a man like Ramsay Adams.

Grace had known several handsome men. She had even dated a few, but the illusion usually wore off rather quickly. Some were simps, some were wimps, some were macho jerks. The really beautiful ones were usually far too impressed with their own good looks to be impressed by hers, which remained totally unimpressive no matter how much moisturizer and milk-of-almond scrub she slathered on.

The plain truth was that Grace found most handsome men to be bores. Until she'd met Ramsay Adams. Tall, dark—too rugged to be called classically handsome, but all the more striking for the strength and angularity of his features—he had immediately set fire to her imagination.

They hadn't actually met until the party after the wedding. Grace, having found a secluded spot on the sidelines, had been nursing her second glass of champagne while she'd watched the dancers. Just as Ramsay Adams and one of the bridesmaids had danced past, someone had lurched into her from behind. Instinctively, she'd flung up her hands for balance and watched in horror as the wine struck Ramsay full in the face and slowly trickled down to soak into his starched white collar and bib.

"Aw, for gawd's sake," his gorgeous redheaded partner had whined. Glaring at Grace, she brushed a few drops from her skirt while Grace prayed to be transported to some other planet. Retroactively!

The music ended to a scattering of applause. Ramsay, every bit as debonair as if his hair weren't dripping down his forehead and his shirtfront sticking wetly to his chest, excused himself to escort his partner back to her table.

Grace was almost out the door when he caught up with her. "You're Coral's sister, aren't you? I'm Ramsay Adams, Tom's best man. I don't know how we happened to miss being introduced earlier, but now that you've gone to such great lengths to rectify the situation, the least you can do is tell me your name."

He was even more devastating up close, where she could see the texture of his skin and the odd golden flecks in his dark gray eyes—where she could feel the warmth of his body and catch a drift of some subtle masculine cologne. "Gr-Grace O'Donald," she whispered. "I'm so sorry. If there's anything I can do— I'll pay for your dry cleaning, of course, and your, uh—"

"You could dance with me," he said, with a quirky half smile that set her heart to hammering so hard she could hardly breathe.

"I'm not very good. I'd end up owing for your podiatrist's bill, too."

He held out his arms and laughed aloud, and Grace stood by helplessly as her brain gave one last feeble flutter and shut down. He danced her through the wide, arched doorway into the anteroom. They were alone but for a passing waiter carrying a tray of empty champagne glasses. Neither of them spoke. Words weren't needed.

The last time Grace had danced had been at her senior prom, three years before. It had been nothing at all like this. Not slow and dreamy, like floating on clouds. In Ramsay's arms, she was no longer clumsy, no longer stiff and awkward. Plain, practical little Grace O'Donald—the runt of the litter, the cuckoo in the nest—had been suddenly, magically, transformed to a swan. She was waltzing as if she'd done it all her life, with the handsomest, most sophisticated man in the universe, and he was holding her as if she were every bit as lovely and desirable as the other two O'Donald women. By the time the second number ended, both his arms were around her, and her head was on his chest, and she was breathing in the warm, intoxicating scent of champagne, sandalwood cologne and healthy male flesh.

"Who *are* you?" he murmured, a slight frown drawing his dark brows together, and somehow, Grace sensed he was asking more than the words implied.

With perfect honesty, she answered, "I don't know."

And then Coral was there. "Ram! Where on earth did you disappear to? Melanie's waiting for you to take her in to supper. Come on, come on—the lobsters are getting cold! You're at our table, you and Mel. Grace, I've put you with the Reverend and Mrs. Cahill over there by the door, all right, sweetie? Be a dear and look at their grandkids' pictures, will you? Mrs. Cahill's been chasing me around with her billfold for hours! You've always been good with old people."

A hacking cough from the next pew jerked Grace back to the present, and she looked around guiltily. The last thing she needed now was to lose her objectivity.

All right, so she was about to meet Ramsay Adams again after nine years. He wouldn't remember her. There hadn't been a single hint in the letter he'd written after the plane crash that he even remembered meeting her, much less . : .

Whatever.

He'd addressed her as "Dear Miss O'Donald:". Colon. Not even a *semi*colon. And the letter itself had been dictated. But that didn't matter. What mattered was that he had taken possession of Chad, and for six weeks he'd been playing lawyer games with her. She had written, she had called, she had even gone to his office, all to no avail. He hadn't written back, he'd been out when she had made a special trip to see him, and if his secretary had passed on her messages, he hadn't bothered to respond.

Grace tugged angrily at the seams of her pigskin gloves. She'd worn them not only to cover her rough, red hands, but to mask—she sincerely hoped—the smell of fatback. She had fished her pots at first light that morning, and the bait had been riper than usual. She'd showered afterward, of course, and scrubbed her hands extra hard, first with soap and then with vinegar, slathering on gallons of scented lotion. Even so, she half expected someone to turn and demand to know where the stench of dead fish was coming from.

Sniffing experimentally, she smelled only dust, furniture polish, flowers, and that chilly, chalky scent that always seemed to linger in empty churches and unused classrooms. No fish. Thank God for small favors.

Where was that blasted lawyer, anyway? And where was Chad? At this rate, she'd have to spend the night in Norfolk, and she wasn't sure she had enough money to cover the cost of hotel accommodations for two.

Was a boy of eight too old to share a room with a female relative he hardly knew? Was he too young for a room of his own? In spite of the fact that she taught beginning piano three afternoons a week, the things she didn't know about children would fill a library.

Eventually the sparse crowd of mourners began to rise and edge out of the padded pews, pausing in clumps to speak in hushed undertones. Grace stood, too, noticing for the first time that her feet were like blocks of ice. Evidently the church's heating system didn't reach to the back row. She waited impatiently, her eyes searching the congregation for a glimpse of a tall, dark-haired man with a child.

Or maybe with a wife and several children.

Chad would have changed—children did—but Ramsay Adams couldn't have changed that much. Unless he'd lost his hair and gained a lot of weight. She almost hoped he had. It would be easier to get through these next few minutes if she could keep her mind on why she was there.

Light from the stained-glass windows spilled over the chilly interior, catching dust motes like falling angels, and unexpectedly, Grace's eyes filled. Her chin began to quiver.

Coral was gone. Her beautiful, golden-haired sister was dead at the tragically young age of twenty-six, victim of a plane crash between Las Vegas and Palm Springs. Victim of a stupid ass of a husband who thought all his millions enabled him to drink and fly his private jet with impunity.

Ram kept his seat until the church had cleared. He had briefly considered bringing the boy to the service. According to some experts, such rituals served to bring home the realities of death to a grieving child.

But the more he got to know him, the more Ram was beginning to believe that Chad Chancellor was not your typical grieving child. For one thing, he scarcely knew his parents if Mrs. Bullard, the woman who'd been hired to look after him when he wasn't in school, could be believed.

Knowing the provisions of Tom's will, Ram had arranged for Mrs. Bullard to retire. He had put the Palm Springs house in the hands of a competent real-estate agent and flown east with the boy, where he had turned him over to his own housekeeper, Edith Suggs.

There was a lot to be said for routine, and considering the fact that Chad's young life had been totally shattered by the sudden death of his parents, the small routines the three of them had managed to establish over the past six weeks were the best thing for all concerned.

Actually, Ram had begun to look forward to going home each day to something more welcoming than a scrupulously clean house and a prepared casserole left in the refrigerator.

"Uh, Mr. Adams, if you'd like to, you may use my office to, uh, to collect yourself?"

Distracted from his own unfocused thoughts, Ram glanced up at the minister and shook his head. He'd completely lost track of time. The church was all but empty. "Thanks, Dr. Handscomb, but that won't be necessary. It was a moving service."

"Well, I know Mr. and Mrs. Chancellor haven't lived in Norfolk for some time now, but they still have friends here. Mr. Chancellor's grandfather donated all the windows in the west wing, and Mrs. Chancellor's mother was buried from this very church not five years ago, in July, if memory serves. Cancer of the liver, I believe it was. Poor woman, she was still quite beautiful, but then they both were, weren't they? Lovely women, lovely..."

"Yes, they were." Both beautiful and both cold as an Arctic sunrise.

"I'd like to take this opportunity of telling you that the church very much appreciates your memorial donation, Mr. Adams. We've been needing a new furnace for years, and I wondered if—"

"Fine, fine, whatever you want to use it for." Ram extended his hand, shook the minister's limp, dry one briefly, and said, "Thank you again for everything, Dr. Handscomb." Quite suddenly, he

had to get out of there. He'd had all he could take
of air that smelled of lilies, furnace oil and furniture polish. Of unctuous sentiments murmured by
people who were obviously dying to find out just
how much the Chancellors had left, and who was
the beneficiary of their will, and wasn't there a
child?

There was a child. There was also a sister. A sister he had spent far more time than was reasonable,
under the circumstances, thinking about after their
one brief meeting. He had tried to call as soon as
he'd been notified of the fatal crash, but there were
hundreds of O'Donalds in the phone book that
covered the entire northeast corner of the state, and
not a single Grace among them. All he'd had was a
post office box number. Evidently the island didn't
run to street numbers. In the end, he had written,
hoping she would receive his letter before she heard
the news through the media.

In the middle of a protracted, fiercely fought legal battle, Ram had been distracted by getting the
boy settled in a new school and several rush trips to
California to wind up Tom's affairs. But he had instructed his secretary to write and assure her that
Chad was being well cared for, and that a memorial
service was being arranged.

Grace O'Donald. Funny, she wasn't exactly a
memorable type, yet...

It was odd, too, because he'd started seeing a
woman shortly after the wedding. He'd been at-

tracted enough that eventually he'd even bought an engagement ring, but somehow he'd never quite gotten around to giving it to her. The time or the mood had never seemed quite right. There'd been other women since then, but Addie Blake had been the only near miss.

Oddly enough, however, it wasn't Addie's elegant body and flawless features that visited his restless dreams. For reasons he was at a loss to explain, it was always Grace's small, tanned face, her clear, amber eyes with their dreamy, unawakened look, that drifted in and out of focus at times when he was too tired to work but too stressed out to sleep soundly.

Funny, the way the mind worked. He had seen the woman once, and then only for a few minutes. Over the years he had picked up a few stray bits of information. For instance, he knew that when Irene O'Donald had left her husband, her oldest daughter had chosen to stay with her father. Evidently she'd been living down there on the Outer Banks ever since. Once or twice he'd actually toyed with the idea of driving down for the day and looking her up on some pretext or other, but for one reason or another, he never had. It was a crazy idea, anyhow.

Over the years he'd nearly forgotten about her, but it had all come back when Coral and Tom had been killed, and he'd had to go bring the boy back east. As Tom's attorney as well as his friend, Ram knew for a fact that any expectations the sister might have had were doomed to disappointment. Once he satisfied the creditors—and there were a surprising number of those, including the IRS—what little remained would be put into a trust fund for the boy. Ram was already in the process of setting it up.

Surely she didn't intend to challenge the will.

Standing in a side door that faced out onto a sodden playground, Ram breathed deeply of the early March air. Dammit, he almost wished she would! Right now he could do with a good fight, something to vent his anger, his frustrations and—oh, hell, his grief! He and Tom went way back, and while they'd disagreed on a lot of things over the years, they'd remained friends. Tom had always insisted that he needed one person in his life, private and public, that he could trust implicitly. For better or worse, Ram had been that man.

Waiting until he was certain all the others had left, he closed the door behind him and followed the flagged walkway around the corner of the tall stone structure. Instead of returning to the office, he was tempted to go directly home, collect the boy and drive down to his cottage at Sandbridge. A good stiff salt breeze just might blow away the sickening sweetness of lilies.

"Mr. Adams?"

Ram turned slowly to stare down at the woman who accosted him just as he was about to head for his car. Eyeing her warily, he nodded.

"You probably don't remember me, but I'm Grace O'Donald, Coral's sister. Chad's aunt?"

He remembered. He remembered far too well. "Miss O'Donald," he said noncommittally. She was smaller than he remembered, but otherwise, she matched his memories perfectly. At the wedding, she'd worn beige, and it had occurred to him then that she was all one color.

Now she wore tan, and she was still all one color. Tan hair, tan skin, tan coat, tan stockings.

Good legs, though. Damned fine legs, in fact.

She was holding out her hand, and he shook it and made himself let go. She had a firm handshake for a woman. Somehow that didn't surprise him. Steady eyes, as well—even when she was embarrassed, he recalled with an unexpected wash of tenderness.

Her eyes, too, were tan. Coral's had been light blue, her hair platinum blond. There was certainly no family resemblance, but then, Coral Chancellor had been a stunning woman. Not even her worst enemy could deny her that. Her sister barely missed being downright plain, and for the life of him, Ram couldn't figure why she had stuck in his memory for so long. Nine years. Two brief waltzes nine years ago, and he could still remember the way she had felt in his arms, the way she had smelled—even the way she had gasped and blushed when he'd deliberately thrust his leg between hers for a quick turn.

You're non compos, *Adams. Back off!* "Was there something you wanted to see me about, Miss O'Donald?"

"Something I wanted to see you about? Mr. Adams, you didn't answer a single one of my calls. I wrote and called until I was blue in the face, and you never answered, and when I drove all the way to Norfolk and tracked you down to your office, all I got from that dragon who guards your moat was that Mr. Adams had left for the day and couldn't be reached!"

"You could have called me at home."

"Your number is unlisted, as if you didn't know. The Doberman who answers your phone refused to give it to me!"

"Hmm, yes, well...my staff does have orders not to give out my home number. I'm sorry if you were inconvenienced."

"If I was *inconvenienced?* When you're deliberately keeping my nephew from me at a time in his life when he needs me? What I want to know is, *why!*"

"If you'd quit whining long enough, Grace," Ram said with the sardonic lift of brow, "I just might tell you why."

"Whining!" Grace's mouth fell open. She had never whined in her life. Not once! Not when her mother had taken her sister and gone off and left her without even saying goodbye. Not when her father had dropped dead of a heart attack out on the reef

while he was setting stakes for a new pound net. Not
even when some scumbag from up the Banks had
cut loose half her brand new crab pots just before a
three day nor'easter, and she'd been out hundreds of
dollars, not to mention the income the pots would
have earned her. Eyes glittering like newly polished
brass, she said, "What have you done with my
nephew?"

"I told you, Chadwick is doing as well as could be
expected under the circumstances. I simply saw no
reason to upset him further."

"You saw no reason to—? The last thing I would
ever do is upset him. All I want to do is take him
back to his grandfather's house and make a home
for him. He needs a home and family now more
than ever."

"The boy has a home. He's being well cared for."

"By strangers! I'm his aunt! Tom didn't have any
family, so there's no one on that side to take him in.
Why are you deliberately keeping him away from
me?" She was practically shouting, and that wasn't
like her. Grace wasn't given to strong emotion, including anger. She was like her father in that.

But then, Ramsay Adams would try the patience
of a saint. Which she wasn't. God! To think of all
the hours she had wasted in daydreams—and night
dreams, too! It just went to prove what she'd already known. Good-looking men weren't worth the
air they breathed! Give her a plain, hard-working
fisherman any day.

For a single moment, she felt again the sensation of breathlessness she had experienced when Ramsay Adams had held her in both his arms and waltzed her across the empty anteroom. It had been like stepping into a fairy tale, and for a moment she had been Cinderella, Snow White and Rapunzel all rolled into one.

But even fairy tales had a downside. It was called reality. The eyes she had remembered as warm and caressing were the color of ice on a black-water creek and every bit as cold. Curling her fists in her pockets, Grace forced him to meet her gaze, and then she let him see just what she thought of a man who would heartlessly prevent a child and a relative who desperately needed one another from being together. And all over some piddling little technicality of the law, no doubt.

He didn't back down. Reluctantly she gave him credit for that much, at least. Neither did he speak, and she couldn't think of another thing to say. At least nothing that wouldn't make matters worse. It seemed they were going to fight, and the odds were definitely in his favor. He was a fighter—she wasn't. She wasn't even on her own turf, which gave him still another advantage.

She shivered. The temperature had dropped several degrees just since they'd been inside the church. The sun, which had been shining brightly in a clear blue sky when she'd left home this morning, was now covered by a skein of buttermilk clouds. A chilly northwest wind whipped her coattails around her knees, bringing with it the scent of damp concrete, early jonquils and exhaust fumes. Feeling uncomfortably out of her element, Grace burrowed her fists deeper into the pockets of her coat and hunched her shoulders.

Damn the man, he wasn't giving an inch! He wasn't even feeling the cold! But then, men who wore topcoats over three-piece suits wouldn't. Probably insulated by his overblown ego. Too bad she wasn't holding a glass of champagne. She might just dampen that ego of his for him.

"Exactly when were you planning to let me have him?" she said through clenched jaws. "You know very well I came here to take him home with me. I told your secretary to tell you to bring his things to the service. I'm not leaving here without him." Powerful words. Unfortunately she was shivering so hard her voice shook, and Grace purely hated showing any sign of weakness, especially around a cast-iron type like Ramsay Adams.

"Look, we can't talk here," he said. "There's a place a couple of blocks over where we can talk over coffee. Have you had lunch?"

It was going on one in the afternoon. The service had been scheduled for the noon hour for the convenience of any nine-to-fivers who cared to attend. Grace hadn't had lunch. She also hadn't had breakfast, but she wasn't about to mention the fact. "I'd just as soon you directed me to where I can collect

Chad so that we can get home before dark. I have work to do."

As if she had never spoken, he took her arm in a firm grip and steered her toward the only car left in the parking lot, which happened to be a sleek black sedan. Her own pickup truck was parked half a block down the street, as all the slots closer had been taken by the time she'd finally found the right number on the right street in the right area of Greater Norfolk.

Grace told herself she was going along with him because he was her only link with Chad, and if she walked away she'd be giving up the battle. That was the only reason. "I'd call the law, but then, you *are* the law, aren't you?" she muttered. "Are you going to let me have him or not?"

Ram glanced down at the woman who marched beside him. Her hair, which he'd thought of as tan, glinted with streaks of warm color as sunlight briefly pierced the veil of clouds. She was livid. He couldn't much blame her. He honestly hadn't known about the calls and letters. His secretary, who was going through some heavy personal problems, was inclined to be overprotective ever since an irate welder had stormed into a nearby office and shot his estranged wife's attorney in the groin at close range.

But this was too much. He'd tried to be understanding when she'd screwed up his files, but he was going to have to have a serious talk with the woman if this was the way his clients were being dealt with.

"Well? I'm waiting," Grace reminded him. While he unlocked his car, she crossed her arms over her chest and lifted her chin defiantly.

"Pity you don't have a glass of champagne."

For a single instant as she raised her eyes to his, he glimpsed the same vulnerability, the same desperate dignity, that had made him sweep her into his arms and waltz away with her nine years ago. "We'll talk about it over coffee," he said gruffly. "This place has great sandwiches if you happen to be hungry."

"No, thank you," she said, but not even the sound of a passing city bus could hide the rumble of her stomach's response. Ram grinned. Suddenly, in spite of the somber occasion—in spite of the raw March weather and a bunch of off-the-wall memories that only complicated matters—he felt good. The odd restlessness that had haunted him with increasing frequency these past few years was strangely missing.

He wondered briefly if it was the money she was after. If it had been Coral, or even Tom, he wouldn't have had any doubts. Money had been important to both of them. The boy had taken second place.

Make that third place, he amended. Where the beautiful Chancellors were concerned, the pursuit of pleasure had run a close second to the accumulation of wealth. They'd been two of a kind, Coral and Tom. Hedonistic, heedless—the kind of people who should never have had a kid in the first place.

But Tom had liked the idea of having a son to inherit, to carry on the family name, for what it was worth. And Coral had sure as hell made him pay through the nose for her nine months of inconvenience!

"All right, but after we talk, will you take me to Chad?"

Ram adjusted the rearview mirror and fastened his seat belt, checking to see that hers was fastened, too. "Why are you so eager to have him? I know for a fact that you two haven't seen each other in several years. Is it the money?"

She winced. Pride stung, she led with her chin. "What if I said it was?"

"I wouldn't believe you." Without knowing anything more about her than that she was the sister of a woman he had come to despise, Ram knew that much.

With a sense of anticipation that defied reason, he eased into the center lane and pressed the accelerator. He felt good. Damn good! On a cold, wet day in early March, following a memorial service for his oldest friend, with nothing more exciting to look forward to than a job he had come to despise—with a woman beside him who was determined to fight him tooth and nail for what they both wanted—he felt *good?*

Yeah . . . he felt good.

Chapter Two

The coffee shop was short on atmosphere, but the aroma was so rich you could cut it with a knife. Coffee, smoked fish and other unidentifiable delicacies. Ramsay led Grace to a booth with a view of the parking lot and helped her off with her coat. He subdued the urge to keep on unwrapping and satisfied himself with appreciating the brown jersey dress and gold paisley scarf. Both were obviously inexpensive, yet surprisingly becoming to the slight, understated figure. The lady had style, he mused, seating her before taking his place across the scarred varnished table. He had forgotten that about her, remembering only the way she had felt in his arms. For all her seeming fragility, there was a strength about her that had surprised him.

"Two colombians and a plate of pastries," he told the waitress. "Make that decaf," he added, and to Grace, "I don't think either of us needs the extra jolt at the moment."

Grace knotted her hands in her lap and stared out the steamy window at the darkening sky. It was impossible to relax, even with the warmth beginning to seep into her bones. She sat erect, her back barely touching the vinyl-covered bench, and waited for

Ramsay Adams to fire the first shot. Lawyer or not, he wasn't going to intimidate her. Justice was on her side.

"So, tell me, Grace, just what is it that you do? I don't think we ever got that far at our first meeting, did we?" His tidewater drawl was dark, rich, and deceptively smooth. Grace reminded herself that this man probably made his living persuading other people that black was white and wrong was right. "I believe you said you had to get back home so as to go to work?" he prompted.

"Mostly, I fish, Mr. Adams."

"Ramsay. Or Ram, if you prefer. And no, it has nothing to do with my disposition, believe it or not. Did you say you fished, or did I hear you incorrectly?"

She forced herself to speak calmly, rationally, unwilling to give him an opening to question her emotional stability. Not with Chad's whole future at stake. "Three afternoons a week, I teach beginning piano. The rest of the time I run two hundred crab pots. Later on in the season, when the price of crabs drops off so that it's hardly worth the cost of bait and fuel to fish them, I'll bring those in and set out half a dozen or so gill nets."

For a long time, there was no response. Another lawyer trick, Grace told herself as she fought against her own lack of confidence. "You're a musician and a commercial fisherman. Isn't it, uh, an unusual combination?"

"I don't see anything unusual about it. I'm qualified to teach music, and I fished all my life with my father when I wasn't in school. Look, you don't need to know all this. All you need to know is that I own my own home and I earn enough to support a child. If you want character references, I can supply those, but I don't think I will. After all, I'm the one entitled here. You're only a lawyer."

"Ouch," Ram said softly.

The waitress appeared beside them and set out two plates, a platter of assorted pastries, a carafe of steaming coffee and two thick mugs. Grace poured, praying that her stomach wouldn't embarrass her by growling again before she could appease it. She hadn't set out this morning to fight a custody battle. She'd simply meant to meet Chad and take him home with her, where he belonged.

She might have known it wouldn't be that easy.

Glowering at the muted design of Ramsay Adams's silk tie, she nibbled on a Danish and wondered what was the best way to deal with a man like Ramsay Adams. The only way she knew was the direct approach, and so far, that had got her exactly nowhere.

He was looking at her, studying her under those crow-black brows of his, and she placed the unfinished pastry back on her plate and swallowed hard. It didn't help that his necktie alone had probably cost more than her entire outfit. Money didn't matter. Self-confidence did, and hers was leaking fast.

In a custody case, a clever lawyer could use her modest means to his advantage. If he knew just how modest those means really were—and how unpredictable—she wouldn't have a snowball's chance in hell!

"By the way, I thought it best under the circumstances to remove Chad from his boarding school in California and enroll him in a private school a few miles from my home for what's left of the spring term. He's adjusting pretty well. I don't think he cared for boarding school."

"Boarding school! But he's only a baby!"

"This was his first year. However, I think he'll be happier in a good day school."

"Hatteras schools are excellent. We even have a private school on the island. He'll do just fine there."

Ram's eyes narrowed. "My housekeeper looks after him as if he were her own."

Grace moved in for the kill. "But I can look after him better, because he *is* my own."

"You're not going to give an inch, are you?"

There was something in his voice that sounded almost like admiration, but Grace couldn't allow herself to be thrown off guard. She didn't know all his tricks. She didn't know *any* of his tricks, but she knew enough not to trust him. She also knew that he affected her in a way that had nothing to do with Chad.

"I don't have to give an inch," she said with quiet determination. "You're the one who's in the wrong, and if I have to fight you for him, I will, but Chad's the one who'll suffer. It takes a real mean man to treat a child that way."

"A real mean man?" Ram repeated softly. He leaned back with every appearance of composure, the stoneware mug cradled between his large, well-kept hands. Amusement flared briefly in his slate-colored eyes. "You seem to have lost sight of a few basic facts, Grace—or maybe you never knew. I happen to be Chad's godfather. I was there when he was christened." One dark brow lifted sardonically. "Where were you? I was there to help celebrate his first birthday. Where were you?" He continued to hammer with soft relentlessness. "I had the privilege of launching him on his trial ride the day we took the training wheels off his bike. Were you there? Did we somehow manage to miss each other the way we nearly did at the wedding?"

Half a Danish suddenly turned to concrete in her stomach. Carefully, she set her mug down and prepared to defend herself without revealing the fact that she had never been invited. "It's my understanding that a blood relative takes precedence over a godparent." She could only pray she was right. "As for not being there for all the milestones in my nephew's life, it's expensive to fly all the way across the country. As much as I might've liked to, I couldn't just hop on a plane and go visit whenever I felt like it.''

Once Tom and Coral had moved west, when Chad was two months old, she'd barely even heard from them. She hadn't even known when her nephew was christened until after the fact, but this man didn't have to know that.

"That's just my point," Ram said quietly. "It takes money to raise a child these days, especially one who's accustomed to a—uh, certain standard of living, shall we say? Of course, your nephew happens to be worth rather a lot of it, doesn't he? You do know that? Maybe you were counting on it when you made your claim."

Grace felt the color drain right out of her face, leaving her cold and shaken. "Think whatever you want to, Mr. Adams, that doesn't change the facts. And the facts are that I have every right to take Chad home with me, and you don't have any right at all to keep him from me—against his will, for all I know. Did you even tell him I was coming to fetch him home?"

"But I didn't know you were coming to fetch him home, did I?"

"I told your secretary I planned to take him with me today."

Ram spread his hands, palm up. "The message never reached me. Did you call or write, and if you wrote, did you send it to the firm, or to me?"

"I wrote! I knew calling wouldn't do any good! I copied the name and address off your letterhead. You must have got it!"

"The firm must've got it. Did you make it clear where to direct it? It's a fairly large firm."

Exasperated, Grace cried, "I called you 'Dear Mr. Adams,' not Dear Mr. Adams, Cornwall, Stover and Haymes! All you had to do was open it!"

"Thank you, dear Miss O'Donald."

Grace, fingertips drumming on the tabletop, tried to intimidate him by staring him down, the way she had intimidated the men at the fish house when she'd fished her first season alone after her father had died.

The devil didn't even flicker an eyelash. If he had one iota of humanity in him, it wasn't in evidence. His hands were relaxed on the table, the planes of his hard face totally without emotion. It occurred to her that if he happened to be a trial lawyer, he probably insisted on having all-female juries, knowing that not a one of them would be able to think her way out of a paper bag by the time he got done with her.

"Give up?" he asked with a lazy smile. She felt like kicking him under the table.

"Not in a million years," she shot back, wishing she had worn something newer, brighter. Wishing she had done something more interesting with her hair than clip it back with a barrette. Wishing she had at least retouched the lipstick she'd chewed off while she circled one block after another looking for the right church.

Challenged, she reacted, not for the first time in her life, with more pride than common sense. "Regardless of what you think, Mr. Adams, I came to say goodbye to my sister, which I've done, and to fetch my nephew, which I fully intend to do. You can cooperate, or you can explain to the police why you're holding a child and preventing his family from taking him home. Your choice, Mr. Adams."

"It's Ramsay, and I've always admired courage, Grace. Combined with enough common sense, it can make up for a lot of shortcomings. Chad, however, is right where he's going to stay for the foreseeable future. If you rip him out of school for the second time in two months, away from the only stable influence in his life right now, you're asking for the kind of trouble I don't think you're prepared to handle. Believe me, I have only the boy's best interest at heart."

Leaning forward, Grace gripped the edge of the table, her eyes pleading. "But I—"

"Listen to me, Grace, and then tell me if what I have to say doesn't make sense. Will you do that much for me? For Chad?"

Her shoulders slumped. There was a look of defeat on her small, plain face that should have made him feel triumphant. It didn't. Those clear tan eyes of hers were too easy to read, and what he was reading there now didn't make him feel particularly noble.

His gaze dropped to her hands. They were beautifully shaped, the short nails unpolished. They were also badly chapped, her poor knuckles painfully so. There was a strip of adhesive at the base of her thumb. Ram had always appreciated feminine hands on a woman. Soft, smooth, well-manicured—teasing him with the scent of some exotic and erotic fragrance.

Acting purely on impulse—something he hadn't allowed himself to do in more years than he cared to recall—he reached for her left hand, and before she could jerk it back, he turned it over in his own, touching the row of calluses across the base of her fingers.

Hearing her gasp, he came to his senses and dropped her hand as if it were on fire, but not before he felt a current of awareness shoot through his body, right down to the soles of his feet.

The same thing had happened to him nine years ago when, again on impulse, he had returned his dancing partner to her table and gone back to waltz with the woman who had just tossed a glass of champagne in his face.

You're overdue for some serious R and R, Adams. "All right, here's what I propose," he said brusquely after clearing his throat. "School will be out about the last of May. I suggest you leave Chad in my care until then so as not to disrupt his life any more than it has been already. He's known me all his life, and right now he needs a familiar face more than anything else. Visit him on weekends whenever you have business in the area. Get to know him again. Later on we'll talk about allowing him to spend a week or so with you during the summer. What do you say to that?''

Grace started to protest, but he cut her off. "Before you give me your answer, Grace, you may as well know that not only am I Chad's godfather, I'm the trustee of his trust fund, the executor of Tom and Coral's wills, and I intend to apply for legal guardianship." He hadn't intended to tell her that just yet. "I have no reason to think it will be denied."

He gave her full marks for guts. She didn't collapse, neither did she throw a tantrum, the way Coral would have done in those circumstances. He wondered briefly why he didn't feel more satisfaction. Everything was turning out just the way he'd planned it. He watched her slide her hands off the table into her lap. Smart woman. Obviously she knew when she was licked.

"Then I guess that's all there is to say. For now, at least." Her voice was the kind that in a woman made him think of candlelight and slow music. Low-pitched, a little on the husky side. Nothing at all like her sister's had been. Coral's voice had been inclined to go shrill when she was crossed. It had been one of several things he had come to dislike about her, but then, this was hardly the proper time to dwell on the shortcomings of the deceased.

"Look, why don't you come home with me," he heard himself saying. "There's plenty of room, and my housekeeper lives in now. You could visit with Chad and get an early start home in the morning." The words had come out of the blue. Better than most men, Ram knew the dangers of getting too friendly with the opposition. It was the quickest way to blow his objectivity.

"No. Thank you, but no." With a dignity that caught him on the raw, she gathered her purse and gloves and stood. "It's two blocks down and one block over, isn't it?"

"The church? I'll drive you, of course." He tossed several bills down onto the table. Thank God, she hadn't taken him up on his offer! He was acting wildly out of character. Maybe he was coming down with whatever it was that had been laying low his office staff for the past six weeks. Two days ago there'd only been three people at work all day.

"That isn't at all necessary. I can—"

Taking her by the elbow, he steered her through the crowded room, jerked open the steamy glass door, nearly colliding with another couple just entering. On the sidewalk, he halted, feet braced apart, jaw set at an aggressive angle. "I brought you here and I'll drive you back, is that understood?" His narrowed eyes dared her to argue.

She didn't, but her militant stance told him pretty much what she was thinking. She was thinking that the battle might be lost, but the war sure as hell wasn't over yet.

So be it, he thought with an undercurrent of anticipation.

March weather on the Outer Banks of North Carolina was notoriously fickle. Inlets were cut, beach cottages washed away, highways flooded and tempers tested in the perennial battle between commercial fishermen, sport fishermen and the occasional nearsighted wind-surfer or jet-skier who couldn't handle sharing the waters of the Pamlico Sound with a variety of nets and crab pots.

Grace had dealt with it all before. She dealt with it now, pragmatically as always. The market for crabs was at its peak. Jimmies and sooks alike were bringing a dollar a pound, and with her new pot puller she could fish her two hundred pots, rebait, get weighed and ticketed and be home by the middle of the morning. She was averaging three to four hundred pounds a day—sometimes more—and the weather was holding fair.

It wouldn't last, of course. It never did. There would be days when it was blowing too hard to go out. Days when the fog would roll in so thick she couldn't see her 55-horse outboard from the bow of her Carolina skiff.

Those were the days she dreaded—the days when she couldn't go out. The crabs would keep, but there was too much time to think. It had been two and a half weeks since she'd met Ramsay Adams again after nine years of having him crop up in her fantasies with depressing regularity. But it was Chad she was worried about, not Ramsay. Not a single day passed that she didn't wonder if he was well, if he remembered her at all, and if Ramsay had even told him that she had gone there to bring him home with her.

Not an evening passed that she didn't include him in her prayers, unstructured and informal though they were. Grace had never asked for much, in her prayers or otherwise. The way she saw it, she'd been blessed with a strong back, good health and a competent brain. The rest was up to her.

But in areas where she had no control, such as the case of Chad, she had to rely on something larger than herself. It wasn't easy, because Grace wasn't born to be a leaner, but there were times when one had to borrow strength from a greater source.

She had finished putting a new worm shoe on an old boat of her father's, and it was all ready for copper painting. As for the house, it was so clean it echoed. With time on her hands—three days of unrelenting gale-force winds and two of thick fog—she had gone into a cleaning frenzy until everything waxable gleamed and everything scrubbable smelled of pine oil, temporarily disguising the lingering nuance of decades of collard greens and fried mullet. Between trying to instill some sense of timing in the youngest Shoemaker boy, hearing the five hundredth stumbling rendition of "Für Elise," and devising clever schemes to teach Cecil Ann Williams, who could hear something once and play it by ear, to read music, she cleaned.

The windows gleamed, and even the curtains had been taken down, washed, starched and ironed. Grace wasn't much of a hand at ironing. Her father had never set much store by it, and neither had she. Still, it helped to keep away the loneliness.

The loneliness. There. She had finally admitted it. With her father gone and no special person to fill the empty spaces in her life—and none on the horizon, either—all she had to look forward to was year after year of teaching beginning piano until her ears and her patience gave out, of crabbing, fishing and gardening until she was too arthritic to hang a net, dump a crab pot or fork over a compost pile.

Until she got too old and too discouraged to dream anymore, much less to fantasize.

As for her social life, lately it had consisted mostly of her volunteer work as a driver for social services and reading to those whose eyes were no longer up to the task. It should have been satisfying. It *was* satisfying. So why was she suddenly feeling so dissatisfied?

Bartram O'Donald had buried his grief in work when his wife had walked out, taking his youngest daughter with her. Irene, although born on Hatteras, had been too beautiful and too ambitious to be content as a fisherman's wife. She'd wanted to move away and Bartram had refused to go with her. After one last blazing battle, she'd left, taking her beautiful baby with her, leaving Grace behind. Grace had never understood, but she'd been given no choice but to accept. Recognizing her father's pain, she had done the best she could to make up for his loss. He had needed her.

But she'd been only a child, and she'd been hurting, too.

Now someone needed her again. A child. A boy with Coral's blue eyes and pale hair, with his grandfather's high forehead and square jaw. The week he had spent with her here when he was five had been wonderful. Once he'd crept out of his shell, they had played together, just the two of them. The empty old house had seemed to come alive. Chad was the closest thing to a son she was ever likely to have. Ramsay Adams didn't need him. He already had everything. Looks. Money. A profession and a social life. For all she knew, he already had a dozen sons of his own. If not, it couldn't be from lack of opportunity!

Dammit, this was one battle she intended to win!

A renewed glint of determination in her eyes, Grace switched off the weather radio, collected the latest copy of *National Fisherman* and sat down to a supper of leftover ham and yesterday's cold biscuits. She was halfway through when someone knocked on her front door. Most people used the back door.

Most people didn't even bother to knock, simply cracking the door to call and see if she was home.

"Who on earth...?" she muttered, hurrying through the house.

And then she knew. As impossible as it was, she knew a moment before she opened the door who would be on the other side.

Chad had grown much taller since she'd last seen him, but she would have recognized him anywhere. Those blue eyes. Those golden curls. Her father's chin was even more pronounced and— Oh, God, she wasn't going to cry!

He was shyly poking his toe at a battered old decoy that guarded the front porch. She wanted to touch him, but didn't dare—not yet.

Instead she looked up at Ramsay Adams, and then was almost sorry she had. Both times she had seen him before, he'd been more or less formally dressed. In casual clothes, his raw masculinity was overwhelming. Her fantasies hadn't done him justice.

"Maybe I should have called first," he said. "I tried this morning, but there was no answer."

"Um—the lines have been crazy lately. Beach flooding," she murmured. He was wearing a thick, ivory sweater over a dark, denim shirt, and a pair of worn corduroys, but it might as well have been a loincloth. She gripped the doorframe and fought for composure. ''I was working outside on my nets for a few hours this morning. Maybe—''

''Yes, well . . . may we come in?''

She stepped back and saw for the first time that he was carrying a nylon backpack. It was purple-and-lime green with comic characters on the sides. Just the thing for a distinguished attorney-at-law from the commonwealth of Virginia.

''If it's not convenient, you have only to say so. There are several motels open for the season.''

Ignoring him, Grace addressed the silent child who now seemed determined to attach himself physically to the long, corduroy-clad thigh. ''Chad, I'm your Aunt Grace. You probably don't remember, but the last time I saw you I taught you how to play 'Kitten on the Keys' and how to tie a bowline.'' Her eyes devoured the boy she hadn't seen in three years. His hair was darker. On closer examination, she thought that there was less of Coral and more of her father in him now. Nothing at all of Tom, so far as she could see.

''Shouldn't you be in school?'' she asked him. It was the last Wednesday in March. Most schools had at least another two months to go.

''There was an epidemic at Chad's school,'' Ramsay said. ''He'll be expected back on Monday, but we thought it might be a good time to pay a visit. If it's not inconvenient?''

Grace shifted her gaze from her silent nephew to the rather grim-faced man towering over them both. She knew precisely what he was up to. He was obviously trying to catch her off guard, showing up this way with no warning. Trying to prove that she was unfit to be a guardian.

Suppressing a sudden urge to giggle, she wondered what he'd expected to find. Men crawling out of the woodwork? A rowdy party in full swing? Maybe she should be flattered, but she wasn't. "It's not at all inconvenient. Chad, are you hungry? I was just starting supper. There's ham and biscuits, or I have some hot dogs—or we could have spaghetti. It's out of a jar, but—"

"Hot dogs sound fine," Ram said. "How about it, son? Can you handle a couple of wieners?"

She saw the boy glance from one adult to the other before nodding uncertainly. Her heart went out to him, for she knew how confusing his life must have been these past few weeks, losing his parents, his home, all his young school friends. Being transported from one coast to the other to live with a man who wasn't even kin.

And now coming down here, to a place he barely remembered, to a relative he barely knew. For the first time it occurred to Grace that Ramsay might have been right all along.

One of her piano students was just Chad's age. At eight, boys were supposed to be curious and noisy and rowdy. She did know that much. Chad was tall for his age, but he'd always seemed so young. At five, he'd been alternately too quiet, too well-behaved, or given to tantrums, bedwetting and tears. He was still too quiet.

Suddenly she wondered if she was capable of dealing with whatever problems he brought with him this time.

"Hot dogs it is, then," she said brightly, leading the way to the kitchen. "If you'd like to wash up, it's the door on the left. Do you remember the last time you were here, Chad, when the cat got shut up in the downstairs bathroom and we searched all over the neighborhood before you finally heard her crying?"

"And you thought it was only a gull," the boy said with a shy grin that melted her right down to the marrow.

As soon as the door closed behind him, Grace risked a smug look over her shoulder at the man behind her. In the narrow hallway, his shoulders looked impossibly broad, and Grace told herself it was the bulky sweater. Conscious once again of the vast differences between their circumstances, their backgrounds, she cautioned herself to be on guard. Not that it did much good. She still had an uncomfortable feeling that Ramsay Adams was playing her the same way her father had once played a fifty-seven-pound channel bass on ten-pound test line.

The contest had taken forever, but eventually Bartram had won the battle, landing his record fish alongside the Frisco pier to the cheers of some dozen or so fishermen who'd reeled in their lines to watch.

Pausing in the act of placing five wieners in the skillet, it occurred to Grace to wonder which of them she was identifying with—under-equipped fisherman or unlucky fish.

In the long run, would it even matter?

Chapter Three

You will not make a fool of yourself over that man. You will not make a fool of yourself over that man, you will not! There, put that on your music stand and play it until you know it by heart!

Grace glanced at the driveway one last time before pulling away from the pier her father had built the first year she had gone off to college. By now the planks were silvered and sagging, but still as sound as ever. "Ready? Hold on, we're off," she said, setting the throttle at considerably less than her usual speed.

By the time they got back a few hours later, Chad had lost the last vestige of shyness. She had to remind him more than once to keep his seat until they were tied up at the pier again.

"Boy, them jimmies are big, aren't they, Aunt Grace?"

"*Those* jimmies, and yes, they are, Chad. But wait'll you see a sook with her pocketbook full."

"Pocketbook? Crabs don't carry pocketbooks. You're only teasing!"

Which led to a discussion of the comparative anatomy of the male and female hard crab—which lasted until they met Ramsay coming around the corner of her house to meet them.

"Uncle Ram, Uncle Ram, do you know where a lady crab carries her pocketbook? On her stomach! And do you know what that long, skinny thing on a jimmy crab's stomach is? It's where he keeps his—"

"Chad, you left your cola cans in the boat. Better bring them up to the house."

The boy was off like a shot, and Grace, her face pinker than could be accounted for by the fresh northwest wind, carefully avoided looking at Ram, who was grinning broadly.

"Anatomy lessons this early in the morning?" he queried.

"Biology lessons."

"What's the difference?"

"I don't know, and you can just stop laughing!" Grace snapped, half irritated, half amused that she should react like a puberty-stricken girl at the mention of a hard crab's reproductive equipment.

Ram laughed even harder, but it cost him. He'd woken up with a pounding head, which hadn't improved over the morning spent waiting for the two of them to come in. He had arrived just in time to see them pull up to the first float, and watched for a while. Then he'd headed toward Hatteras village to find a coffee shop, where he'd downed a couple of aspirin. Which, so far, hadn't done the job.

"In the recycling basket," Grace directed when Chad raced up with the empties. Turning to Ram, she asked if he'd found a place to stay the night before.

Ram named a motel a few miles up the highway. He'd had a lousy night, partly due to the fact that he always slept better on his own turf, partly due to his headache, and partly—mostly—due to the fact that he couldn't get the woman off his mind long enough to relax.

The night before, he had stayed only long enough to eat and to hear Chad bungle his way through the brief piano piece he had learned three years before, and then left before he started begging her to find him a place in her house—preferably in her bed.

"I thought maybe we could go out to lunch," he said.

"I put on a pot of ham bone soup this morning."

"It'll keep."

"Or you could share," she suggested, cutting him a sidelong glance that was far different from her usual direct gaze. Accustomed to reading body language, Ram was intrigued by her reaction. She was perfectly natural with the boy, but something about him was bothering her. He'd like to think she was as attracted to him as he was to her, but more than likely she was merely suspicious.

With just cause. He wasn't going to give up the boy so easily.

"What do you say, son, soup or hamburgers?"

Chad, seated on the bottom step, tugging off his filthy sneakers, grinned shyly and said, "I helped with the vegetables for the soup. I didn't even cut myself, either. I was real careful, wasn't I, Aunt Grace?"

"Very careful. You were a big help."

"See, we had to hurry, 'cause if we didn't, the crabs might eat each other, and the price might drop at the market, and anyway, I only cried over the onions, not the carrots and celery and potatoes."

Over the crop of short, golden curls, bent assiduously over a knotted shoestring, Ram met Grace's eyes in shared amusement. The look held warmth and a bond of caring, with no hint at all of the conflict of interest between them.

Ram was struck by the directness of those clear amber eyes. By their honesty. The lady was not into game-playing. His own life, on the other hand, was built on games to the point that sometimes it seemed as if everything he had accomplished in his entire thirty-seven years was an illusion. He had played a game with his father and lost, leaving him stuck in a profession for which he had no real affinity. More often than not, he played games with his partners, occasionally with a client. He played games with the women he occasionally saw, some of whom were interested in a commitment he wasn't ready to give, some of whom were more interested in what he could do for them in a professional capacity.

For a little while, as Grace and Chad set out bowls, buttered and toasted leftover biscuits and ladled up a rich, steamy concoction that Grace apologetically explained was really her weekly potlikker soup with the addition of a ham bone, Ram felt curiously light-headed, as if he had somehow managed to shed all his emotional baggage.

When Chad insisted on knowing what potlikker soup was, Grace explained that she saved the juice of all the vegetables she cooked during the week—especially the liquor left in the pot after cooking greens—and added whatever she had on hand to make a savory soup.

Ram's interest in food diminished still further.

The vegetables were unevenly cut, but no one seemed to care. Having helped in the making, Chad was enthusiastic about the end product, pressing his Uncle Ram to finish his bowl and have more.

Ram did his best, but the truth was, he was feeling worse by the minute. Not only was his head still pounding, now his stomach was threatening rebellion.

As for Grace, she was still amazed by the fact that he was actually here, in her shabby, familiar kitchen, eating from her everyday dishes and drinking coffee from one of her mismatched mugs.

She'd be willing to bet his mother had never cooked a pot of greens in her life. Maybe braised endive, or possibly buttered spinach. La-la vegetables, not homegrown ones like turnips and turnip greens, or good, frost-nipped collards. Much less, made soup from the leftovers. Men like Ramsay Adams lunched at fancy restaurants. With clients. With fancy cocktails and wine.

Should she offer him some of Aunt Manie's scuppernong wine? Aunt Manie had passed away years ago, but Grace still had a few jugs of her sweet homemade wine. If the corks hadn't disintegrated and the whole works evaporated by now. Or turned to vinegar.

Chad heaped fig preserves on another biscuit, gobbled it down in three bites, and asked politely to be excused so he could go play on her piano in the front room.

"You may be excused, but wash your hands before you touch the piano. I don't want you sticking to the keys. I have a student coming tomorrow afternoon for a lesson."

"Yes, ma'am! I mean, thank you, Aunt Grace. Yippee!"

Ram winced as Chad slammed the door and raced down the hall.

"Your head hurts, doesn't it?" Grace asked quietly. She got up and removed the soup bowls and silverware. "Have you taken anything?"

"Aspirin. Evidently, not enough." His words were clipped, but this time Grace wasn't put off. The man was hurting. That was an excuse anyone could understand. He had made a show of enthusiasm, finishing a single toasted biscuit and half a bowl of soup, but either he didn't like her cooking or he was feeling a lot worse than he let on.

"If you'd like to lie down, I'll take Chad outside for a spell. Isn't it great, the way he got over his shyness so quickly?"

"Yeah. Great," Ram said dully. "I'll just run on back to the motel—maybe I'll come by later on and take the two of you out to dinner."

"You'd be better off sleeping as long as you can. Chad and I can bring you something for supper so you won't have to bother with going out. Maybe some stewed flounder. That's certainly bland enough."

Was it her imagination, or did Ramsay actually flinch at the offer? It was definitely not her imagination that made him look paler than normal. The faint beard shadow on his angular jaw stood out in dark relief against his sudden pallor, and she was about to remark on it when he muttered a hasty apology, shoved back his chair and fled. A moment later she heard him being violently ill in the bathroom just down the hall.

Chad met her outside the bathroom door. "I guess it's my fault," he whispered dolefully. "I was sick last week. All the kids at school had it—some of 'em got sick right in school. Mickey McCarthy threw up all over Samantha Poole's homework, and the teacher said she had to do it over again. I think that's pretty rotten, don't you?"

"Pretty rotten," Grace agreed distractedly. Should she go make up the bed in her father's room first, or see if she could get hold of a doctor?

Ram emerged before she could make up her mind, his face gray except for two patches of color high on his cheekbones. His breathing was ragged, as if he'd run five miles uphill. Grace found herself wanting to gather him into her arms, pull his head down onto her shoulder, and comfort him forever—which was a pretty bizarre fantasy, even for her.

"I'm sorry," he said.

"I'm sorry, too. If you can hang on a minute, I'll make up the spare bed for you and then get the doctor on the line. He'll know what's going around and what to do about it."

"No, thanks. Motel. Sleep it off. Be fine in a few hours."

"Don't be ridiculous." She urged him toward a chair, and he didn't resist. "Sit right there until I call you. Chad, come help me make the bed."

"Please don't bother," Ram called after her. "I'm embarrassed enough as it is. I'd much rather go back to the motel."

Hands on her hips, Grace stared him down. A weaker-looking, more miserable creature would be hard to find, but she schooled herself against showing sympathy. "If you go back to the motel, Chad and I will just wear out the highway checking on you, so you may as well be considerate enough to stay here. If, as you say, all you need is sleep, then you won't be putting us out any. There's plenty of room.''

It was an easy victory. Ramsay was too weak to fight. Grace felt almost guilty and tried hard not to show it. All the same, it was encouraging to know that she could win any victory at all over such an opponent. It didn't take a law degree to know that she was vastly overmatched.

What was even more encouraging was the fact that Chad had taken to her like rust to a barbed-wire fence.

''Ma'am—I mean, Aunt Grace—do you remember those things we played with that had dots all over them? Do you still have any of those left?''

''If I do, they'll probably be in the closet under the stairs where I keep things I seldom need anymore. Why don't you look while I get Mr. Adams settled? Once he's feeling better, he'll need something to keep him from climbing the walls. Dominoes would be perfect.'' Ramsay Adams play dominoes? The mind boggled!

After her patient was bedded down, Grace left a glass of cola, a towel and a plastic-lined bucket beside him. She drove to the motel, a matter of five minutes, and retrieved his unpacked bag, hurrying back to her two men.

Her two men. How wonderful that sounded, she mused.

And how utterly impossible.

Grace and Chad played dominoes quietly until suppertime, making up rules as they went because it had been years since Grace had played and the instructions had long since been lost. Shortly after supper, she settled her young guest in his own room with a stack of books that had once belonged to her father, looked in on her other guest, who was sleeping soundly, and tiptoed back downstairs to put away the supper things.

Ramsay Adams was actually sleeping under her very own roof, his all but naked body lying between sheets she had washed and mended with her own hands. He'd been lying on his stomach, his legs sprawled apart under the covers, and his bare arms crossed over his head on the pillow when she'd looked in. She'd been tempted to stay and watch him sleep, just for a little while, but common sense had won out. She had trouble enough keeping her fantasies in their proper perspective without that.

And anyway, wasn't this just another fantasy? Any minute now she would wake up, grab a cup of reheated coffee, climb into her clothes, throw on her slicker and her boots and go crank up her outboard for the run out to her pots. She was *not* merely a foolish female who had fixated on a certain male ideal some nine years ago and now couldn't tell fact from fantasy.

Drying the last soup bowl, she added it to the stack in the cabinet, hung up the towel, locked the back door and turned out the light.

But once she'd washed up and changed into her nightgown—a hopelessly unglamorous cotton affair straight out of a mail-order catalog—she felt compelled to take one last look at her patient, in case he had taken a turn for the worst.

He had rolled over onto his back. Stretched out on her father's old iron bed in the front room, his muscular six-foot carcass completely nude under the covers for all she knew—his clothes were draped over the back of the rocking chair—he looked so handsome, so virile, even with a slightly greenish pallor, that Grace was embarrassed by her own prurient thoughts.

"Get real, O'Donald," she muttered. "No more romances for you, lady. From now on when you want to read, stick to *National Fisherman* and the *Coastland Times!*"

Chad was still reading when she looked in one last time. "Better get some sleep," she said softly.

"Are we going to fish something in the morning?"

"Crab pots at dawn, but I'm afraid—"

"I know. You can't take me with you." His small face turned sullen, and her heart went out to him. How many times had he been left behind in his young life?

"We'll go together lots of times," she promised him, vowing that somehow she was going to keep that promise. Only not tomorrow. "But one of us needs to stay here to keep an eye on Mr. Adams. I wouldn't feel right leaving him all alone, would you?"

"No, ma'am." He hid his disappointment, and Grace found herself almost wishing he would argue. He was too young to accept disappointment so readily.

Of course, Coral had always been obedient, too. Unlike Grace, Coral had been the perfect child—beautiful, smart, and quick to seek her mother's approval. Grace, older by four years, had been her father's child, happier with boats than dolls, more interested in learning how to trap muskrats than in learning how to apply pink lip pomade and scented lotions.

"Maybe when Uncle Ram wakes up he'll want me to play dominoes with him," Chad said with a sigh of resignation.

"Maybe he will," Grace agreed softly, although she seriously doubted if the man would feel like playing anything any time soon. "Better get some sleep now, sugar. I'll take you to the fish house with me if your Uncle Ram's feeling better when I get in." She switched off the light, placed the book on top of the stack and leaned over to kiss her nephew on the forehead. He smelled just the least bit fishy, but she decided that going to bed unwashed, uncombed and unbrushed for once wasn't going to do him any irreparable harm.

At his age, she'd been known to smooth the surface of her hair without even unbraiding it and put a pair of clean socks over dirty feet before crawling between the sheets, unlike Coral, who had invariably slept in pink ruffled pajamas and scented dusting powder, with Barbie on the pillow beside her.

With Chad, she'd settle for the basics to start with. Time enough to establish a healthy, wholesome bedtime routine once she had him all to herself.

Ram was sick again in the night. He made it to the bathroom, and afterward, dashed cold water over his face, liberally splashing his pajama top in the process. He was shivering. Burning up and freezing at the same time. His head felt as if six jackhammers were doing a job on his skull.

When he was sure he could walk without reeling, he headed for his bed again, only to find Grace O'Donald waiting for him. She was wearing a cotton nightgown that had obviously been designed by a missionary sometime in the late nineteenth century. Her hair drooped in a single, shaggy braid over her shoulder, and she looked so damned sweet he groaned.

"Get out," he growled. "Please." The last thing he wanted was for her to see him like this.

She ignored him. With a few deft sweeps of her small, capable hands, she smoothed his bed and plumped his pillow. Ram knew he ought to be grateful, but all he could do was grunt something unintelligible and crawl in. God, he was miserable!

He couldn't remember the last time he had felt so wretched.

"Next year, take your flu shots," she said, calmly drawing the covers up over his chest.

He sent her a resentful look, but his teeth were chattering too hard to try to defend himself. He was too young to take flu shots, dammit! Besides, this was probably some rogue variety that hadn't even been typed yet. These days, bugs mutated so fast that as soon as a new cure was developed, they'd already changed identity so that it couldn't touch them.

"Don't have time to be sick," he muttered.

"Fine. Then get yourself well."

"Busy. Lost a lot of time flying—"

"Next time let someone else fly. You stay home and take care of yourself."

"You poisoned me. That stuff I ate for—"

"I did not. You were already sick when you came here, so don't talk foolishness."

He glared at her, his fever-bright eyes daring her to argue with him. "Don't think this changes anything. I'm keeping the boy."

"We'll talk about it when you're in your right mind."

"In my right mind I wouldn't have come within a hundred miles of any damn piano-playing female fisherman!"

"Then you're obviously not, because you obviously did, so be quiet and go back to sleep." She smiled. Actually *smiled* at him!

Ram groaned and rolled away from her, determined to ignore her until she went away.

He knew when she stood, and he hoped she would leave—and hoped she wouldn't. When he felt her cool hand on his cheek, he couldn't prevent himself from turning his face toward her palm. Who would have believed a hard, calloused hand could be so comforting?

"Y'ought to stay 'way," he said, slurring his words. "Might catch it."

"I had it last month."

"This—rogue variety."

"Naturally. What other kind would you have?" she asked, her voice resonating with humor, sympathy and just a hint of triumph.

Ram reached up and caught her fingers, pressing her palm against his forehead. She was so warm and he was so cold. If he didn't feel so rotten, he'd be tempted to—

Fever talk. He must be running a temperature, because the thoughts churning around in his pounding head were totally irrational.

"Doesn't change anything," he warned her again, in case she started getting the idea that she could take advantage of his momentary weakness. "Head hurts like the devil."

"Don't try to talk. You probably couldn't keep aspirin down, but an ice pack might help."

"Hell, no! F-f-freezing!"

"I know, and I'm sorry, but let's see what we can do with an ice bag at one end and a heating pad at the other, all right?"

He wanted to tell her that if she'd go on touching him, talking to him in that soft, husky tone until he fell asleep, he just might live through the night. The trouble was, one small part of him—call it masculine pride for lack of a better term—hated like the very devil for her to see him lying here, helpless as a newborn babe.

Grace checked in on her patient the minute she got in from fishing her crab pots the next morning. She stepped out of her boots and yellow slicker on the back porch, washed and lotioned her hands, and tiptoed up the stairs. Chad had greeted her at the back door with the news that "Uncle Ram" hadn't been sick again, and that Chad had made himself some breakfast, and that there were cartoons on TV, so could he watch?

In her jeans, with her hair still wild and wind-blown, her cheeks still flushed from the stiff breeze that continued out of the northwest, she peered in at the sleeping man. Not until she saw him lying there, looking so alien, yet somehow so right, did she allow herself to admit that she'd been afraid he would leave before she got in.

It might have been better if he had, she thought ruefully, tiptoeing closer to gaze down at the sleeping figure. He had thrown off the mound of covers, kicked the heating pad to the floor, and now he lay there, his bare chest moving slowly with his regular breathing. His chest was hairy, but not excessively so. All too clearly she recalled the impact of seeing him stagger back into the bedroom last night wearing only a pair of briefs. Even sick as a dog, he was magnificent.

Collecting the lukewarm cold pack, she knelt to retrieve the heating pad, switched it off and unplugged it. When she turned for one last look, he was staring back at her. He hadn't moved a muscle, and she could have sworn she hadn't made a sound, but he was watching her, his eyes no longer fever-bright, but no less intense.

"You're pretty with your hair like that."

Her hand flew to her hair in a self-conscious gesture that was totally unlike her. "Thank you," she managed, wondering what his motive was. She'd never been pretty in her life. Her mother had seen that she didn't suffer any illusions on that score. "Would you like some breakfast?"

His lips, which were thin but sensuously carved, quirked in wry amusement. "I want to say yes, but defense counsel advises against it. Maybe after I've been up for a while..."

"That'll be tomorrow. You'll need something before then."

"That will be in about two minutes, max. Trust me to know what I need."

"Fine. Act like a stubborn mule, then, and see how far it gets you."

"All sympathy, aren't we?"

His eyes glittered up at her, and Grace was suddenly acutely conscious that, having come in straight off the sound after emptying and rebaiting her traps, she probably smelled to high heaven and looked even worse! Back rigid, she stalked from the room, hearing his soft laughter behind her. It was all she could do not to slam the door, but she refused to give him the satisfaction of knowing he could get to her so easily.

"Ready to go to the fish house?" she called through the door. She'd poured herself a cup of coffee, made toast and cut herself a wedge of cheese. "Our patient's recovering nicely. I think he'll be all right until we get back, don't you?"

Several hours later, the crabs having been weighed and ticketed, they returned. Chad had a circle of chocolate around his mouth and Grace had an earful of boyish confidences. They had stopped to buy groceries and to let Chad see the lighthouse, and she'd more or less promised him that one of these days he could climb to the top, the way she had as a child, although the tower had been closed for repairs for the past several years.

Ramsay, dressed in his corduroys and a pedigreed navy flannel shirt, had made his way downstairs. Seated in the comfortable old armchair that she'd recently slipcovered in denim because it wore like iron and didn't show dirt, he looked pale, miserable and mean as a cottonmouth. When Chad raced in to tell him all about the big fish he'd seen in the ice house, and the wind-surfers they had watched at Canadian Hole, he actually winced.

"I wondered if you were planning to come back," he said after the boy had dashed off toward the kitchen. It was nearly two in the afternoon. He was fuming.

"And I wondered if you'd still be here."

"Count on it. You took something of mine with you, and I'm not about to leave without it."

Grace's hopes plunged. She might have known it wasn't going to be this easy. "Can we talk about it later? Right now I've got to put away these groceries. I thought soup and crackers would be about right for you. Do you like hot tea?"

"We'll talk about it now. As for lunch, Chad and I can stop on the way north." Raising his voice, he called out, "Chad? Son, go get your things together, will you? Time to shove off."

"But I thought—that is, you said he didn't have to be back at school until Monday."

"Did you think I was on holiday, too?"

Angry and disappointed, Grace turned away, almost tripping over the leather flight bag she had retrieved from the motel just yesterday. It was packed, zipped and ready to go. Damn him, if he'd intended to turn right around and go back home, why had he bothered to come in the first place? It wasn't fair, either to Chad or to her, to tease them this way!

She slammed cans of evaporated milk onto the pantry shelf, crammed marshmallows and fresh vegetables together into the meat drawer of the refrigerator and crumpled the bag instead of folding it neatly. She'd bought Chad's favorite Popsicles, the kind of juice he liked in little boxes, and an expensive pre-sweetened cereal loaded with fruits and nuts, plus more milk than she would use in a month. She'd even bought three boneless, skinless chicken breasts, a luxury she seldom afforded herself, thinking she could do something with them that wouldn't offend Ram's sensitive stomach.

"Aunt Grace, can I come back sometime?" Chad said from the kitchen doorway. His face was a mile long, but he was clutching his colorful backpack in one hand and his coat in the other.

"You bet you can, sugar. Any time at all. And once school is out, your Uncle Ram has promised you can come stay with me."

He brightened immediately. "Honest? For keeps? I can help you fish and make my bed and everything. Mrs. Suggs says I'm a big help around the house."

"I'm sure you are. With two of us to go at it, we'll be done with our work in no time, and then we can play dominoes or read your grandfather's books."

"Yea-aah!"

"Say goodbye to your aunt, Chadwick. Thank her for her hospitality."

Grace's eyes flew guiltily to Ram's. For a big man, he moved surprisingly quietly. Like all successful predators, he had a talent for sneaking up and catching his prey off guard.

"You can leave him here with me. I could drive him back on Sunday afternoon," she said after hugging her nephew and watching him carry his bag out to the car.

"No."

"You're in no condition to drive to Norfolk. What if you have a relapse halfway there? Have you thought about that?"

"I won't."

Exasperated, she flung down the dish towel she had just snatched off the rack. "You don't know that! Not even your pigheaded brand of omnipotence can guarantee you won't—"

"Grace, don't make this any more difficult than it has to be. I told you I intend to let the boy visit with you. I'll be as generous with him as possible, but I won't have him being tugged back and forth between the two of us. He's had enough to deal with without being handed more."

She stared at him helplessly, feeling guilty, feeling confused, feeling angry, praying she wouldn't disgrace herself by crying and begging. When she could trust herself to speak unemotionally, she said, "Chad needs a woman. Coral was my sister and I loved her, even though I hardly knew her, but I'm not sure she was always the most attentive of mothers. And housekeepers can be unreliable."

"Mine's been reliable for six years. But you're right. Coral was a lousy parent and Tom was no better. There's nothing that can be done about it now. Chad thinks his parents were forced to send him off to boarding school because they were away so much on business trips. You and I know better. They were both spoiled brats. The quest for pleasure was the most important thing in their lives, and eventually it killed them."

Hearing the words spoken so dispassionately by someone who knew them far better than she ever had, Grace had no choice but to accept the truth. But it hurt. "I thought you and Tom were friends," she said. Suddenly cold, although the day had turned out quite warm, she drew her old yellow cardigan more closely around her, wishing now that he was leaving that she was wearing something newer and more flattering.

"We were friends. We grew up together under more or less similar circumstances. A series of nannies, boarding schools, summer camps. We attended the same prep school and the same university, although once we got past puberty we discovered that we didn't agree on very much."

"I knew you were Tom's attorney and his best man, but—"

"And you were the sister of the bride—the woman who toasted me with champagne."

She could feel herself flushing. "I hoped you had forgotten that."

"I never did." Leaning against the doorframe, he looked very different from the sophisticated, fashionably dressed man she had waltzed with in an empty anteroom a long time ago. And even more dangerous. "Not for want of trying," he added.

That hurt, although Grace told herself she shouldn't have been surprised. "No more than I tried," she shot back, and then could have bitten off her tongue. She could tell that from the sudden flare of interest in his eyes that she'd given away her guilty secret. "Look, if you're going, just go!" she snapped. "You might think you've recovered, but believe me, you're going to be feeling pretty shaky by the time you get home, so the sooner you—"

"What was it you tried so hard to forget, Grace?"

"Nothing!" She flung out her hands, exasperated, embarrassed—wishing she had never had that second glass of champagne at the wedding. The air between them seemed to pulsate, making it difficult to breathe. "Nothing at all! For goodness' sake, what was there to forget?"

"You tell me. However, I'm just beginning to wonder if there might be a way we can work this out."

"Work what out? Oh ... with Chad. Well, I wish you'd let me in on it."

The hand he held up, palm outward, was not quite steady. "This isn't the time to discuss it. My head still feels like it got caught in an avalanche, but I promise you I'll take good care of the boy. I'll have him give you a phone call sometime next week, and later on we can get together and discuss how we're going to divide him up."

"We're not going to divide him up. He's mine. He belongs with me, and I mean to have him." When he continued to study her as though she were some new life-form he was just now discovering, she said, "Ram, I don't *have* anybody but Chad, and he doesn't have anyone but *me*. We need each other, can't you understand that?"

He gave her a long, enigmatic look and then picked up his flight bag. "If I weren't afraid I'd be passing on something you wouldn't thank me for, I might try to change your mind."

"It wouldn't do you any good."

"About a lot of things," he went on as if she hadn't spoken. "Later, Grace. We'll settle things later."

"Come back here! Don't you walk away from me, Ramsay Adams!"

But it was too late. He already had. Grace watched in impotent fury as he sauntered down the long, narrow hall, looking impossibly tall, lean and dangerous despite the fact the he obviously wasn't back up to fighting trim.

Turning away, she wandered into the living room and sank down into the chair he had recently vacated, burying her face in her hands. "Damn the man," she whispered. "Damn, damn, *damn* the man, anyway!"

Chapter Four

There were no lights on in the front of the house when Ram got home, meaning that Mrs. Suggs had been busy in the kitchen since before dark. As a rule, he was home earlier. At least he had been for the past couple of months, since Chad had come to live with him and he'd prevailed upon his housekeeper to live in. Before that, he had often stayed at the office until hunger had driven him out for food, after which, exhaustion had usually forced him to go home.

Tonight he'd stayed late to wind up a *pro bono* case he'd been involved with for the past two months. He was tired, but for once it was a good kind of tired. For a change, instead of helping some corporate entity cover its corporate rear end against some obscure eventuality, he'd been dealing with real people with real problems. In this particular case, it was a handicapped veteran with a diabetic wife, who'd been the victim of a greedy landlord, an unscrupulous exterminator and a run of bad luck. The couple was now installed in a new and well-run complex, with an iron-clad lease. Thanks to the settlement he'd been able to get for them, they would have access to better medical care and sufficient job training to launch them both on new careers.

Ram was locked into a profession he hadn't chosen, but days like this made it easier to bear. His name was still listed first on the firm's letterhead in deference to his late father, but as a junior partner, he usually got stuck with the scut work.

Instead of going on through to the kitchen, where he was pretty sure he would find Chad doing homework while Mrs. Suggs put the finishing touches on dinner, Ram opened the door to his study, closing it quietly behind him.

In just a few short weeks the house had lost much of the emptiness that had characterized it for so long. One of these days he was going to have to pick up a few more pieces of furniture—maybe some paintings and rugs and the kind of personal knick-knacks that most houses accumulated. He'd bought the place when he had stepped into his father's shoes at the firm, but somehow he'd never got around to furnishing it beyond the basic necessities.

Nor had he realized just how barren it looked until he'd experienced the cheerful clutter of Grace O'Donald's old, white-frame house.

With a sigh that he wasn't even aware of, Ram shrugged off his jacket and rubbed the back of his neck. He was tired. God, he was tired! It wasn't his work, per se—although he had long since faced the fact that, given a choice, he would have been doing almost anything else in the world rather than what he was doing.

Charles Ramsay Adams. He had barely known the man. They had argued for years over Ram's future. They'd still been arguing when, during Ram's third year at the university, his father had been diagnosed with a slow-growing, inoperable brain tumor. After that there had been no question of following his own interests, which had included botany and marine geology.

"Name me one marine geologist who ever made a dime!" his father would say when Ram tried to broach the topic. "Or a single damned tree-hugger who ever got rich, unless he specialized in growing illegal crops."

Cashing in had not been among Ram's priorities at the time, although he readily admitted that it might have been more important had his entire life not been cushioned by his father's money.

That had been nearly fifteen years ago. By the time Charles Adams had died, his wife having preceded him by eighteen months, Ram's future had already been determined.

He'd put his father's house on the market and looked around for something more to his own taste. He'd been seeing Addie Blake at the time, with some vague idea of an eventual marriage. Sexually, they'd been well suited. Intellectually, Addie was more than his equal. But when she'd got involved with a wildly radical group and tried to recruit him to the cause, even to the point of bringing her social activism into the bedroom, Ram had begun to back off.

Eventually, Addie had moved to the west coast and gone into politics. Ram had settled in at the firm, although it was no real secret that his heart wasn't in corporate law. But by then, he'd already invested too many years to start over in a new field.

Sighing, he loosened his tie and settled into the chair that, along with a desk, a computer and a set of built-in bookshelves, was the room's only furniture. The walls were white. All the rooms in the house were white, but after seeing the eclectic clutter of Grace's home, he found it all rather sterile.

Ram's living room furniture consisted of a black leather sofa and a black lacquer coffee table. Period. Mentally, he compared it to a wallpapered room with a sagging, slipcovered sofa, an assortment of chairs and tables, a piano littered with sheet music and a glass jar of red hot cinnamon balls, an overflowing bookshelf and a lumpy, hand-crocheted rug. Grace's coffee table had been hidden under books, magazines, several stray dominoes and a half-finished section of jigsaw puzzle. The place had a lived-in look that only generations of living could produce.

Ram couldn't possibly compete with that. No wonder Chad had twisted around to gaze wistfully over his shoulder as they'd driven away. It had been all Ram could do not to turn around and go back himself—back to Grace's warmth, her caring, her gentle good humor. Back to her comfortably cluttered nest.

His own nest had been decorated by a professional. At least as far as it went. He had cut short the process when it had occurred to him that the place was beginning to resemble a five-star hotel instead of the comfortable home he had envisioned, but he'd never got around to finishing the job.

"Sir? I mean, Uncle Ram?" The door opened silently, allowing a stream of light to fall across the gleaming parquet floor.

"Yeah, come on in, son." Ram stretched and pressed his fingers against his throbbing temples. "Switch on the light, will you? I was just sitting here resting my eyes while I waited for you and Mrs. Suggs to get dinner on the table."

"It's chicken and pineapple upside-down cake."

"Chicken pineapple cake? Don't believe I've ever sampled that particular flavor before."

"Aw, you know what I mean, Uncle Ram! Fried chicken and cake with pineapple and cherries and stuff on it. I helped Mrs. Suggs put the trimmings in the pan and pour the raw cake on top."

Ram ruffled the boy's curly hair as they headed for the formal dining room. Like the rest of the house, the dining room boasted of no more than the bare essentials. Teak with black leather, top of the line, yet it couldn't hold a candle to a certain scarred pine table surrounded by mismatched chairs and a homemade sideboard where a root-headed decoy vied for space with cookbooks, a marine band radio and a bunch of houseplants.

Suddenly he felt such an intense need to be there, to see her, to hear her voice—to hold her and feel with his own arms that warm, resilient strength that was so surprising in one so small.

"Oh—what? The chicken? Delicious."

With a snort of impatience, the housekeeper reached past him and helped Chad to a second piece, sending Ram a look that made him wonder how long he'd been staring into space.

"Sorry," he muttered. "My mind was back at the office."

Correction. His mind was nowhere near his office. Hadn't been in complete attendance, if the truth were known, since the day of the memorial service. Since he'd come face-to-face with a woman who had haunted his dreams like a persistent ghost for more than nine years.

And then, just when he was getting used to dealing with her in the flesh, he'd had to go and get sick practically on her doorstep.

Which was a terrific way to make a favorable impression on the woman of your choice, he thought wryly.

Chad's chatter was all about school and radio-controlled aircraft and Bart Simpson. Mrs. Suggs filled in the few brief silences with a few remarks about the rising cost of bananas and her sister's kidney stones.

Ram thought about Grace O'Donald. He thought about the way her hands had felt on his face in the middle of the night. He thought about the soft, husky sound of her voice, about the unlikely fact that she was both a piano teacher and a licensed commercial fisherman, and the even more unlikely fact that she had been Coral Chancellor's sister.

Grace was sound asleep when the phone rang. She glanced automatically at the luminous dial of her alarm clock. Eleven-ten. Who would be calling her at this late hour? An emergency trip for social services?

Stumbling from her bed, she hurried to the phone in the hall. She'd been meaning to have a jack installed in her bedroom, but like a lot of things, she never seemed to get around to it. Sometimes it was hard to drum up enough motivation.

"H'lo?" she mumbled. "O'Donald residence."

"Grace, I was thinking—"

Ramsay Adams? Like a two-hundred-watt bulb being snapped on, suddenly she was wide-awake.

"...Not too late to call? I should have waited, but I figured you'd be out—uh, fishing your crab pots in the morning, and I'll be tied up most of the day tomorrow unless we can get a continuance or the—"

"Ramsay, is Chad all right? Has he caught whatever it was you had?"

"The twenty-four-hour thing? No, he's fine. I caught it from him, matter of fact. That's not why I was calling. The thing is—"

Grace waited, curling her toes against the gritty feel of sand on the strip of linoleum that had covered the upstairs hallway for as long as she could remember. That was another thing she intended to do one of these days—replace it with a runner. Her mother had wanted to carpet the whole house, upstairs and down—it was one of the things they had fought about—but Bartram had hated to walk barefoot on anything that couldn't be scrubbed clean with a mop and bucket. It had been just one more in a long line of irreconcilable differences.

"So what about it? You want to drive up on Friday and spend the weekend with Chad and me? You can see how he's doing, check out his school, and maybe we can run down to Sandbridge for a few hours. He enjoys that." And when the silence had crackled for too long, he heard himself almost pleading with her. Ramsay Adams, the man who could intimidate a witness with silence better than most men could with thumbscrews. "Look, why don't you just think about it? I can call back in the morning with instructions, or even later on in the day if that would be better for you. I didn't realize how late it was."

"No—yes—that is..."

"Or I could drive down and pick you up if you don't want to tackle city traffic."

* * *

"I can't believe I'm doing this," Grace muttered for the third time since crossing the North Carolina-Virginia state line. It wasn't as if she could spare the time. It wasn't even as though this was going to forward her cause, because she knew darn well what he was doing. He was going to show off all the advantages he could afford to give Chad that she couldn't.

So, all right! He had a fancy house and a housekeeper and a high-paying profession. All she had was a house, a piano, a couple of small boats, neither new, a few gill nets and a few crab pots. It was a shaky way to make a living, but between that and her garden, she'd never gone hungry. Her taxes got paid. She'd even accumulated a small savings account.

More important, she wasn't dependent on someone else to look after a child while she went to work, which was more than he could say. Maybe Ram could afford to buy him computers and bicycles and keep him in a fancy private school, but there was something to be said for living in the home where your ancestors had lived, fishing the same waters they had fished, and growing up with a working knowledge of the real world.

On the other hand, this was the real world, too, she thought as she braked to avoid a sudden slow up in the line of traffic along the Military Highway.

Eventually, following Ram's instructions, she located the right address. The neighborhood was depressingly posh. Houses set well back from the street, hidden behind massive hedges or wrought-iron fences or brick walls. Number 143 had a boxwood hedge cornered by brick pillars and an open wrought-iron gate.

"Bloody swank," she grumbled, wheeling her rusty pickup truck into the circular drive. If he thought she was going to be intimidated into parking in the rear, he was about ninety degrees off course. She pulled up in front, set the parking brake and slid stiffly down to the paved driveway just as a streak of red-and-white, followed by a larger streak of blue, darted out the front door and met her with shouts and yaps.

"Aunt Grace, Aunt Grace, I've got a dog! See? His name is Katie—I mean her. She's a she, and Uncle Ram says she's a registered Brickany. Her name's Katie, you can call her that and she'll come. Most of the time, anyway. And she already knows my voice, don't you, Katie?"

Grace survived Katie's enthusiastic greeting, and Chad's. She met the redoubtable Mrs. Suggs, suffered the older woman's suspicious scrutiny, and did some scrutinizing of her own. So this was the live-in housekeeper who looked after her nephew while Ram was at work. Well, we'd just see about that.

"Chad can show you where to put your things, Miss O'Donald. I've put you in the room next to his.

Mine's next door, if you happen to need anything in the night."

In other words, Grace interpreted, amused, don't go playing musical bedrooms. "Thank you," she said. "Then if you don't mind, I'll go now and freshen up. Chad's Katie gave me a big welcome."

"Might's well drop your skirt down the stairs, I'll see if I can get them muddy paw prints out. It's washable, isn't it?"

"I don't own anything that isn't washable. I'd appreciate it, Mrs. Suggs. I only brought the one skirt, one dress and a pair of jeans."

The housekeeper seemed to thaw a bit, and Grace found her way upstairs with Chad as an eager guide. He had to show her his room, and his Uncle Ram's—information she could have lived without. "I'll meet you downstairs as soon as I've washed up, all right?"

Ten minutes later she was being given a tour of the house. "This is the kitchen. Mrs. Suggs makes real good cakes. I help her sometimes. This is the dining room. We eat in here, breakfast and all. This is the, uh, sumerium? Someralum?"

"Solarium?" Grace provided, and he nodded eagerly.

"Yeah, that's it. There's nothing in there but a bunch of empty boxes. Mrs. Suggs says you're supposed to plant stuff in them, but why would you want to do that? Hey, you wanna go outdoors with me? I've got a new basketball hoop on the garage.

We can play basketball. Katie likes to play—she runs after the ball, but she can't get her teeth around it, and maybe when Uncle Ram gets home from work we can go to his cottage down at Sandbridge and skip shells and stuff on the water! I bet you'd like that, huh? We can get ice-cream combs on the way, too, only don't tell Mrs. Suggs, 'cause she says it'll spoil our appetites, only it never does.''

So Ram had a beach cottage at Sandbridge. Something else he could offer that she couldn't—a vacation home.

"Come on, Aunt Grace, you will, won't you? You'll like Uncle Ram's cottage, only it's 'bout to fall overboard. Uncle Ram says it's corrosion. Is that like the juice that leaks out of old batteries?''

"*E*-rosion, not *cor*-rosion—although I suppose there are certain similarities.'' Which she proceeded to explain. When she thought about the solemn child who had visited her three years before, who had said little beyond a whispered "Yes, ma'am" and "No, ma'am" for the first few days of his stay, Grace couldn't help but be impressed at the way he had bloomed under Ram Adams's care. He seemed happier and more confident just since the last time she'd seen him.

Which, as much as she hated to admit it, meant that Ramsay Adams must be doing something right.

Which meant that Grace just might not be able to fight him, because Chad's happiness was the most important thing of all, not her own. And if he would be happier here than with her...

A weight of depression settled over her, and she fought it by laughing a little louder and jumping a little higher with the ball. When she collided with Chad under the hoop, she swept him up in an impulsive hug and kissed him noisily on the cheek.

"Aw, jeez, Aunt Grace, you didn't hafta do that," he complained, but she noticed that he didn't wipe it off, either.

She resisted the urge to hug him again, and it occurred to her that it had been years since she had hugged anything other than her pillow.

The ball ricocheted off the backboard, and Chad chortled as she scrambled backward to catch it. When she tripped over the excited spaniel, landing flat on her rear end and elbows in the middle of an unplanted flower bed, she began to laugh. She laughed until tears ran down her cheeks. Until her throat ached and her heart ached. And still the tears flowed.

"Hey, hey, what's going on here?"

At the familiar tidewater drawl, Grace looked up through her dirty fingers to see Ramsay leaning over her, resplendent in a steel gray suit with a muted rust, gray-and-turquoise silk tie. He held out an impeccable hand and grasped one of hers, which was filthy, pulling her to her feet and catching her against him before she could step back.

"Don't touch me, I'm all muddy," she said breathlessly.

His eyes seemed to devour her in the instant before he released her. Feeling as if she'd somehow been branded for life, Grace looked away and began busily brushing the dirt off the seat of her jeans. "I tripped over Katie," she muttered.

"Whoa—look here," Ram said, and she looked up before she could catch herself.

He brushed his fingers lingeringly over her cheek. "Dirt. You didn't land on your face, did you?" There was laughter in his eyes, and something else— something that made her feel as if she'd suddenly stepped into a vacuum.

Pushing away his hand, she scrubbed her face with her palms, smearing tears and dirt across both cheeks. "This is right up there with dousing you with champagne, isn't it? You'd think I'd learn."

"Would you care to waltz?" His eyes spoke volumes that Grace dared not even try to interpret.

"Hey, Uncle Ram, could we go to your cottage?"

Ram stared down at the diminutive woman in muddy blue jeans, sneakers, and a white-and-yellow plaid shirt. He couldn't believe he'd been fool enough to invite her here. It was bad enough that he'd seen her in her own home among her own things, and had that memory to haunt his dreams. Now she was going to haunt his lonely house with echoes of her warm laughter, her soft, husky voice and the quick sparks of anger that aroused him in a most inappropriate way.

Temporary insanity. It had to be that. *Non compos mentis.*

In his right mind, would he suddenly be seeing visions of her in his bed, and him in hers—of the two of them walking for miles on the beach in the rain, the fog, coming home to a warm kitchen filled with laughter and the smell of good things cooking and the promise of passion to come?

So it had come to this. He had finally lost it.

Chapter Five

Grace knew too late that she should never have come. It wasn't going to help her case, and it certainly wasn't going to do anything for her peace of mind. The times before had been different. The wedding reception, and the crazy way she had seemed to flow right into the arms of a stranger as inevitably as any river ever flowed down to the sea. The way she had followed his lead without a moment's hesitation. It had to have been the champagne, because she didn't even know *how* to waltz!

At the memorial service—and later, in the steamy little coffee shop—he still hadn't seemed quite real. Not the sweating, swearing, salt-stained, hard-working kind of real that Grace was accustomed to in the men she usually dealt with.

But real or not, Ram Adams was the man she had to deal with if she ever hoped to gain possession of her nephew. And while she might have cause to question his judgment, she couldn't really question his integrity.

The trouble was, he was also the man who had starred in all her choicest fantasies. Other women might dream of movie heroes, but for nine years, Grace had dreamed of a dark-eyed stranger who had held her and waltzed with her and made her feel beautiful and desirable for a few brief moments of an otherwise lustreless life. It had seemed harmless enough at the time. Looking back, she thought the trouble must have started that day at the coffee shop, because that was when the man and the fantasy had begun to merge.

But it wasn't until the fantasy had appeared at her front door, dressed in faded corduroys, a denim shirt and a bulky sweater, his hair all windblown, with the shadow of a beard darkening his angular jaw, that she'd finally, irretrievably, lost her grip on reality.

Sitting with him through the night while he slept off the worst ravages of the twenty-four-hour flu, she had dared to dream a different kind of dream. A dream not based on champagne and waltzes, but on sickness and health, better and worse, richer and poorer, and laughter and tears.

Once upon a time Grace had dared to dream of a man who would take her lukewarm, amateur fantasies and turn them into flaming reality. Now, remembering a few of the warmer of those fantasies, it was her face that flamed as she stripped off her mud-stained jeans and put on her last clean outfit, a pink chambray dress with a red braided belt.

"Living alone finally got to you, old gal—either that or you've got yourself a premature midlife crisis," she whispered to the mirror as she brushed her hair into obedience and tied it back with a scarf.

One thing was clear—she was going to have to snap out of it if she wanted to get through this weekend with a single shred of dignity intact.

Freshly washed, dressed and brushed, she stalled for time by examining the room she'd been given. It was probably the best guest room, but it could have been a furniture warehouse for all the warmth and personality it revealed. No scarf on the dresser, no pictures on the walls, not even a bedside rug. The walls were stark white, as were the venetian blinds and the candlewick bedspread.

There were three windows, one overlooking a brick-paved courtyard bordered by several empty planters, the other two overlooking what was probably intended to be a garden, only nothing was growing there except for a few scrawny shrubs.

What she wouldn't give for a truckload of that rich, loamy soil to mix with all the sand in her own garden! With dirt like that, she might even try her hand at growing roses, something she'd always wanted to do.

"Grace? Are you all right?"

Fighting the sudden rise of panic at the sound of that deep, rich accent, she took one last glance in the mahogany-framed mirror. "I'm fine," she said hurriedly. "I'll be down in one minute." She wasn't fine, she was shaking like a jibstay in a hurricane. *This is your fantasy speaking, Grace Elizabeth O'Donald. If you had the brains God gave an oyster, you'd have stayed home where you belonged!*

Without warning, the door opened and Ramsay stepped inside. "I, uh, wasn't sure if you'd skinned your hand when you fell. I thought you might need an antiseptic cream."

"No, thanks." But maybe a little digitalis or nitroglycerin to take care of my palpitations, she added silently.

"Remember I told you there might be a way?" At her puzzled look, he turned and stared down at the barren courtyard. "To share Chad. We could, you know—more or less evenly." He turned away from the window and moved restlessly around the room, looking out one window after another. Then he crossed the bare floor to stand before her.

Grace wrapped her arms over her chest. He was so close she could see the tiny crow's feet at the outer corners of his eyes, smell the subtle hint of citrus and sandalwood and something else—something musky and masculine and threatening. "I don't want to share."

"Have you considered that a boy might need a man in his life?" Looking away, Ram hooked his thumbs into the back pockets of his custom-tailored suit pants. If Grace hadn't known better, she would have thought he was ill at ease. He had shed his coat, loosened his tie and unbuttoned the top two buttons of his shirt, yet he looked as if his collar was too tight.

"I deal with men all the time. It's not as though I wanted to take him off to a convent. Anyway, it would never work with you living here and me living on the Banks. I take it you mean joint custody. One week with you, the next with me and so on. We might split the holidays—I get Christmas and Thanksgiving, you get Columbus Day and the Fourth of July, but what about school?" She sighed. "It just wouldn't work, Ramsay." The hair that she had brushed and tied neatly with a scarf began to slither free, and she shook it back impatiently.

"You didn't give me a chance. Look, this is going to sound crazy, but hear me out before you condemn my idea out of hand, will you?" When she started to turn away, he reached out and clasped her by the shoulders. "Grace, I've been doing a lot of thinking."

He'd been doing a lot of thinking! All Grace could think of at the moment was that if he didn't take his hands off her shoulders, she was going to melt all over him like butter on hot corn. "I'm listening," she said evenly, praying he couldn't hear her heart pounding in her breast. Unable to meet his eyes, she stared at his throat, mesmerized by the jerky movement of his Adam's apple as he swallowed. His skin, which was firmer and darker than she would have expected in a man who supposedly led a sedentary life, suddenly filmed with moisture. A wisp of crisp black hair curled in the vee of his shirt, and she fisted her hands at her sides against the urge to reach up and twist it around her finger.

"I'm talking about marriage."

Her eyes widened. Now she was the one who was feverish! Had he really said—?

No, she was fantasizing again. Or maybe she was having auditory hallucinations, which were probably a symptom of some dreadful, obscure disease. "Muh-muh-muh—" she stammered, her gaze clinging helplessly to his eyes.

"Dammit, don't look at me like that!"

"Like what?" she wailed.

"You're asking for this," he muttered just before his mouth came down on hers. After the first few moments of fierce, grinding force, the pressure eased. His arms came around her just before she collapsed, and she slipped into her old fantasy with the ease of long years of practice.

It felt so real. Melting, she clung to his shoulders, her body pressed tightly to his. He tasted better than champagne, better than anything she could have imagined in her sweetest dreams. After that first wild moment of teeth grazing teeth, lips bruising lips, his mouth began to move softly on hers, and she was lost.

Fleetingly it occurred to her that for a man who supposedly worked behind a desk, his arms were remarkably hard—as was the rest of him. When she tried to pull away, they turned to steel. He pressed her face to his shoulder, and his lips brushed her hair and strayed to her temple. They were both panting as if they'd been running, his breath warm and moist against her skin. Imprisoned by his gentle strength, she sighed and closed her eyes, surrendering to feelings more intense than anything she could ever have imagined.

It had to stop. She couldn't even think! "Ram—"

"Don't talk. Just don't say anything just yet, will you?" he whispered unevenly.

But she had to. Feelings got all mixed up in a fantasy, but words—words had meaning. Words were real.

Marriage. Had he actually uttered the word *marriage?*

"I didn't hear you," she said.

"I didn't say anything," he replied, still holding her so close she could feel the hard edge of his rib cage, the jut of his arousal.

"I mean—I meant—before."

"Before what, Grace?"

Was he teasing her? She didn't know him well enough to be sure.

Then why did she feel as if she'd finally come home after a lifetime of wandering? "I'm serious, Ramsay."

When he chuckled against her ear, raising goose bumps down her flank, she shoved at his chest. "Dammit, I'm serious!"

"You think I'm not?" His arms still held her captive. She could have broken away if she'd really wanted to, she thought guiltily. She might be small, but she was no weakling. Which meant she didn't really want to break free. Which meant she had lost and he had won.

Before she could force herself to react, his tongue traced the rim of her ear. Hypnotically caressing her back, he brushed her hair aside to trail his fingertips over her exquisitely sensitive nape and then slowly moved his hand down her spine to press her against his groin, where a telling tension still throbbed.

"Ram, whatever you think you're doing, it's not going to work."

"Isn't it? I think it's going to work better than either one of us ever dreamed it could."

"You're talking gibberish."

"Maybe. Maybe not," he said, and before she could argue he brought his mouth down on hers once more, with even more devastating results. This time he left no small part of her mouth unexplored. When he lifted his lips a long time later, Grace felt as if she'd been thoroughly, if lovingly, ravished.

Her hands flew to cover her burning cheeks.

"Look at me, Grace," Ram said gruffly.

"Stop it! Whatever you're doing to me, just stop it," she cried, wondering what had happened to her free will. With the gentle strength she was coming to associate with him, he forced her face up so that she had the choice of meeting his eyes or closing her own, and she didn't dare close her eyes. Not again.

"Ram, I can't think when you look at me that way!"

"How do you think I'm looking at you? As if I'd like to take you to bed?"

"Don't say that!"

"Well, you want me to level with you, don't you? How do you expect me to feel after the way you kissed me?" At her look of consternation, he began to chuckle. "Oh, yes, you did, too," he taunted softly. "I'm not so out of practice I can't recognize a woman in lust when I kiss one."

Grace groaned. She shut her eyes tightly, but it didn't help. How could it when he could read her mind? Knew all her secrets, all her most private fantasies?

That day at the wedding reception, when he'd pulled her into his arms and forced her to dance with him, he had to have known how vulnerable she was. The proverbial wallflower, in her brand new beige silk dress—her mother had graciously told her just before the wedding that beige wasn't her color, that it made her look sallow. With her hair, which she'd spent ages torturing with a hot curling iron, coming undone around her shoulders, and her poor aching feet in those wretched new high-heeled pumps...

Oh, yes, he had known exactly what he was doing. She must have been a barrel of laughs!

Only what was he up to now? She stepped back so that their bodies were no longer touching, but he didn't release her. Not entirely. Instead his hands caught and held hers, and short of making an issue of it, she couldn't pull them free.

"All right, you said wanted to talk, so we'll talk, but not here," she told him.

"Running scared?" he taunted softly, his slate-colored eyes gleaming with an unholy light.

"Of you? Don't be absurd. I don't know what your game is, but I can assure you you're not going to make me give up my claim."

"Is that what you think this is all about, Grace?"

"Isn't it?" She took another step back, and his hands fell away. It took every shred of courage she possessed to meet his eyes directly, but she did it, daring him to deny it.

Neither of them heard the clatter outside until Chad thumped on the door and called out, "Uncle Ram? Are you in there? Is Aunt Grace okay?"

Ram swore softly under his breath. "Yeah, son, she's fine. Tell Mrs. Suggs I'd like coffee served in the study, will you?"

"Can Aunt Grace and me play more basketball while you drink your coffee? It's still plenty light outside."

It wasn't. Dusk had fallen quickly as rain clouds gathered overhead. Ram looked at Grace with a rueful smile. Back to earth, his eyes seemed to say, and she tucked her hands under her arms.

Before she could agree, Ram shook his head. "No more basketball," he said as the boy opened the door. "Your Aunt Grace is going to be sore enough as it is after that tumble she took."

"Could we take her to the cottage? I bet she'd like to see your pictures and all that stuff."

"Tomorrow," Ram said, the tone of his voice leaving no room for argument. "Meanwhile, why don't we challenge her to a game of Chinese checkers after dinner?"

"Yip-peee!"

When the sound of Chad's hightops clattering down the stairs diminished, Ram moved to the window once more. "I hope you don't mind. You probably will be sore—I'd recommend a long, hot soak."

"I'll take it under advisement," she replied, thankful to be back to a world she understood.

"Yeah, you do that. And if you need any help," Ram said softly, a wicked grin on his face, "just sing out." Before she could think of a suitable retort, he added, "The boy loves games. Got a real competitive streak. I reckon I'm going to have to start following sports."

"Fishing is a sport."

"Commercial fishing? Come on, Grace, you're reaching."

"Well, it is!"

"Sure it is. Cast your net and haul 'em in."

"You make it sound so easy. Believe me, it's not. There's always an element of risk involved, but for some men, it gets in the blood—like gambling or football. Always waiting for that one big haul, just knowing it's going to be this time. And if not this time, then next time. Fishing can be a lot more exciting than fighting over a silly little ball.''

Ram leaned against the tall mahogany chest of drawers, his lean, muscular legs crossed at the ankles. "Is that why you do it, Grace? For the thrill of it?" There was an openly teasing light in his dark eyes.

"Hardly," she admitted wryly. "I fish because it's all I've ever done."

"What about your music?"

"Oh, that." She shrugged. "Three-quarters of a degree in music doesn't really prepare you for much in the way of making a living. So I take a few students and I substitute at church. Look, hadn't we better go downstairs before Mrs. Suggs comes up after us? I've more or less been warned about—you know."

"Hanky-panky?" he asked with a broad grin that subtracted years from his normally stern features.

Grace managed to murmur something unintelligible and all but bolted through the door, but Ram caught up with her on the stairs.

"Tonight, after Chad's turned in, we'll continue where we left off," he said quietly. "We still have some details to work out."

"I think you're mad," she shot over her shoulder, and at the sound of his low chuckle, she warned herself not to allow his madness to displace thirty-one years of her own pragmatism.

As it turned out, they didn't get around to settling any details until much later. First there was a phone call, which Ram took in his study. It lasted more than half an hour. Then there was dinner, and afterward Chad insisted on his game of Chinese checkers, which turned into a rout—two males against a single female. She beat them both hands down.

"I suspect you've played this game before," Ram teased as he tipped his chair back on its hind legs.

"Did I say I hadn't?"

"You didn't warn us you were a champ, did she, Chad?"

"Boy, I bet you're real good at a lot of games, aren't you, Aunt Grace," the boy said admiringly.

On the verge of modestly admitting her skills, she intercepted a look from Ram that brought hot color flaming to her cheeks. "Not all of them," she muttered, and started gathering up the popcorn bowls.

"Say good-night, Chad."

"Do I have to, Uncle Ram?"

"You have to, son."

Grace wondered briefly what had happened to the child who used to go to bed without a murmur, spoke when spoken to and stared down at his toes when someone asked him a direct question.

"Tomorrow we'll show your Aunt Grace our own beach, shall we? You can challenge her to a shell skipping contest, but I wouldn't count on beating her. I'm beginning to think the lady has a few surprises up her sleeve."

When Grace rose to follow, he called her back. "Don't go yet. We still haven't had that talk."

"Can't it wait until morning?" She was tired, but that wasn't the reason she needed to escape. "It's been a long day."

"You fished your traps this morning?"

"Pots. Yes. They'll hold until I get home tomorrow afternoon, but if they're full and I don't get out there for several days in a row, they'll start eating each other."

"It's a dog eat dog world."

"Or in this case, crab eat crab." She began gathering up glasses. "I'd better go put this stuff in the kitchen."

"Mrs. Suggs can take care of it in the morning."

"But—"

"Grace, sit down. A few hours ago, I proposed to you. I'd like an answer now, if you don't mind?"

Warily, Grace lowered herself slowly to a chair. "Exactly what was it that you proposed?"

"What was it that I—? What kind of question is that?"

He looked irritated. If Grace hadn't known him better, she might have thought he even looked embarrassed.

"I proposed marriage, dammit! What the devil did you think I was proposing?"

Chapter Six

Grace clutched the empty popcorn bowl in her arms and stared. Not until color began to flush his cheeks did it occur to her that Ram might be as uncomfortable as she was.

"You really meant it, then—what you said upstairs? I thought that sort of thing went out in the last century," she said finally.

"Marriage?"

"Marriages of convenience. The kind you're talking about."

He shrugged, not quite meeting her eyes. Which was just as well, as she couldn't bring herself to meet his for fear of what he might see there. "Most marriages are," he said gruffly. "Convenient, that is. For one reason or another."

"I suppose. I only meant—"

"Yes or no, Grace?"

"What if I said no?"

"Then I suppose we'd have to work out some other kind of arrangement."

Grace started to speak, cleared her throat, and then tried again. "And if I said yes?"

Something bright and hot leapt in Ram's dark eyes and was quickly extinguished. "Then we work out the details and go on to the next step. But you might as well know now that convenient or not, no wife of mine is going to sleep in a separate bedroom."

Trying to appear as composed as if she weren't on the verge of hysterical giggles—or tears—she said, "So you expect me to close up my home, sell off my boat and nets, take in my crab pots and—"

"I didn't say that."

"Oh? Then you intend to give up your law practice and move down to Hatteras and fish with me? Do you, by any chance, know enough music to teach it? We could share my piano."

"That's not all we'll share," Ram muttered. His mouth thinned to a hard line as he stood and slammed the lid on the game box. Fixing her with a scorching look, he said, "Just sleep on it! We'll talk again tomorrow. Meanwhile, I'd advise you to forget about it for tonight. If I know you, you'll only dig in your heels. By morning, you'll be ready to renege on the whole deal."

Grace rose with all the dignity at her command—which admittedly wasn't much at the moment. "There's no deal to renege on, and you *don't* know me. And I don't know you. And that's the real problem, isn't it?"

"Is it? Or maybe we know each other better than either of us wants to admit."

"We've seen each other exactly four times over a period of nine years. That's hardly enough to base a—"

"Nine years is a long time."

"Four times! A few hours, at the very most."

"Go to bed, Grace. Another day or so after all this time isn't going to make that much difference."

Much later, staring up at the glow of a security light reflected on the bedroom ceiling, Grace wondered if he honestly expected her to be able to sleep after being proposed to for the first time in her life.

He was probably an old hand at proposing, she thought with bitter amusement. Only, in that case, where were all his wives? Because she couldn't imagine any woman actually turning him down. He was everything a woman could want in a mate—strong, intelligent, kind and successful. He had a whimsical sense of humor—at least when he wasn't sick or trying to get his own way. As for the way he looked, tall, dark and handsome didn't begin to do him justice.

The wretch! No doubt he was sprawled out in bed right this very minute, snoring peacefully while she lay here stiff as an old beached croaker. Dammit, this was no fantasy, this was a blooming nightmare!

Early April was a time of contrasts. Wet, naked tree trunks silhouetted against banks of colorful blossoms. Sweet-scented breezes sifting flurries of leftover leaves across newly green lawns, while everywhere tender shoots thrust through crumbly dark earth in search of the sun.

Grace rose early from force of habit. Feeling pale and cross, she took her coffee outside and perched on the edge of one of the empty planters while her mind skittered frantically over one irrelevant topic after another, like a skater racing past patches of thin ice, desperately trying to keep from breaking through the surface.

Idly, she pulled up a stem of chickweed, the only thing that grew there. If they'd been hers, they would already be overflowing with pink and purple petunias, or maybe nasturtiums, with mounds of silvery artemesia and—

But they weren't hers.

Grace insisted on driving her truck to the cottage so as to leave directly from there after lunch. It wasn't the way Ram had planned things, but he didn't complain. He rode in the truck as navigator, leaving Chad and Mrs. Suggs to follow in his car. The day was warm and Sunday traffic to Virginia Beach was heavy, hardly the circumstances under which to press his suit. He resigned himself to waiting another week.

The cottage looked more dilapidated than ever after a hard winter. He tried to see it through her eyes. Five small rooms and a wraparound porch perched on stilts like a weathered stork. It was old, it was battered—in another few years, if the erosion continued at its present rate, it would probably be condemned.

Still, it had hung on for the four years since he'd bought it, and if the whole thing tumbled into the surf tomorrow, he would have more than received his money's worth. When it came to putting things in perspective, there was a lot to be said for beach walking in the face of a howling gale, or for reading by the light of an oil lamp when the power went off. Four years of therapy wouldn't have come much cheaper, and probably wouldn't have done half as much good.

"It's sort of, uh, casual," he said modestly, and Grace had to laugh.

"Casual. Right." She could tell he was proud as he could be of the place, and in spite of its obvious shortcomings, it did have a certain ramshackle charm.

"Well, come on up—watch the bottom step." He took her arm and the brief contact sizzled right down to her toenails.

Mrs. Suggs, grumbling about damp rot and mildew, turned to get the picnic baskets from the back seat of the car, and Ram took them from her and carried them upstairs, while Chad and Katie raced down to the water's edge, a few yards away.

"You know the rules," Ram called after Chad. To Grace he explained, "Don't worry, he knows the limits. I'll keep an eye on him from the window."

Ram turned on lights and opened windows in the sparsely furnished living-dining room while Grace examined a row of old photographs on the dark-paneled walls. Those and the collection of memorabilia all seemed to be related to the lifesaving service.

"Was all this stuff here when you bought the place?" she asked curiously, turning to watch as he opened a window facing the ocean. In a black knit shirt, his powerful forearms bare, the play of muscles as he strained to unstick the swollen wood fascinated her.

Everything about the man fascinated her. Therein lay the danger.

"No, it's, uh, I've always been interested in that sort of thing."

It occurred to Grace that he seemed almost embarrassed by the admission. "My great-grandfather was in the livesaving service," she said. "I remember Daddy telling me stories when I was little, about shipwrecks and rescues and patrolling the beach in the fiercest winter storms. Exciting, heroic stories."

Stories, she had come to realize, from a lonely man who was trying hard to convince himself that he'd done the right thing by clinging to his roots instead of pulling them free and following his wife and child to the city. Or perhaps stories to distract the lost, hurt child who had been left behind.

"My grandfather was in the lifesaving service, too—actually, it had turned into the coast guard by then, I believe," Ram said. "That was my mother's father. I never knew him. He died long before I was born."

"I guess we have something in common, after all." Suddenly, in spite of too few hours of sleep, in spite of all reason, Grace felt a rising tide of hope.

Ram leaned against the corner of a battered oak desk. In the warm light reflected from the ancient pine paneling, he looked younger than the thirty-seven years she knew him to be. His hair was wind-blown, his angular cheekbones flushed from exertion, and his thin khakis molded his hips with breathtaking faithfulness. "It would seem so. I might as well confess, though—I never studied music."

"I never studied law," Grace responded, struggling hard to keep her gaze above his shoulders.

"I'm allergic to shellfish."

She shrugged. "I'm allergic to poison ivy."

They both fell silent. Grace, wearing the jeans she had washed and dried the night before, was too aware of her body—and his. Too aware of the way he was looking at her. It was a physical sensation.

Reaching out abruptly, she picked up a corroded brass sextant from a shelf that held several maritime artifacts. "Was this your grandfather's?"

He shook his head. "I'd like to think so, but I doubt it. I picked it up at a salvage place."

"One of my great-grandfathers was a sea captain in the West Indies trade, sailing out of Norfolk.

Wouldn't it be strange if..." Their eyes met and held as possibilities shimmered in the air between them. Struggling to regain her balance, she said, "Daddy taught me how to read a chart and use a compass and a marine radio, but even out on the reef, I'm seldom out of sight of some familiar landmark, even if it's only a particular pound net. Except days when the fog comes up suddenly."

"Days when it's so thick you lose sight of the horizon," Ram said, nodding. "When you feel like you're standing at the edge of the earth."

"Yes," she whispered, suddenly lost in a different kind of fog. A fog that blanketed her common sense, one that dulled every shred of survival instinct she'd been born with. If Ram had opened his arms just then she'd have walked into them forever and never looked back.

The salty, iodiny smell of the ocean wafted through the house, quickly displacing the musty damp smell. From outside, against the crash of the surf, came the joyous sounds of a boy and a dog at play, yet they could have been the only two people in the world.

"Grace—" How had he moved so swiftly? Lifting one hand, he cupped her cheek, his eyes searching hers with a question.

"If you expect me to use this here stove to heat dinner, Mr. Adams, you're going to have to find me some matches. These here is too wet to strike."

For one seamless moment, they stared at each other. Then a wintry smile twisted Ram's mouth and he turned away.

A hot and cold picnic lunch shared the table with all the sandy treasures Chad had dragged in from the beach. Grace didn't have the heart to reprimand him, and obviously, neither did Ram. The meal was noisy, cheerful and impersonal, and soon afterward Grace left. If she felt vaguely unsatisfied, as if she'd been offered a feast and had it snatched away at the last minute, it had nothing to do with food.

During the drive south, she went over every word spoken, every look, every touch, searching for meaning, for possibilities.

In the end, all she found were obstacles.

The week crept by. Chad was involved in end-of-term projects, and Ram was involved in something he had set into motion immediately after his trip to the Outer Banks. Winding up his work at the firm and finalizing the arrangements for further study meant a series of fourteen-hour days and too many sleepless nights, but now that he'd set his course, he was determined to stick to it.

And through it all, at odd moments of the day or night, he found himself thinking about Grace. Dwelling on the way she looked when she was trying not to smile. Warming to the memory of her squeaky, triumphant little laugh when she'd jumped four of his marbles to win the first game.

A commercial fisherman. God, if ever a woman had been miscast, it was Grace O'Donald! He had no trouble seeing her as a music teacher, patiently going over and over something with some kid who wanted only to get through his lesson and race back outside—praising him when he accidentally hit the right note, wincing silently at the clinkers.

But a commercial fisherman? Going out alone in a small open boat in all kinds of weather—doing backbreaking work for damned little pay, risking her life with no one to know or even care if she ever made it back to shore?

Oh, no. Oh, hell, no!

The first time he had seen her had been at Tom's wedding. He'd tried to recall the little he knew about her from what Coral had said, not that she'd mentioned her sister very often. In fact, up until shortly before the wedding, Ram had assumed Coral was an only child.

But since those two waltzes with the "only child's" sister—waltzes during which neither of them had spoken a word—he'd had time to think about all the things Coral had *not* said. Ram had always been good at reading between the lines.

He forced himself to wait until Friday night to call. It nearly killed him. By Wednesday it was all he could do not to strike out on Route 168 south and drive like a bat out of hell until he reached that cluttered, wonderful old house of hers, take her to bed and make love to her until neither one of them had the strength to stay awake, and then wake up and start all over again.

But he didn't. Unfortunately he was a little too civilized to resort to caveman tactics. However he wasn't above using a little strategy.

"Chad's graduation's coming up pretty soon," he said over the phone on Friday night. "I'm afraid I more or less promised him you'd be there."

"You know I will!" She sounded breathless, which he took as a good sign.

"Were you outside?"

"No, I was sitting right by the— I was reading."

"So, anyhow, I thought we might get together this weekend and talk about it. We never got around to our talk last weekend. If you're not tied up, that is. If you are, I guess I could steal some time in the middle of the week to drive down, but—"

"I'm not tied up," she said in that husky little voice that got to him every time.

"Tomorrow, then. Don't worry if I'm a little late, I'll have to clear up a few things at the office first." He smiled. At home in his study, leaning back in his chrome and leather chair behind a desk that was piled high with files, he grinned like a wolf.

Not tied up? That's what you *think, lady.*

By ten o'clock on Saturday morning, the house once more smelled of lemon and pine, with the added bouquet of sweet potato pie. Grace hadn't the least idea when he would arrive, or if Chad would be with him. She did know the drive south would take a little longer now, as beach traffic had picked up.

Her head bristled with curlers, and she'd used a blue mud mask on her face, hoping for once in her life the magic would work.

But it wasn't the effects of any cosmetic sorcery that brought the becoming flush to her cheeks and the glow to her amber eyes when she opened the door a few hours later.

The sun had just touched down on the western rim of Pamlico Sound, spilling its lifeblood across the waters. The branches of live oaks, scrub oaks and leggy yaupons etched a black lace border along the shore. But Ram had eyes only for Grace. The sunset, the gleaming interior, the good smells emanating from the back of the house—none of it mattered. He had been here exactly once before in his life. So why did he feel as if he'd come home?

"I cooked supper," she said almost apologetically. "I wasn't sure when you'd get here—or if Chad...but maybe you'd rather go out. To a restaurant, I mean."

"Chad stayed home. Birthday party for a friend. As for what I want, I want whatever you want," he said, meaning it in a way that left him feeling badly shaken, because suddenly it was entirely true. Nothing else mattered.

The boy, of course, but that would work out. His practice? The home he had bought that had never been a real home? The fact that he was a Norfolk lawyer and she was a Banker fisherwoman?

Irrelevant, all of it. He knew suddenly that only the man and the woman mattered, and if that part of his life was right, everything else would fall into place.

She didn't resist when he reached for her. They made it just inside the door, and then her arms came around his neck, her body swayed against his, and her lips parted just as his mouth came down on hers.

God, he couldn't get close enough to her! Couldn't get enough of the taste of her! He slid one hand between them to cradle her breast, and the feeling swept over him that he was home. It was crazy, but he'd never been more sure of anything in his life.

Eventually they ate. Afterward, he could never remember what. They must have talked, too, because people did. Sane, civilized people didn't sit across a table from each other without uttering a word, lost in a mutual fog.

Ram had left his bag on the bottom step. After rising from the table, clearing away the remains and washing dishes by hand—they must have talked then, if only to say, "Where does this go? and "Where shall I put this?''—they moved toward the stairs by unspoken consent.

Grace's heart was pounding. Her palms were sweaty, and it had nothing to do with dishwashing. Side by side on the steep, narrow stairway, they climbed, hips rubbing hips, arms about waists. Grace could hardly breathe. She knew what was going to happen. They both knew what was going to happen, and were too mature to pretend otherwise.

She wanted him. He wanted her. Against all reason, she was deeply in love with him. He wanted to make a real home for Chad, which was admirable. Marriages had been based on far less and succeeded, only she didn't want to think about that just yet.

"I could swear I hear music," he murmured. "Do you hear a waltz?"

"I hear a flock of cardinals feeding out back—they're always the last ones to eat. And don't you dare remind me of Coral's reception." She buried her face in his shoulder as she led him into her bedroom. "I was so embarrassed. What must you have thought of me."

"I thought—" Ram began, but she covered his mouth with her hand, laughing softly.

What had he thought? That she was utterly lovely, only not in any ordinary way. Not beautiful the way Coral had been beautiful. Grace had the kind of beauty that shone from inside out. The kind that snuck up and walloped a guy before he knew what hit him.

Not until much later had he pieced together the details of her life—the fact that Irene, whom he had met several times but had never particularly liked, had taken her youngest child and walked away from her husband and oldest daughter and never looked back.

It would have been devastating to a sensitive child. God only knows why she hadn't turned out bitter and wild. Instead whatever she'd felt—pain and loneliness at the very least—she had subordinated into making her father's life as complete as it could be under the tragic circumstances. Sharing the rugged life of a fisherman, she had tried to hang on to something of her own—her music—but in the end, even that had been denied her.

And now she was prepared to devote the rest of her life to making a home for her nephew.

"You know what this means, Grace?" Standing beside the bed in the yellow-and-white room, Ramsay was struck by the quiet dignity that had drawn him to this woman from the very first.

"That we're going to sleep together?"

"That we're going to make love together. And then we're going to see about getting married as quickly as possible."

"But I haven't said—"

"But you will," he said, gold lights flashing in his dark gray eyes. "I don't think we have any choice." Releasing her from his arms, he began unfastening the buttons down the front of her shirt. After that, there were no more words until Ram lowered her onto the bed, hurriedly removed his own clothes and joined her there.

Easy, now, don't be in too big a rush.

Yeah, right! You're already shaking so hard you could barely get your clothes off. Go ahead—impress her!

Drawing in a deep, shuddering breath, he let his gaze play over her body. For all her strength, she was delicately made. Made for love, but Ram suspected she'd known damned little of it. He tried to suppress a fierce and unexpected surge of triumph, but was only partially successful.

Grace lay on her back self-consciously, and Ram leaned over her, one hand brushing her hair back from her face, the other at the base of her throat. Deliberately he lowered his mouth to hers, hovered there for an infinite moment before proceeding to kiss her with a thoroughness that left them both shaken.

Lifting his head, he stared down at her. When he continued to stare, silently, doubts crept into Grace's mind. He couldn't go through with it. She wasn't pretty enough. She wasn't experienced enough. If it hadn't been for Chad, he wouldn't even be here.

She wanted to bury her head under the covers, but they were lying on them. "Oh, Lord, how did I get in this mess?" she muttered, and he began to chuckle. She could have hit him! "Better yet, how do I get out of it?" she snarled, and he laughed outright, and then buried his face in her breasts.

"Sweetheart, there's no way you're getting out, not unless—"

"Unless?" she whispered, her hands moving over his silky, naked back.

"Unless you can honestly tell me you don't love me."

And then, suddenly, he wasn't laughing any longer. Lifting his eyes, he stared down at her. "Grace? You do, don't you? Please God, tell me I didn't screw up, because if I misinterpreted the evidence, then I—"

"I do."

"... Might as well go back to—" His eyes narrowed. "You do? You do *what?*"

"What do you want me to say?" she asked helplessly. "You've got to know I'm caught tighter than a gar in a gill net. What more do you want?"

"What do I want? Everything! Only everything, sweetheart! Patience, right now, but I'm afraid it's too late for that." He laughed again, a crow of triumph, and Grace found herself laughing, too. Suddenly his body was hot against hers, hard and muscular everywhere. This time when he kissed her, he rolled her in his arms until she was lying on top of him, his hands tangled in her hair, her hands trapped between them. She could feel the thunder of his heart, feel his thrusting desire, and it was Grace who led the way, shifting and twisting until she was astride his hips.

"Sweet—ah, sweet love, I wanted to go slow the first time, but—"

"You didn't ask what I wanted," she murmured.

"I'm asking now." His lips were asking. His hands were too busy elsewhere.

"You," she whispered. "I want you."

He raised her up until she was positioned, making her hover there while he gazed through her eyes into her very soul. And then, slowly, very slowly, he took her.

A long time later, they got around to talking. Lying in bed, still wrapped in the hazy afterglow of love, they talked about the child they both loved. They talked about her work, which was largely seasonal, about his plans to specialize in maritime law, which would entail more study.

Somewhere between a cold snack and making love again, they spoke about summer homes and winter homes, about growing roses and rearing children, about roots and responsibility.

And love. They both had a lot to say about love. In fact, it would probably take years even to begin to scratch the surface.

* * * * *

SPRING

Spring? A dozen things come quickly to mind. Open windows with the scent of honeysuckle flowing in. Packing away the winter clothes and wondering if it's too soon. (It always is.) Wondering if the ground is warm enough to plant butter beans. Hanging clothes on the line and trying not to step on one of the bees working the violets and creeping Charlie underfoot. Freshly turned gardens, earthworms, cane-pole fishing...

Spring is hope. Spring is promise. No matter how long and hard the winter, no matter how bleak the horizon—no matter how barren the windswept landscape, with its gray patches of ice, its naked trees and drab brown carpet—sooner or later, spring always happens. A shoot of green appears. And then another one. The sun's warmth sends a silent signal, and magically, dormant seeds cast off their hulls and sprout wings of green.

It happens every year to each of us, old or young. No matter how unending winter seems, there's always the promise of spring. In the air, in our hearts, in our souls.

A special spring wish for each of you,

LIGHTFOOT AND LOVING

Cait London

To springtime lovers.
To those who love anytime.
To those who find new loves.
To Gaye, Jeanne, Patty, Helen,
Dorothy, Julie and more.

Chapter One

Morgan Lightfoot allowed himself a tight smile, an unusual event. The April sunshine slid through his 1956 Chevrolet Bel Air's windshield to warm him. The car was a fitting and necessary element in Morgan's quest. He was on his way to exact perfect and exhilarating revenge against his nemesis, S. E. Loving.

He checked the rural Wyoming intersection before easing his car into it. A metallic flash caught his eye and he jammed his western boots down hard against the clutch and the brake pedal. The spotless, recently hand washed and waxed four-door classic beauty squalled; its perfectly tuned motor shuddered, fought for life and died.

A late-model Buick sedan suddenly swerved around him, hitting a series of deep holes, and sped away toward the aptly named small town of Pothole. Morgan closed his eyes and behind his lids remained the face of the woman driver revealed by the small cleared space on the muddy windshield.

S. E. Loving.

Morgan drew a long, slow breath, clamped his lips grimly closed and turned the key of his mechanical pride and joy. The motor hummed, responding to his touch. More than a perfectly tuned carburetor and a humming engine, more than perfect, original upholstery, Alice had been his love since high school. He usually drove a sturdy four-wheel drive Ford pickup back and forth to Laird University, where he was a professor of history, but Morgan had selected Alice to perform this mission. She'd hummed perfectly from Kansas City, Missouri, to the rural, mountainous intersection only to be nearly raped by a mud-covered Buick.

He tapped his fingers on the large steering wheel, then caressed away a speck of dust on the dashboard. He inhaled again, easing the tightness from his lean, six-foot-three-inch body. Ahead of him, the Buick barreled over the unpaved road leading into Pothole, just the way S. E. Loving coursed through life.

Morgan placed his palm lovingly over Alice's passenger seat, the exact area where Loving had once spilled soda. He was sixteen and had just gotten Alice back from her new paint job, the one that concealed her new junkyard fender. At eleven, Susanah Elizabeth Loving was already his nemesis. The day she desecrated Alice, Morgan had been forced by his mother to take Susanah to the grocery store. Since Susanah's mother had not been feeling well and since the Lightfoots and the Lovings were next door neighbors, Morgan's mother had offered his services.

Lacy Norton at fifteen. At sixteen he'd pictured Lacy—budding breasts, long, long tanned legs in short-shorts, a thick fall of blond hair and an inviting lush mouth—snuggled in his arms at the drive-in movie. Just like every teen male in Pritchard, he'd fantasized about Lacy—down on her back on Alice's comfortable front seat. Their private love nest would be shrouded by Alice's steamy windows....

Morgan shot a scowl at the Buick, almost concealed by the dust rising from its tires.

Lacy's back never got to Alice's front or back seat because of Susanah Elizabeth Loving, alias S.E. Loving. Morgan had yelled when she'd spilled her soda on the seat, and she'd cried. Not soft little weeping tears, but raging, tortured, very loud wails, which the whole town heard, including Lacy Norton, who accused him of child-beating.

At forty-three now, Morgan had never forgotten Susanah's contributions to his painful teenage years.

His ex-wife had a bit of Loving's kamikaze determination. After a scalding divorce at thirty, he'd decided to leave commitments to the more savage sex out of the picture. He'd escaped permanent entanglements, though he'd had an affair or two along the way.

Morgan pushed harder on the gas pedal. Susanah's and his life continued to collide upon occasion. While he helped search for unique additions to Laird University's Americana Museum, S. E. Loving was employed by a private museum fostered by wealthy patrons. In the past ten years, she had scooped exactly twelve good acquisitions from his hands using the same kamikaze-style attack with which she now approached Pothole.

Morgan had plans to revenge Loving's last and final coup, the Foster family's antique wooden loom. While Loving had beguiled the Fosters into the donation before Morgan got full approval for purchase, she would not snatch Annabelle Merrill's beloved collection of antique Cutesy-Wootsy dolls.

Morgan allowed himself another tight, grim smile. When the museum gossip dropped the news that Loving was on the scent of a big donation, Morgan's ears had perked up, his desire for revenge surging like a trout after a low-flying spring bug. *This time S. E. Loving was not walking off with the prize.* Annabelle's darling antique Cutesy-Wootsies would clutter the Laird Museum shelves, not Loving's classy little uptown morgue.

Morgan wanted revenge and he was getting those damn Cutesy-Wootsies.

Susanah Loving glanced in her rearview mirror at the gleaming red classic Chevrolet. She would recognize that model anywhere. Lightfoot's broad-shouldered bulk and grim, dark scowl filled the driver's side of Alice's windshield. His eyeglasses were tinted, giving him the appearance of Darth Vader.

"Wolf," she corrected darkly, using the label museum circles had placed on Morgan Lightfoot. Though he taught American Western History, he also was the director of Laird's fine museum. Professionally, he could seduce, invite and ultimately possess a find—a museum acquisition—with methodical precision. Susanah tightened her lips. As her competition, Morgan made her work very hard to obtain her better finds. The last few she'd scooped from his grasp had sent her ego soaring.

She gripped the steering wheel and pressed down on the gas pedal. The car shot forward over the dusty lane as she thought about Lightfoot.

A hard-driving workaholic, Lightfoot's thick wavy hair was prematurely gray. Plain-rimmed glasses shaded those hawkish black eyes and softened his blunt, soaring cheekbones and hard, unsmiling mouth. Susanah skimmed a glance into her rearview mirror and noted the grim set of Lightfoot's dark, unshaven jaw. It lowered into a muscular neck, then there would be that inevitable thatch of dark hair curling at the base of his throat.

Susanah inhaled. He really should shave those whorls of black hair, thus trimming a little of the primitive male image from him.

"The West Was a Man." Susanah muttered the name of the all-male association over which Lightfoot presided. He hunted and researched bits of western lore, such as his recent find, the diary of André DeGermaine, a Taos and Santa Fe shootist.

Her patrons would have paid outrageously for the DeGermaine diary, but Lightfoot had gone on an all-male hunting and camping trip with the owner to insure the donation.

Lightfoot was good at hunting, she decided, frowning as she glanced in the mirror. While she recognized his ability to scour out a good find, she detested that smug little curve to his lips. She always had, especially when he'd told her that Oscar, her goldfish, had committed suicide rather than live with her.

She was just six that summer vacation, and her parents made her leave Oscar with Morgan Lightfoot. Lightfoot was then eleven, and a bike-riding fiend who ran her off the sidewalk when their parents weren't watching and who disdained knowing her when his friends surrounded him.

He still did that during their occasional meetings—lifting his left, thick, arrogant black eyebrow to stare aloofly down at her. Her need to throw something at him hadn't diminished in thirty years. The past few occasions they had met in museum circles, the black eyes behind Lightfoot's lenses had a peculiar gleam. Rather predatory and vengeful, as though he was waiting for something. For the past year, there was an aura of a gunfighter waiting for a showdown. At the Jennings's last party to celebrate the acquisition of the Foster loom, she'd caught him staring at her. Lightfoot's jaw had locked then, a primitive little muscle jerking beneath his dark skin.

She knew that he was out for revenge. No doubt he'd grumbled over the way she'd cooked dinner for the Fosters and served it on a lovely hand-loomed tablecloth. Susanah couldn't help it if the Fosters believed she had actually woven it herself. She hadn't, but she had once used a child's hand loom to make a pot holder. The experience had served her well.

Susanah sniffed and tilted her head, scanning the small town's streets for the house Annabelle Merrill had described. Mentally running through her checklist for the look that would appeal to the almost ninety-year-old lady, Susanah decided her neat navy blue skirt and cotton blouse perfectly matched the April day. She eased a strand of long, light brown hair up into the neat chignon she always wore and straightened her practical glasses. The neutral frames were sedate to perfection. The little antique cameo at her throat would appeal to the older woman and Susanah would use it to note how she meticulously cared for anything in her possession.

The Cutesy-Wootsies would be in her possession, or rather, in the Jennings's private museum.

She blinked, her body suddenly chilled with a dire premonition. *Why was Morgan Lightfoot's cherry red, classic Chevrolet cruising in Wyoming, far from Kansas City?*

The frozen chill squeezed her heart just as she spotted Annabelle's house. The two-story, white gingerbread house with a picket fence was just as the elderly lady had described it on the telephone.

Susanah's eyes jerked back to the mirror and found Alice right behind her. The massive gleaming bumper blinded Susanah when it wasn't dulled by the shade of the tall pines bordering the road.

"Blast!" Susanah took a last lingering look at Annabelle's house and drove past it. Lightfoot might not recognize the Buick, but she didn't want to take chances. She circled the block and parked in the driveway of a house. The elderly man and woman rocking on the front porch watched her with curiosity. She waved to them, commented on the nice warm day, and waited until Alice slid by, then circled the block to park behind Annabelle's house. Susanah gripped the steering wheel with sweaty hands.

There was only one reason Pothole would attract Lightfoot—the Cutesy-Wootsies.

Susanah closed her eyes. She envisioned the adorable little porcelain dolls' delighted grins. Then she saw Lightfoot's big, possessive fingers closing around them. Her heart pounded and she shuddered. "Oh, no..."

She wouldn't let the Cutesy-Wootsies fall into Lightfoot's fist. Taking a deep breath, she smoothed her neat chignon and slid out of the driver's seat. Because it wouldn't do to approach Annabelle from the back of the house, Susanah was forced to walk to the front gate in the picket fence. She looked stealthily up the street. With just a heartbeat's grace ahead of Lightfoot, she could sway Annabelle to donate the dolls to the Jennings private museum.

She glanced down the empty street, opened the gate and walked to Annabelle's house. The slight chilly wind from the mountains tinkled in the wind chimes on the porch as Susanah walked up the steps. The hairs on the back of her neck lifted just after she turned the old-style door knocker. Susanah glanced back to see the cherry red Chevrolet glide up to the sidewalk in front of the house. Her heart stopped when Alice's finely tuned engine died.

"Oh, hello," a woman's kindly musical voice said when the door swung open. Susanah pivoted to the woman, smothered a panicked urge to push her back into the safety of the house and lock the door. Standing in the huge doorway, a small, elderly lady with a wispy gray topknot peered out at her. She smiled graciously and blinked behind the glasses that perched on the tip of her nose. She glanced past Susanah's shoulder to the big man walking toward the house. When Lightfoot was at the first step, Annabelle waved to him. "Oh, dear. I just love a man who drives a red classic Chevrolet. Henry, my poor departed husband, would have adored it."

Annabelle beamed from Susanah, who couldn't close her parted lips, to Morgan, who returned his most devastatingly male smile. Susanah knew him better than anyone. When Lightfoot smiled that way, he could be lethal. Her throat squeezed closed when she tried to speak, but Annabelle was delighted. "I'm so glad you brought your husband, dear. Now I can see the two of you together. You're a beautiful couple. I won't let the Cutesy-Wootsies go to anyone but a loving husband and wife, who will love and take care of my beloved precious little darlings just like I have for almost eighty years. I'm getting on a bit, you know, and I want to know that my precious little ones are in hands that would please my husband. I'm afraid my children have failed miserably as Cutesy-Wootsy candidates. Since I advertised in the doll journal for interviews, I've turned down any number of single parents."

She sighed, blinked up at Morgan and laughed. "My, you remind me of my Henry. I promised him on his deathbed that I'd only let the Cutesies go to a loving family. It's not that I've anything against single parents, but Henry made me promise, you see. He was like that, a very old-fashioned, wonderful man."

Susanah held her breath, closed her eyes and wondered why she had never married. Perhaps Lightfoot had scarred her, turned her against males at an early age. No, that wasn't it. She'd had an affair and found the whole event as enchanting as glue. Nothing had ever stimulated her like a good find for her museum. With the sense of falling off a high cliff into a deep, treacherous whirlpool, she glanced up at Lightfoot, who was watching her with that one cocked-high black eyebrow. There was something fierce and angry flickering in his eyes behind the lenses. Then she knew—Lightfoot had appeared to snatch the dolls into his grasp. The smug curve of his mouth challenged her. She swallowed and cleared her throat as Lightfoot walked up the steps to take and shake Annabelle's hand.

While Susanah fumbled for words, Lightfoot bent his head and kissed her lightly. The slight brush of his lips across hers stunned Susanah, who tried to scramble back into the current time zone. Lightfoot took away her options with one sentence in his deep, quiet voice. "Mr. and Mrs. Morgan Lightfoot. My wife, Susanah."

"Lovely couple. My Cutesies need to be surrounded by affection. Come in, won't you?" Annabelle's rippling laughter followed her into the house.

Susanah glared up at Lightfoot. He whoofed when her elbow jabbed his flat stomach. "What do you think you're doing?" she growled.

"Coming?" Annabelle's light, cheery voice prompted from the shadows of the house. "Go ahead and visit with the Cutesies. I'll start lunch. Won't be a moment."

"Shut you up, didn't it?" Lightfoot asked in his gravelly voice. "She wants a married couple, she gets one. We'll work out the details later."

"'We'll work out the details'?" Susanah asked in a low explosion of indignation. *"We?"*

The flat of his hand on the back of her waist startled her, the strength behind it denying her effort to resist. "Get inside," Lightfoot ordered quietly.

Susanah narrowed her eyes up at him. "You won't get them."

His mouth curved slightly. "Stop arguing before I kiss you again."

"Yuk! Phooey! Gag!" Susanah returned, instantly resenting how easily Lightfoot could cause her to revert to a nine-year-old child. She closed her eyes to his slow, wolfish, disarming grin. She ran the tip of her tongue across her dry lips and scowled up at him.

"Mmm," he said thoughtfully, as though he had just tasted something delicious.

"Gads, Lightfoot, you'll get yours," she whispered and stepped into the doily-draped parlor. African violets fused with a variety of plants, lacy full-length curtains allowed the sun to slant down to the polished wooden floor softened by cabbage rose patterned rugs. The scent of apple pie and pot roast mingled with lemon furniture oil. The house was full of love, the enchanting nuance wrapping itself around Susanah.

Startlingly male in the small, cluttered frilly room, Lightfoot wore a red knit sweater that stretched across broad shoulders. His worn jeans sheathed narrow hips and long legs. The comfortable cowboy boots only added to his western aura, one that Annabelle would no doubt find appealing, since her husband had been a retired rancher.

"Cut the act," Susanah said out of the corner of her mouth. She wished her lips would stop tingling from his uninvited kiss.

Behind his lenses, his black eyes slanted down a threat. "Touchy? Moving too long in the slow lane are we? Well, my, my."

She eased around his tall, muscular body under the pretense of examining the Cutesy-Wootsies, which sat in front of a massive dollhouse. The ten bisque dolls were in perfect condition, sitting on individual chairs surrounding a miniature tea set. Only ten inches tall, they looked like chubby little girls dressed in their best dresses and black patent-leather shoes, and giggling enchantingly over an eighty-year-old secret. Each dress had been sewn by hand and embellished with hand-tatted lace. Tiny starched slips with lace peeked from the dolls' skirts.

"So this is all that's left of the great doll-maker, François Bergerac's original handmade twenty dolls," Morgan whispered into Susanah's ear. His body leaned slightly against her back as she bent to the collection, studying it with a magnifying glass.

His husky voice startled Susanah, the warmth of his breath swirling around her ear, and she straightened. Their glasses bumped, jammed against each nose. "Would you stay your distance from me,

Lightfoot?'' she asked between her teeth as she rubbed the bridge of her nose.

Those fierce, black, predator eyes narrowed instantly as he rubbed his nose briskly. "Give me one reason why I should. You're trespassing on my acquisition, Loving.''

He stood there, tall and arrogantly male, with his tilted head. The sunlight passing through a lace curtain deflected off his lenses like a laser spear.

Annabelle swished by, carrying a tray with a teapot and cups and saucers. The little woman barely reached Lightfoot's broad chest. "You know, for some reason, I didn't recognize the name Lightfoot when you called earlier, Susanah. For some reason, I thought your name was Loving.... Oh, dear, I hope my years aren't showing," she noted worriedly.

Susanah smiled weakly. While Morgan wasn't welcome to the Cutesies, she liked the elderly woman immediately and didn't want to distress her. "I kept my name for professional reasons. We're on our honeymoon," she lied.

"You are? How wonderful. I'm so happy for the both of you. Do you have children?" Annabelle placed the tray on a small doily-covered table near an overstuffed couch with more doilies and turned to study the newly married Lightfoots. She clasped her hands dreamily.

Morgan cleared his throat, looking amazingly startled. It was the first time Susanah had seen that expression on his face. "Ah, we hope to have children," Susanah added for good measure and momentarily enjoyed his wary, shocked frown, quickly replaced by a loverlike gaze. Annabelle's bright blue eyes sparkled as Morgan took Susanah's left hand in his big one. Her stealthy, determined attempt to withdraw her fingers from his possession was easily denied. She pushed her lips back from her teeth, feigning a smile.

Annabelle beamed. The lace covering her breasts almost tremored in happiness. "Wonderful! I wouldn't want my Cutesies to be the reason you didn't have children, although they did ease the pain of my two children's passings. I have two other children, but they live a distance away. You see, the Cutesies were beloved by all my family. They have returned that love with cheerful little faces for eighty years. Oh, I didn't have all of them at first, but Papa saw how much I loved them, and he ordered the rest. Lucy was the last. That's her," she said, pointing to the dolls. "She's a bit uppity today because she's wearing her favorite red bow in her hair."

The elderly woman smiled benignly, studying Susanah and Morgan. "My, you're a handsome couple. And on your honeymoon." She sighed dreamily. "This is just perfect. There, sit down on the couch, Morgan. Don't worry about hurting it, my Henry was a large man, too. In fact, you remind me of him, especially the jeans and the boots." She laughed, a merry, lilting sound that Susanah immediately liked. "We'll visit awhile and then the pot roast will be finished. I hope you're hungry. Henry could almost eat a whole roast by himself. I love cooking big meals and miss it, now that I'm alone," she added wistfully.

Susanah flexed her fingers, straining away from Morgan's. He bent to brush a kiss on her hair and whispered, "You're not wearing a ring, Loving. I'm just helping out by concealing it."

Obviously interpreting Morgan's whisper as an endearment, Annabelle tilted her head and waited, her face glowing with a happy smile. Morgan eased himself down into the couch and Susanah sat stiffly near him. The cushions sagged toward Morgan, forcing her to lean against his side despite her efforts to sit apart. His wolfish smile infuriated her; so did the way he rested their joined hands on his hard thigh. The muscles beneath the worn denim shifted as he made himself comfortable. The smell of soap and a unique spicy tang that Susanah interpreted as Morgan's personal scent wafted over her.

Annabelle clasped her hands to her bosom and sighed. "Newlyweds." Her eyes lighted. "I want to see you together with my Cutesies. We just have time before lunch. You sit right there, Susanah—what a lovely, old-fashioned name—and Morgan—such a strong, masculine name, a perfect match. I'll bring the Cutesies to you. I want to see how they react to you and you to them."

She scurried back and forth, the scents of sunshine and ironed clothing clinging to the dark navy cotton dress with its pink flowery sprigs. Eventually all ten of the dolls were evenly split on Susanah's and Morgan's laps. Morgan looked distinctly uncomfortable, which pleased Susanah.

She noted that he eased Lucy away from his zipper and carefully placed the doll's cheery smile toward the huge potted fern. Annabelle continued chatting merrily along, stopping periodically to sigh and lovingly study the picture of Susanah, Morgan and the dolls. She introduced Lucy's friends, Magnolia, Jessica, Betty, Mary, Elizabeth, Rachel, Opal, Fay and Belle. Each doll had unique characteristics and Annabelle pointed them out as they sipped their tea.

Careful not to indispose the dolls, Susanah was forced to rest her body cozily against Morgan's hard one. From the dark gleam behind his lenses, he was no more happy about the play than herself. Because he was uncomfortable, she took a small bit of revenge and allowed her head to rest a moment on his shoulder. His body tensed immediately, the padding of muscles tightening beneath her cheek as she looked adoringly up at him. She smiled lightly, while inside her a happy little voice of experience told her his expression concealed a nasty bit of temper. She made a mental note of "Score one."

While Annabelle continued her melodic, happy dialogue about the individual characteristics of each doll, Morgan smiled and bent to kiss Susanah. Not the brush of his lips at the doorway, but a full-fledged teasing play of his mouth across hers. The wooing, seductive light caress caused Susanah to stop breathing. She blinked, startled as her mouth began to lift to his. Before she eased away, she noted a dangerous flare to Morgan's nostrils, his eyes narrowing behind his lenses.

She studied the incredible gleam, shocked at the sensual hunger within it. *Lightfoot had wanted to deepen the kiss. Lightfoot! Her archrival!* The kiss had nothing to do with acting, which was even more shocking. She blinked again, trying to ease her body away from his hard one. Her efforts served to nudge her breast against Morgan's upper arm. It tightened instantly, and something leapt deep in his black eyes.

The doll tumbled into his lap again; Morgan jumped and Annabelle laughed merrily. "That imp, Lucy did the same thing to my Henry. It took him a bit to get used to my Cutesies. But he did because he loved me."

Throughout the tea, Morgan said little and once Susanah caught him looking at her broodingly.

She fought the slow, steady flush that worked its way from her throat to her cheeks. She licked her lips and Morgan's narrowed black gaze jerked to her mouth.

Her heart thudded in her throat. She placed her fingers over the cameo and found it throbbing with a wild beat of her pulse.

" . . . You'll stay with me," Annabelle was saying when Susanah returned to the conversation. "I've always liked young people staying here. I'm thinking about opening a bed and breakfast, specializing in newly married couples. Just the other day, I was saying to Fanny Lemon that Pothole needs a new industry. The church's little bazaar every week isn't enough to keep me busy."

She sipped her tea, and smiled smugly. "You see, Fanny has always been a competitor—Henry and she, well, once . . . seventy or so years ago, she tried to woo Henry away from me. I put a stop to that, I can tell you. But now she's determined to have the first honeymoon bed and breakfast in Pothole. She scooped my idea! Oh, now, don't think I'll charge you. This will be a wonderful week or more, depending on how much time it takes you to know the Cutesies. Usually it's about a week, though." She clasped her hands and sighed. "Young people in love always make me feel so happy. I'll cherish every moment you're here. Of course, you must make yourself at home."

Annabelle's thin finger shook teasingly. "Don't think you youngsters need to spare those little hugs and kisses around me. Love is a wonderful thing to see." She beamed beautifully. "I'm looking forward to your visit. The bedroom upstairs is all ready for you. Now, don't worry about your size, Morgan, dear. My Henry and myself were quite comfortable on that four-poster bed and I'm certain you are his same height.''

A wisp of hair escaped her gray topknot as she whispered, "Why, Susanah, you're blushing. You remind me of myself as a bride. If Morgan is as much like my Henry as I think he is, you'll keep that lovely honeymoon sweetness all of your lives. Shall we have lunch?''

Chapter Two

After lunch, Morgan glanced down at Susanah as she walked by his side. Her head was high, her mouth tight and her hand was stiff within the confines of his. Annabelle waved from the porch. "Have fun, darlings," she called in her delightful, musical voice. "See you in a little while. We're having peach cobbler, steak and potatoes tonight."

Susanah eased into Alice's front seat when Morgan opened the door. He crossed to the driver's side and slid inside. "Scoot over here, Loving. You're supposed to be my bride, remember? You should *want* to be close to me," he said between his teeth.

She stared at him menacingly from behind her lenses. He noted that the honey brown shade of her eyes darkened into rich chocolate brown when she was angered. "You want those dolls, don't you?" he pushed, resenting his surging sensual hunger when he had kissed her earlier. "Scoot over here."

Her fingers tapped her thigh. Then, taking a deep breath, she gingerly eased across Alice's seat to sit near him. Morgan resisted the urge to snap at her. Instead he reached out his right arm, firmly captured her stiff shoulder and jerked her against him. Susanah's lips pressed together and a dangerous gleam shot up at him. "Will you stop?" she demanded.

Morgan concentrated on the firm, resisting hand she had placed against his ribs, pushing him away. He tried to ignore the nudge of her soft hip against his as he started Alice.

"You've gotten us into a neat little mess here, Lightfoot," she began. "A fine kettle of bass."

"Fish," he corrected, looking for the jewelry store that Annabelle had recommended when he shyly admitted to forgetting the ring Susanah had placed on the windowsill while doing dishes. They'd driven two cars, Susanah had supplied, because at times, Alice needed towing. Morgan caressed Alice's steering wheel. "Alice has never failed me yet," he said in her defense.

Susanah snorted delicately in disbelief. "So you're going to buy me a simple gold ring to commemorate our honeymoon, eh?"

"Worked, didn't it? We need the time to talk." Morgan suddenly realized that S. E. Loving was the only woman who had every truly resisted his plans. He avoided confrontation with females whenever possible; now it seemed that S. E. Loving, confrontation female summa cum laude, could not be avoided. He pulled Alice up to the curb in front of the small jewelry store.

Susanah eyed him warily. "If I have to wear a ring, you have to wear one, too."

"You're being childish, Loving. Reminds me of when you made me taste that slime medicine when you had pneumonia that time. You wouldn't take it unless I did," he returned, uncomfortable with the memory of the lingering softness of her lips and the knowledge that just for a heartbeat, they had clung to his. He looked at her now, all five feet six inches of Viking War Maiden, gathering herself into a ball to maul him. Since she weighed ninety-five pounds less than himself, the tussle wouldn't last long.

He eyed her warily and reconsidered the tussle. From all her constant fidgeting, he deducted she was fast and wiry. The thought of pinning her beneath him slid across his mind, shocking him.

"I'm not sharing a bed with you, Lightfoot. Much less a bedroom." She crossed her arms in front of herself and stared at an elderly man using a cane to cross the street.

Morgan smiled with all the nastiness only Loving could draw out in him. "We're honeymooning, remember? Annabelle loves hugging and kissing."

"Yuk. Phooey. Not with you," she returned, sliding across the seat and jerking open Alice's door. Morgan grimaced when she slammed the door.

He walked to her. "Fine. Let Annabelle know that we're an unhappy couple. That my bride refuses me my lawful rights in her bed. There goes the dolls."

"Cutesies," Susanah shot back, looking up at him. Her chignon had begun to loosen in its moorings, and she jerked the pins away, leaving her honey brown hair loose. "They're mine, Lightfoot. Find an excuse and leave."

He pushed his lips back from his teeth. "No, honey, sweetheart, baby. *You* leave and I'll explain to Annabelle something or another."

" 'Baby'? Is that what you call those floozies you used to park with up on Moonlight Ridge?"

"Jealous?" he shot back.

She sniffed again delicately and walked toward the jewelry shop. Morgan was left studying the interesting full sway of her backside. He frowned as her skirt swished around her shapely calves, his gaze sliding down to her slender ankles and small feet. "I'm losing it," he muttered as he followed her into the store, reluctantly admitting that he'd always been attracted to women with nice legs.

They purchased two cheap rings with quiet, terse determination, and Morgan forced himself to quietly close Alice's door on Susanah's grim stare. He crossed to his side, opened the door, and found her furiously pumping Alice's clutch. "I've always wanted to drive a clutch car," Susanah said while she concentrated on scooting the seat closer. "I'll drive us back to Annabelle's."

Without thinking, simply defending his beloved Alice from Susanah's marauding little fingers—one of which wore a new solid gold band—Morgan bent, lifted Susanah, and plopped her down in the middle of the seat. "Stay there," he ordered tightly and slid gently into Alice's seat.

Alice purred beneath his touch, easing the tension that seemed to spring into him at each touch of Susanah's soft body. On the way back to Annabelle's, she sat dutifully close to him, fiddling with her new band. "I like this, Lightfoot. It will be my trophy when the dolls are in Jennings' showcases," she said, studying the gleaming gold on her pale finger. "I'll reimburse you the difference between your band and mine when this is over. I think I'll keep it as a reminder of making you eat crow."

"You won't get the Cutesies by being nice," he returned. "They're mine."

"Wrong."

Morgan inhaled to steady his worn nerves, then moved Alice off the highway onto a private shaded glade. He stopped the motor and turned slowly to Susanah. "Get this straight. You mess up this donation and the museum circles won't be big enough for the both of us. When I really want something, I get it."

"Wrong, again." Susanah smiled grimly. "I like Annabelle. She's delightful. I wouldn't hurt her for anything. But if you kiss me one more time, Lightfoot... I won't be responsible."

Her challenge was too much. Morgan opened his door, caught Susanah by the waist, eased her to her back and laid his full length on top of her, just the way he'd wanted to do with Lacy Norton.

Maybe it was the sight of Susanah's long, tanned legs that reminded him of his hormonal days. He didn't know. He just knew that Susanah had tossed him a challenge he couldn't refuse.

Susanah didn't move. She stared up at him with her calm honey brown eyes, her lips pressed together tightly.

He noted that her skirt was wadded between them and the jostling had popped a button from her bodice. A lacy pale pink bra shimmered across the swell of Susanah's soft breast. He noted the peak surging against the cotton blouse, and the scent of her body wafted up to him. She still used baby powder, he realized distantly.

"Our legs are dangling out the door," she said in a husky, low voice. "Nice. Very professional look for museum curators."

"Uh-huh," he returned, watching the slight breeze slide a silky honey gold strand across her hot cheek. He eased it back with the tip of his finger, enchanted by the shy, wary gaze.

"A fine kettle of bass you've got us in," she whispered unevenly, her fingertips gently squeezing his shoulders. The timid pressure excited him. The sensual emotion coursing through him, tightening his body, startled Morgan. He discovered his hips pressing into the gentle cradle of her thighs.

She inhaled suddenly as though she had not breathed in several heartbeats. The motion brought her breasts up to his chest. Morgan couldn't stop his gaze from sliding down to the soft contours, nor his chest from gently settling down on hers.

Susanah cleared her throat. "Ah...what's this supposed to prove, Lightfoot? I won't be intimidated. I won't leave because of threats to my person and being squashed in Alice or on an antique bed."

Morgan closed his eyes and tried to stop the pounding need in his body. His body wasn't listening. The need to taunt Susanah just as he always had rose too sharply to be denied. He slowly lowered his head to kiss those surprisingly tempting lips. They rose a tiny fraction to meet his. "Do you know how to kiss, Loving?" he asked huskily. "We'll have to practice a bit to put Annabelle off the scent."

"Wouldn't want Annabelle to be unhappy with us," she whispered back unevenly, her fingertips tightening on his shoulders. "But we're a little old, and you're definitely too tall to be lying in Alice's front seat."

"We could try the back," he suggested gallantly, stealing a tiny, tempting kiss. He noted that Susanah didn't play games; she regarded him steadily from behind her glasses. He took them off, and his own, and placed them on the dashboard. They were steamed, anyway.

Morgan placed his cheek alongside Susanah's just as he had done when she'd been really upset at four years old. She'd been crying about a dead bird, one he'd just shot with his slingshot, and had crawled up into his lap, nearly upsetting him. He never shot birds again or anything else, her heart-racking sobs disintegrating his killer instinct. Even back then, she had managed to topple his "cool."

The rise and fall of her breasts ceased. "You're heavy, Lightfoot," she whispered unevenly against his ear.

The gentle, wispy, husky sound tore at him and he turned his head slightly. Their lips brushed. Again. Morgan closed his eyes with the sweetness of the caress. A haunting ache slid through him, a warm sense of coming home. It curled inside him, filling all the empty, cold corners.

He felt as though rose petals, the deliciousness of Mom's apple pie, spring sunshine and rainbows enclosed him. He wanted to wallow in the warmth, grab it with both fists, sniff the happiness and snuggle deep in it, letting it pour into every scar of life and cleanse his deepest, most secret being. He wanted children laughing as they tumbled into his arms, a wife doing the same, and the long empty nights filled with cuddles and caresses and lovemaking. *Lovemaking....*

His eyes jerked open. S. E. Loving lay beneath him, her mouth moist and parted, her cheeks flushed and her eyes heavy with sensuality. "Taking a status check, Lightfoot?" she asked huskily. "You won't scare me off with these tactics. I can hold my own," she said, her voice catching in a whimsical little breathless way that excited him.

"Can you?" he asked gently before taking her mouth in the way that he had wanted.

Morgan puttered around the house that afternoon, noting the supplies needed for bracing up the front porch. He tightened several loose shutters with the grim determination not to think about S. E. Loving's soft body beneath his in the big four-poster bed in Annabelle's upstairs bedroom. S. E. Loving was a tough-minded hoarder, scavenger, and had taken away his last acquisition, the Foster loom. His reputation was at stake; he needed revenge.

His body was at need. He was tense and the sudden sensual awareness that plagued him intensified every time Susanah came near. As he sat in a wooden lawn chair, Annabelle had posed them for her camera shot, seating Susanah, clad in jeans, on Morgan's lap. Clad in jeans, her soft derriere nestled against him set off a dangerous, sensual awareness that he'd never had with another woman.

S. E. Loving, he thought grimly, while Annabelle scurried closer to better drape Susanah on his aroused body. "Just a kiss now for my album. I'll want to remember how much in love you two were when you first met my precious darlings."

Susanah inhaled impatiently, her hand tense on his shoulder. "Get on with it, Lightfoot," she ordered, squirming slightly on his lap to get more comfortable. She stopped, stared thoughtfully at Annabelle's sundial, blinked, and frowned up at him. "You have a definite problem, Lightfoot," she said warily, easing from his lap.

Susanah adjusted the sheet she had placed across the cord running from the top to the bottom of the bed. She straightened and smoothed the folds of her old-fashioned and beloved long granny gown. At nine o'clock, the old house was settling in for the night. With Annabelle fluttering around the house, making certain that her honeymooners would be comfortable for the night, there was little time to discuss sleeping arrangements. Annabelle had dressed the dolls in their nighties, carefully explaining that Magnolia preferred daisies on her gown, while Rachel liked long sleeves. Morgan and Susanah had silently agreed to discuss the whole matter behind their bedroom door.

Susanah was not leaving Morgan alone with Annabelle for a minute. He was too treacherous and appealing. If he wasn't stopped, he might use Annabelle's love and run with the dolls at midnight. Therefore she was forced into more kisses and contacts with Morgan's huge, fit body. She frowned; he probably smothered his affairs in melt-down kisses and body heat. There was something else—a winsome hunger that would be difficult for any woman to deny.

She listened to the floor creaking and resented the time she'd had to leave him alone in the bathroom.

Only the challenging lift of his black eyebrow at the bathroom door had stopped her.

Before supper, they had just stepped into Annabelle's pantry for a heated discussion of who had parentage rights to the Cutesies. Annabelle's happy humming had startled them and Lightfoot had jerked Susanah to him for a kiss before the pantry door opened. "Oh! Here you are," Annabelle had cooed, beaming happily. "Never mind me, I just wanted a jar of peaches."

Annabelle had patted Susanah on the shoulder as she scurried past to the peaches. "Henry was just like this boy...always showing me how much he loved me. I was quite breathless throughout our marriage."

Annabelle had watched their faces when she showed them the lovely old-fashioned bedroom and huge four-poster. Unable to speak at that moment, Morgan and Susanah had stood stiffly, considering the patchwork quilt and dust ruffle affair. The elderly lady had hummed, reached up to pat Morgan's shoulder, and had gently pulled open a dresser drawer to reveal a wooden mallet. "Just a tap or two and the bed won't creak as much," she had whispered.

Morgan's dark, grim face had flushed, making the bedroom scenario almost worthwhile. When his narrowed gaze had swung to Susanah, searing her, her cheeks heated.

Annabelle had glanced up in passing Susanah, pressed her arm, and whispered, "You'll have to tend those scratches on your neck, dear. My Henry used to have a heavy beard, too." Morgan had grinned wolfishly when Susanah's fingers found the tender abrasions. Right there, in front of the bed and Annabelle, he'd bent his head to kiss her hot cheeks. Then he'd bent to lick the tiny chafed marks below her ear. The moist tip of his tongue had raised chills on her body. Then he had grinned that gotcha grin and Susanah had gritted her teeth behind her smiling lips.

Now, as she prepared for a night of sleeping beside "Wolf" Lightfoot, Susanah's frown deepened as she adjusted the folds of the sheet. Morgan could kiss. He'd used tidbits of tender, seeking, arousing little kisses...or devastating, hungry, sensual kisses that had left her stunned lying beneath him on Alice's front seat.

He'd seemed quite pleased with himself, his hair mussed by her fingers, his lips slightly swollen with the kisses she had returned hungrily. Then there had been that long, slow, devastating look down their laminated bodies, her bare legs cradling his long jeans-covered legs. His hunger had flickered before he'd shielded it from her. He'd kissed her again gently and said huskily, "Why, Loving, I think you may have acquired a new wrinkle or two."

Annabelle's blue eyes had twinkled merrily when they'd returned, though she didn't say anything about Susanah's wrinkled clothing. Annabelle had seemed inordinately pleased when the sheriff had called and asked questions about the cherry red classic car in front of her house. The sheriff had spotted the car in the local lover's lane. He'd spared Annabelle the details of the four feet sticking out of the driver's open door.

Susanah shook her head. Tasting Morgan was like licking a stick of dynamite. Of course he would know how to kiss well. He'd practiced with Emily Zelling at twelve and every girl he could get his hands on since then. Now that Susanah had sampled him a bit, she wondered what moves Morgan had used to get the finds from that widow and the divorcée. She shook her head again. She really didn't want to know his moves. Her own experience had been an attempt to live with a man who'd expected her to be his mother. Their lovemaking sessions had produced frustration and yawns.

She dimly remembered older girls talking about Morgan's legendary melt-down kisses. He'd gone away to college, and had ignored her on their brief, necessary neighborly meetings during the holidays. Through the years, her mother had kept her informed of Morgan's marriage and soon-to-follow divorce. "Poor Morgan. He wanted children so desperately. His wife didn't. He's never been quite the same since. He's in the same business as you are, Susanah. Collecting musty old things and sharing them with museums."

Susanah had to admit that Morgan's professional skills almost matched hers . . . almost. After all, she had the Foster loom to her credits.

She placed four stacks of big, thick books down the center of the bed. Hands on hips, she studied them, then eased the books closer to what would be Morgan's side. She walked around the huge, hand-carved, four-poster considering her workmanship. She studied her long granny gown and decided that no one could term it as inviting. The light flannel covered her from throat to ankles.

Morgan was definitely playing a rough game. Sensuality was the one thing she hadn't been prepared to find in his tactics. Then he'd had the nerve to act as disgusted as he was sensually hungry. He was padding down the narrow hallway now, the old floorboards creaking with his weight. Susanah remembered that weight and the sudden dark flaring of his black eyes as he leaned down to kiss her.

He would stop at nothing to get Annabelle's darlings.

Susanah moved around the bed and got between the sheets. She laid her head back on the pillow and crossed her arms over her chest. She would discuss the matter with Morgan reasonably, and bribe him if she had to stoop to levels he understood. They were both adults . . . or rather, she was, while he— Well, Morgan's aroused body had startled her . . . and surprisingly, had interested her more than the Cutesies.

The doorknob turned and after a slight hesitation, Morgan slid into bed. It sagged, squeaked, and the books began toppling on him. He grabbed the sheet, cursed, and righted the books. "What are you doing, Loving?"

Behind the sheet that separated them, she remained wisely quiet. She'd had enough of Morgan the Melt-down Kisser for one day. She was tired and wanted to chat cozily with Annabelle in the morning. Annabelle planned to start her bread making at dawn. While the lovely little lady kneaded, Susanah had plans to influence her. With luck, she could pack the Cutesies, or at least get Annabelle to sign a release to Jennings Museum before Morgan issued his first yawn. Like Annabelle's beloved Henry, Morgan would not do anything to hurt the adorable woman's big heart.

Susanah sensed that in him, the protector of children and innocents. There was that time he'd fended off a gang of thugs from a helpless grandmother and a child. He'd destroyed eight bullies with some fancy kick-boxing judo thing, then chased down the one that got away. He'd climbed over fences and rooftops, swung through a window and collared the young tough. On a camping expedition, he'd risked his life scaling a sheer bluff to rescue a young woman whose bravado had died.

Susanah sniffed. That young woman probably thanked him in ways Susanah didn't want to consider.

She tapped her fingers on the patchwork quilt and remembered the tense muscles on Morgan's shoulders as he had lain over her in his car. He'd trembled against her, his eyes dark with sensual hunger.

He'd startled her at first. She'd never experienced a man staring at her as if he could devour her, nor with that unique tenderness. What had he muttered as he had sat up about being a "sucker for baby powder"?

Susanah closed her eyes. She recognized the incident for what it was—Morgan testing her, foraging out her weaknesses to make her leave. She smiled grimly. She'd foraged out a few of his weaknesses and strengths during that little bout. Whatever he wanted, however badly Morgan Lightfoot wanted something, he would not do anything hurtful. Deep down, she knew that. He would just work and chip—as he had done with those melt-down kisses—until he got what he wanted.

Her eyebrows jerked together. *Not this time.* The Cutesies were hers and the Foster loom had proven she was much faster than Morgan in getting what she wanted.

The moon shifted through the budding aspen tree beyond the bedroom window to paint shadows on the rosebud wallpaper. The house creaked, the front porch wind chimes tinkling musically in the gentle spring breeze. Susanah drifted off, listening to the music, contemplating the arrangement of the dolls in Jennings' showcases.

Morgan shifted slightly and the books toppled over on him. He grunted unpleasantly, muttered a curse and began placing them on the floor. Susanah sat up, clasping the sheet to her chest. "What are you doing?" she demanded as the old bed squeaked with Morgan's efforts.

"Researching data," Morgan retorted in a flat, disgusted tone. He jerked the draped sheet aside and peered into the shadows at her. "Loving, if you think that this little mess—" he tugged at the rope "—would stop a man from taking a woman, you're not in the real world. Maybe you should take that little thought back to Jennings with you in the morning."

She smiled nastily at him. "Maybe that won't be all I'll be taking back to Jennings."

He stared at her hard, looking disgruntled, rumpled, and thoroughly disgusted. She noted the moonlight skimming from the window across his broad shoulders and down the inevitable thatch of hair that covered his chest. With his evening stubble, Morgan looked dark, primitive and challenging.

Susanah blinked. Little tingles of awareness shot through her as she remembered that warm, hard body over hers on Alice's front seat. His gaze traveled over her face, her hair, and he scowled at the sheet drawn protectively to her chest. His expression was one of absolute disgust. "I bet you sleep with a bra, Loving," he muttered before slashing the sheet closed and lying down. "Though you're obviously not in the training bra stage now. Why don't you just get to sleep now so you'll be rested for your trip home tomorrow?" he suggested.

She eased back to the rosebud pillowcase, trying to dismiss the scent of freshly washed male stretched out beside her. The bed creaked as she moved and again as Morgan shifted. "If you don't stop moving, Annabelle will think we're—"

Morgan completed her sentence in a slow, gravelly, back-of-the-neck-hair-raising drawl, "Making love? You and me, Loving, kissing and rolling and sweating on the sheets? My, my—"

Her fist into his shoulder stopped the taunt. His fingers around her wrist warned. The bed creaked rhythmically, gently bumping the wall, while she tried to dislodge his grip. Morgan whipped off the separating sheet and flung it at the wall. "I'm making my bed on the floor," he said quietly, staring at her.

"No, you're not. I am," she returned and tried to reclaim her wrist. She noted suddenly that Morgan's expression had changed to a puzzled frown. His fingers were caressing her skin.

Between his teeth, he said, "Fine. Then it's settled. You're sleeping on the floor."

Her eyebrows lifted. Morgan had pushed her into a corner and had gotten his way—just like he wanted to do with the Cutesies. "I wouldn't move off this bed if a herd of tarantulas inhabited it."

"This won't work," he said finally after a brief silence of wills. He lay down and placed his hands behind his head as he looked across to her. That wary, hungry, flickering sensual heat swirled from him to her. She shivered as his gaze flicked down her quilt-covered body. "Do you always wear granny gowns?"

"You can't scare me off," she returned, easing back to her pillow. Her throat wouldn't let her breath escape. She licked her dry lips. "Keep your comments about my bras to yourself, please."

"I sleep naked," he returned slowly, watching her. The moonlight played around the cords and muscles of his chest and Susanah experienced the dizzying need to rummage her fingertips through the hair there. "I've changed since you watched me skinny-dipping at the lake," he said.

Susanah closed her eyes and behind her lids remained the image of Morgan's youthful lean body swinging from a rope and plunging into the lake. If he hadn't killed Oscar, she would have thought Morgan beautiful just then. Fish murderers weren't beautiful—

She discovered she had said her last words aloud. Morgan stared at her. "Oscar committed suicide rather than live with you. I knew it when I found him belly up in his fishbowl."

Susanah inhaled, the grief over Oscar's death still shimmering a bit in her adult heart. She knew then that nothing could keep her from attacking him. She surged at Morgan with a fierceness she could not deny. The bed creaked fiercely as he deftly turned her squirming body under his and pinned her wrists to the bed. "So here we are," he said in a deep, raspy voice.

"Let me up," she whispered desperately, aware that her body was responding to his. The bed creaked pleasantly, rhythmically, as she squirmed beneath him. Morgan's heavy thighs easily weighted hers.

"You're a soft little thing, Loving," he said huskily. Then, startling her, he simply placed his head next to hers on the pillow. "You always were, and always so fierce in your beliefs, protecting and cuddling everyone who needed it, except me."

"You never needed me, Lightfoot," she whispered, uneasy with this new gentle turn to him. To fight her uneasiness and the fluttering in her heart, she said, "You were callous. You said you flushed Oscar out to sea."

He nuzzled her throat, causing her heart to flutter faster. His lips edged aside the high nightgown collar to rest against her skin. "I did. When my mother found out that you were sick over mourning Oscar, she wouldn't let me have her apple pie for a month. I remember feeling like the scum of the earth when you looked at me after Oscar's demise. One tear plopped out of your eye—" He gently kissed her left eye. "Just there. An eleven-year-old boy can't always hug and make things better.

Sometime he's so unnerved that only a macho burst of cruelty can cover what he's really feeling. I'd forgotten how shattered you were."

She breathed lightly, warily absorbing this new Morgan. While she had hated the boy, something inside her wanted to hold the man. "I'm tired, Loving. Very tired," he whispered sleepily against her throat.

"Get off me," she ordered breathlessly, totally aware of every inch of Morgan's well-defined arousal between her thighs. "You won't get the Cutsies this way. I can't be bought."

His body tensed and his head went up. "Bought? The word implies that you might find my lovemaking to have bargaining power."

"Romeo," she tossed at him.

"Juliet," he returned, bending to kiss her gently. She noted with distraction that Morgan was always very careful how he kissed her, as though he was tasting a tempting new sweet. The bed creaked as he pressed down gently on her hips, his tongue prompting her lips to open. "Did that precious little live-in teach you how to kiss, Loving?" he asked unevenly.

"You're squashing me," she said breathlessly.

"You could be on top," he offered, watching her intently.

"This isn't game time," she whispered when she managed to push away the image of her body accepting Morgan's big one. While she'd wondered about the enthusiasm of lovemaking, she hadn't really tested any limits. When his hand slid slowly down her body, she bolted with the sensation of being claimed, possessed, desired. Her head hit the headboard, the bed creaked loudly twice and crashed to the floor. Morgan's heavy body remained on top of her, though he had braced his weight from her.

They lay there, in the depths of the monumental headboard, footboard and four posts, and stared at each other.

"There's no way Annabelle could have not heard that," she whispered finally.

"No way," he repeated, still staring at her with that penetrating stare, as if he were trying to understand something dark and mystifying. "You look shattered, Loving. As if you just discovered something. What was it?"

She didn't want him to know how badly she wanted to experiment with a sensual delight she had never known...but somehow knew that Morgan would make love to her very gently, very thoroughly, and that he would not walk away when it was over—their lives were intertwined. The news had startled her. Unnerved her. Frightened her.

"If you'll get off of me, I think I'll just go jogging now," she managed, desperate for time and space away from Morgan.

He grinned, looking very rakish and pleased with himself. She blinked at his devastating, appealing boyish look, and something shifted inside her heart. "Up," she said.

"Annabelle locked the house. She's afraid Fanny will steal her honeymooners," Morgan whispered, easing off her to lie at her side. She contemplated his lazy grin and jumped to her feet. She picked up the hem of her gown, then stepped across his prone body onto the floor.

Dressing in a small closet wasn't that easy. Eventually she was victorious and stepped back into the room wearing her jeans and a sweater. Morgan watched with interest while she tied her laces. "How are you planning to get back inside, Loving?" he asked in a taunting drawl.

"The same way I'm going out," she said, opening the window and stepping through it onto the old roof.

Chapter Three

Morgan scraped his back, grimaced with the slight pain, then wedged his body through the open window. He didn't want to be responsible for damage to Susanah's body. From the rooftop, he scanned the number of pickups slowly prowling by Alice. The shiver of fear that he always felt when his car was in danger doubled and swung to the agile woman making her way across the many angles of the old house. The roof creaked warningly beneath his weight while Susanah nimbly crossed to an antiquated rainspout. "Get back here, Loving," he ordered in a hushed yell.

"I need air that Oscar's murderer isn't breathing," she returned in a hiss, leaping to another angle of the roof and squatting to ease herself over the edge.

"I did not overfeed that sardine," Morgan muttered, then remembered her other accusation of the murder method. "And I did not spit chewing tobacco into his bowl." Morgan found his heart had stopped beating. Fencing with Susanah had become deeply ingrained in his life. If she were hurt, maimed, or that beautiful little neck snapped— He inhaled sharply and decided instantly that he hadn't

had his fill of grazing on that silky neck or listening
to the purrs coming from within it. Dressed in jeans
and a sweater, Morgan eased his worn jogging shoes
gingerly across the roof. The mountain breeze
chilled the sweat on his forehead and he fought the
nausea of fear as Susanah expertly shimmied down
the rainspout.

She dusted her hands in the garden's shadows,
placed them on her hips and stared up at him.

That pale little face challenging Morgan stilled
him suddenly. He realized as he eased cautiously to
the rainspout that ran to the earth that no one had
ever tested him like Susanah. The strange part was,
he was relishing the idea of catching her—like
tracking down a really good "find." While he tested
the ancient guttering and the rose trellis, she jogged
in place, stretched her hands to her toes and then
above her head. He noted distantly that two cars had
stopped by Alice now, their headlights shooting into
Pothole's vacant streets. He scowled at them. Little
Pothole was an interesting place after eleven o'clock
in the evening. Carefully easing his foot to the wood
trellis, Morgan clung to the roof as he worked his
way down. Eventually he had to release the roof and
clench the rainspout. He managed to descend to the
last angle of the roof before the trellis broke and the
rainspout creaked and pulled free. He snagged a
branch, which bobbed with his weight. The thought
of his six-foot-three-inch body dangling like a sheet
in the wind caused him to close his eyes. Images of

his American Western History students laughing up at him passed by his lids. He opened them when the branch popped and began tearing free from the tree.

Morgan leapt the last five feet to stand at Susanah's side. "You'd make a pitiful cat burglar," she said, grinning at him. "Maybe you're too old for this. You weren't very good at it when you were fifteen, either. I used to watch you wait until your parents' bedroom light went out and then you met Matty Johnson. I could have beaten your time then, too."

"Now, I wonder how my mother found out about that..." Morgan murmured, fascinated by the woman grinning impishly up at him. He was startled to find himself bending down to kiss her lightly. Her lips gently pushed at his.

Morgan found his hands gripping her upper arms and his head slanting to deepen the kiss. The wonderful aura of coming home steeped through him again. Rose petals dusted his shoulders, baby powder caused him to think of children, and Susanah's timid answering response was lifting his hormonal level with lightning speed. She inhaled gently, placed her hands on his waist, and her sweet, untutored lips demanded that he follow his basic instincts. He jerked her to him, wanting her to be a part of him, to be a part of his life.

The second time the man cleared his throat, Morgan forced himself to lift his head. Susanah's face caught the moonlight—her lips were soft and swollen, slightly parted, and she looked...she looked well-heated. Morgan closed his eyes, opened them, and tucked Susanah's trembling body against his. Whatever happened, whoever had cleared his throat, Morgan knew that he would protect Susanah. "Yes?" he said to the man pinning them in the bright beam of his flashlight.

A barroom voice issued a slow, deadly growl. "I'm the sheriff. I want to see some identification. Now."

Morgan glanced down at Susanah, who had wrapped her arm around his waist as though she would never let him free. Then she stepped in front of him, but kept one hand latched to his belt. He had the incredible sense of being protected by her one-hundred-plus-pound body. Despite the scenario, he rather liked that feminine strength anchored to him. "Sorry to cause all the disturbance. I left my identification in our room. We were just heading out for a little run."

"This is Annabelle Merrill's place. We had a report—two people were seen climbing out of her window." The flashlight beam shifted up to the window and Morgan saw the outline of a burly man wearing a big western hat.

"We're honeymooning here," Susanah said, draping herself around Morgan and snuggling closer. Morgan noted that his chin fit exactly over the top of her head. The breeze teased him with a strand of her silky hair. For some unexplainable reason, he liked the idea of how well they fitted together—except on the ownership papers of the Cutesies. He blew the strand and the light flowery scent away.

"We'll see about that," the man growled, motioning for them to approach the front porch. Moonlight glinted on the gunmetal in his hand. Morgan noted that the sheriff was almost seven feet tall and the size of a brick wall.

Annabelle opened the door before the sheriff rang the doorbell. "Why, Buster. How nice to see you," she cooed in her musical voice.

Morgan noted that the sheriff, stooping beneath the roof of the porch, winced uncomfortably.

"Annabelle, we had a report of someone crawling out of your upstairs bedroom window. These two were smooching in your garden when I arrived. Do you know them?"

"Of course, Buster. They're my honeymooners ... my first customers in my bed and breakfast. *I* have the first bed and breakfast in Pothole, not Fanny. You know, they're the ones you saw parked in the lover's lane in the car with the steamed-up windows. Come in, children. You'll get cold, just standing there. You may go home now, Buster," Annabelle said firmly with the air of retrieving lost kittens.

The burly, mountainous sheriff shifted uneasily. "Uh ... Annabelle, would you mind calling me 'sheriff'? Most folks stopped calling me Buster before I was twenty. That was forty years ago.''

"I'll work on it, Buster. You were always such a sweet boy," Annabelle said cheerfully. "Come in, children. Some people don't understand how newly married people like to cavort a bit, but I do. Henry and I cavorted every chance we got. So did the children with their spouses. Scampering down the roof, kissing in the pantry, never leaving each other alone for a minute—it's wonderful to have all that activity back in the house again."

She drew Susanah into the house and beamed at Morgan. "My, you do remind me of Henry. He broke that rain gutter more times than I can remember. It never seemed to mind my weight. We spent some of our nicest making-up times after we fixed the rain gutter. You can fix the bed in the morning," she said, standing on tiptoe to kiss Morgan's cheek. She bid the reclining Cutesies another good-night, then kissed Susanah's hot cheek. Annabelle whispered something dreamy and wistful about young, heated blood and moonlight as she passed them. Humming a big band of the '40's tune, Annabelle sailed off into her bedroom directly beneath theirs.

Morgan turned to Susanah, his jaw grinding rhythmically. Because he looked wary and sheepish each time the breeze banged the bent rainspout against the house, she reached up to pat his stubble-covered cheek. "You're not in my league,

Lightfoot. Give it up. Kiss the Cutesies goodbye. Night, night.''

Then she raced up the stairs, took her time dressing in the closet, put on the nightgown and stepped into the fallen bed.

Her foot hit his hard, flat and naked stomach. He grunted, jerked her ankle slightly away and placed it onto the mattress. "Don't talk," he ordered grimly when she settled and pulled the quilt up to her chin.

Morgan turned his back to her, taking a good share of the quilt. Rather than disturb him, Susanah lay still, grinned with her minor victory and plotted the layout of the Cutesies in the showcases. The foot that had landed on Morgan's stomach tickled from the light dusting of hair. She rubbed her arch on the sheet and stilled when Morgan's two feet enclosed hers. He didn't turn, and for a good hour she contemplated the safe feeling of those two large, warm feet cradling hers. If her bedmate wasn't Morgan Lightfoot, she could grow to like the gentle capture.

The next afternoon, Susanah sat on a sun-warmed rock near the riding path. While the horses grazed nearby, she studied Morgan. He stood outlined against the Wyoming blue sky like a cowboy from yesteryear, all hard angles, long legs spread wide, his western hat shadowing his face as he stared out into the rocky buttes. Morgan looked as solitary and distant as his namesake, "Wolf." There was a sadness in his life alone; he could have cuddled daughters; he could have passed on wonderful little boy skills to sons—like spitting distance contests, gauging the wind for the best results. Of course, the times had changed and she had been one of the first girls in town to make the five-foot distance.

She rubbed her abused, jeans-clad derriere, and sucked on a shaft of new grass. She resented Morgan's easy strength when he'd lifted her down from the saddle, the mocking darkness of his eyes as he looked at her. Oh, she wished she could have stopped that one grimace of pain, but he'd caught it, the hard line of his lips smothering a smile.

While she couldn't manage to arise from the confines of the fallen bed at dawn, he'd been puttering around Annabelle's house happily, hammering and sawing and repairing doodads with gusto. If she didn't know his real reason for remaining at Annabelle's, which was to take revenge for the Foster loom coup, Susanah would have thought Morgan to be relaxing. He seemed to cherish forcing her to fetch and carry for his repair jobs. He was an excellent actor, tasting her lips seductively when Annabelle was near. When he'd seen her struggle sleepily with her cup of coffee at breakfast, he'd scooped her into his lap and cuddled her.

Susanah spat out the grass. His cuddling was marvelous. But then, her resistance had always been down in the morning. Then there was the way he'd held her hair to the light, as if watching it catch the sunbeams, and wrapped it around his dark fingers, running his thumb along the strand while his eyes watched her expressions carefully. Though the gesture had been for Annabelle's benefit, it had caused Susanah a weak moment. *She had the worst need to snuggle into Morgan Lightfoot's arms.*

Susanah tilted her head and plucked a new grass blade as she studied the man she had known all her life—yet hadn't known. She respected his skills as a forager. They'd been testing each other, circling warily, finding excuses to visit with Annabelle privately. Since they didn't trust each other, they were constantly together. She refused to run his errands to the lumberyard; he refused to leave the kitchen when Annabelle cooked, which she loved doing for a "man with a good appetite." Susanah studied Morgan's lean, muscular body, and resented the way the instant something passed her lips, inches went to her hips.

She was uneasy with this man who could reach inside her with a dark, hungry look. She resented the need to soothe something deep and aching inside Morgan. Those emotions were treacherous where Morgan was concerned. He'd take any softening and run with the Cutesies.

"I'm ready to go," she said, standing and testing her legs.

He looked at her, his face shadowed within the broad brim of his hat. "Is that so?"

"You could have gone riding by yourself. You didn't have to force me into a position of coming with you. Annabelle thought we needed privacy and sent me off without a second thought."

Morgan walked to her and her heart skipped a beat. She looked up at him warily. "Honeymooners always go riding together, Loving," he drawled in that deep, raspy voice. "You know I couldn't leave you alone with Annabelle. You're treacherous. I personally know you can't cook—your mother told my mother that exactly one week ago. Yet you're bellying up to cookbooks and asking Annabelle's advice for making jam."

"You are deliberately cultivating your Henry look," she accused, backing away a bit to study him critically. "You meticulously checked what western style hat brand he loved and you bought one. No telling what disgusting methods you used to age it. You're endearing yourself to her by puttering and by appearing loverlike with me. You'll stop at nothing. Low... Lightfoot... very low."

He braced his weight on one long leg, tipped back his hat, and looped his thumbs in his belt. The effect jarred her senses, caused her heart to flip-flop, and her legs to weaken. "That's right, Loving, I won't stop," he agreed, methodically drawing off his leather gloves and tucking them in his belt with an ease borne of practice. "But you're not making things easier. The smell of baby powder and you sprawled all over me isn't the easiest wake-up call for a man. For some reason, this morning felt a lot different than when you fell out of your tree house and flattened me when I was seventeen. I've always thought the tree house incident wasn't an accident...that you were spying on me while I talked to Sissy. I'm not too certain that this morning wasn't a repeat of you doing anything to get your way."

Susanah backed another step, closed her eyes and pushed away the image of Morgan in the morning, his hair mussed, stubble covering his jaw, and eyes dark with sensuality. Then there was the unmistakable thrust of his body up to hers. For protection, she dredged up a thought that had angered her. "You had no right to intervene when Annabelle and I were discussing new clothes for the dolls. Honestly...sitting there and commenting on their new bonnets, though I can imagine you've judged a few very private modeling sessions. As I said, you'll stop at nothing."

He lifted that left, mocking eyebrow, reminding Susanah of how she had maneuvered Annabelle into a playing-doll session. She had wanted to check every inch of the Cutesies' little bodies for flaws and mentally inventory them during the tea party. No righteous male would have even been in the same room with grown women tea-partying with dolls. Murmuring quietly to Annabelle while they'd talked about Easter dresses was the perfect opportunity to suggest that she may have to leave suddenly—without Morgan. She had been confident Morgan would be at a disadvantage, but he seemed comfortable with the whole scenario in the doily- and African violet-filled parlor. When he'd snorted at the discussion of bloomers, shook out his newspaper and checked the sports section, he'd reminded Annabelle even more of her Henry.

"You could leave," he suggested lightly, running a slightly rough fingertip around her lips, then across her bottom one. He pushed slightly, testing the softness. "Why haven't you ever married? No biological nesting urges?"

Susanah tried to breathe. When she did, her breast brushed Morgan's thick wrist. She pushed the air from her lungs instantly. He had that dangerous, hungry-male look and she didn't want him foraging into the deep, untested layers of her femininity. Now, faced with Morgan's closeness, she wondered fleetingly if they had ever been fully tested. "Though it's none of your business, I'll tell you why. I've never found anyone who could keep my interest. Finds have always been much more exciting than..."

He supplied the word she hesitated to say. "Lovemaking? Lifetime commitment? You're the kind for lifetime commitment, aren't you, Loving?"

She looked away, toward a deer in the pines. "I'm dedicated to my profession."

When she turned to watch Morgan, she found his gaze and fingertip strolling down her cheek to the fast-beating pulse in her neck. His fingertip rested in the quickening pulse at the hollow of her throat, then slowly slid to the tip of her breast. The slight pressure against her softness caused more sensual awareness than anything in her life. The thought that Morgan, his eyes shadowed and narrowed behind his lenses, could arouse such intensity, such pure need to throw herself on a man and revel in tenderness and mind-blowing passion, frightened her. She eased away and swallowed. "Could we just stick to the subject of the Cutesies, Lightfoot?"

He shrugged lightly, still watching her with that intent quiet stare that caused her stomach to clench, her legs to weaken, and warning little soft quickenings to dart this way and that in her heart. She saw then exactly how attractive, how devastating "Wolf" could be when he wanted to reactivate his male-on-the-scent aura. "Jennings can provide a much better habitat for the Cutesies," she began after taking a deep breath.

Why was he looking at her with such incredible, sweet sadness, such longing, though quickly shielded?

He smiled then, slowly, confidently and replaced his gloves. "We'll see who gives first, Loving," he said quietly. In the next instant he grabbed her jacket lapels and jerked her to him. She had expected a forceful devastation, a proving of his dominant strength and experience, but Morgan carefully placed his hard mouth against hers, as if testing the fit for lifetime use. The kiss seduced before she could move away, a gentle brushing of lips, of tasting. Susanah moved into the magic—she thought she heard children laughing. She smelled rose petals and long, summer nights. She heard crickets by the pond, and the steady, familiar beat of a man's heart beneath her cheek.

With a long sigh, she gave herself to the kiss, standing on tiptoe to stretch herself out against Morgan's hard, safe, familiar body. Her arms wound around his neck, and she arched up into him, searching for the hunger that flamed between them. His hair was cool beneath her fingers, his heart beating safely, rapidly against her when his arms enclosed her slowly, tenderly, as if she were the most precious thing in his life.

"Don't cry, Susanah," he whispered unevenly against her cheek, sheltering her face in the curve of his throat and shoulder. He rocked her gently and she clung to him, shockingly aware that she had never experienced anything so beautiful. There was a sadness too, because so many years had passed without this tender trespass. She shivered, aware that Morgan gently kissed her lids, her nose, brushing his lips against hers almost reverently. She felt as if she'd been running all her life, fighting something so terrifyingly inevitable and beautiful.

The unique experience of having one ankle tied to a four-poster was balanced by the sense of safety provided by Morgan's two large warm feet around her free foot. At one o'clock in the morning, Susanah had awakened when she'd tried to turn on her side and her ankle wouldn't move. She had tugged sleepily at it and then found her other foot held in a comfortable, loose, warm vise. She awoke quickly to find Morgan's broad bare back inches from her nose. Her hand rested on his naked, hard buttock.

She eased her fingers away from him, and rested them against her suddenly knotted stomach. "Morgan!" she whispered. "Morgan!" This time more desperately. When he didn't answer, she eased upright and began trying to undo the intricate knotting of clothesline cord from her ankle. She raged mentally about Morgan's falling asleep instantly, a guise to awake later and imprison her. She had lingered for hours in the scent of a freshly bathed male and wondered desperately why her one experience with a man hadn't affected her as deeply as Morgan did.

He was devious, calculating, she thought furiously, working desperately now at the fancy knot. It wouldn't budge, no doubt tied by a champion Boy Scout. The bed creaked a bit and Susanah stilled, deciding to wait until she had escaped his noose before she hit him with her pillow. When he didn't awaken, she continued working, the old bed creaking gently and bumping the wall.

Morgan inhaled slowly, then drawled sleepily, "You know what this must sound like we're doing, Loving. Lay off."

She skipped freedom and grabbed her pillow. "I'm not into bondage, Lightfoot," she stated before she hit him with the rosebud pillowcase. His feet tightened a bit on her foot, but he didn't turn. "You better not ignore me, Lightfoot, because I can do real damage. You'll be barred from the Cutesey exhibit for life."

"Gosh. You're scaring me," he murmured with a yawn.

Susanah began beating him with her pillow, the bed creaking beneath their weight. Morgan pulled his pillow over his head and ignored her. She resorted to something she had discovered about him before Oscar had made his death journey to sea; she jerked up his big foot, tucked it between her thighs and tickled his arch. He shouted, gave a rusty chuckle and tugged at his foot twice. The bed creaked, bumped the wall once and plummeted to the floor.

Morgan flipped over, pinning Susanah beneath him. "That was dirty pool, Loving," he said in a low, menacing tone.

"Get off me, Lightfoot. What's the idea of tying my ankle to the bedpost?"

"Being returned to Annabelle's protection by Buster the Human Wall isn't going to be repeated."

"Buster is adorable."

"The guy is an overgrown gorilla, Loving," Morgan murmured.

"Are you related?" she asked sweetly.

Morgan shot her one of those dark, hungry male looks that stopped her heart. When it began beating again, it raced beneath his wide palm. "You're trouble, Loving," he said warily, his voice gravelly.

She tried to shift the subject and Morgan's aroused body. Her efforts were unsuccessful. He was very solid. She closed her eyes briefly and wondered how he would withstand her flying leap at him, the intense need to have him and quickly. Morgan was tough, mentally and physically. She knew that he could withstand the onslaught of her startling, wild passions. They hadn't been fully aroused, she realized suddenly, and allowing them to explore Morgan's sensuality would be like opening Pandora's box. To cover her thoughts, she dredged up an old wound. "I won't lie beneath Oscar's murderer," she tried loftily, but her voice came out in a sultry whisper.

"That was twenty-seven years ago, Loving," he said between those light, gentle, sweet kisses. "We've changed." Bending his head and laying his rough cheek along hers, Morgan sucked her earlobe. His uneven, warm breath swirled inside her ear and the erotic motion of his hand caused her to close her eyes and slowly melt into the rosebud sheet. Morgan trembled and stroked his hand gently down her body. "You're shaking and hot, Loving," he whispered softly. "You remind me of a volcano about to erupt."

"Anger," she lied between her teeth, mentally sitting on the lid of her sensual Pandora's box. "I won't become one of your floozies," she whispered desperately. *Why Morgan Lightfoot?*

His lazy smile curved against the side of her throat. " 'Floozies.' That's old-fashioned, like you and baby powder." Then very gently, he eased himself from her.

In the next moment Susanah found herself being tucked beneath the rosebud sheet and quilts very carefully, very tenderly by her rival, Morgan Lightfoot. He untied her ankle, smoothed her arch with his thumb, and tucked her foot beneath the covers. Then he kissed the top of her head, tucked his chin over it, and drew her into the cove of his body.

Susanah was left to deal with her thoughts and the steady beat of Morgan's heart beneath her cheek. Unfortunately, it was a sound she liked.

"I've always wanted babies," Morgan stated the next afternoon, slanting a dramatic and wistful look down at Susanah from the shade of his western hat. "Girls. Lots of them."

Susanah recognized his ploy to endear himself to Annabelle, and ignored him, keeping her chin high. Her hands tightened on the handle of the giant, old-fashioned baby buggy that they pushed down Pothole's main street. Walking beside her, Morgan's big hands shared the handle. Since the dolls rested beneath the shade of the hood, Susanah did not want Morgan pushing them alone. The promenade to Wilson's Emporium on Pothole's only street pleased Annabelle immensely. She walked beside Morgan, her small gloved hand tucked into his elbow. Her other hand waved to the residents of Pothole who stopped to stare at the unlikely threesome with interest.

While Annabelle introduced them gaily to her friends—which was all of Pothole—Buster tracked them from the shadows of his parked patrol car. He watched them while Annabelle seated them on a bench outside the small post office and dry goods store. She went inside to do her business.

Morgan tapped his fingers on the handle of the buggy. Susanah wrapped her fist around it. She listened to his finger tapping for a moment, sucked in her breath, and issued the thought that she had been nurturing since dawn. "Okay. I'll trade you the Foster loom. You can place it on exhibit for a time each year in the Laird Museum. But you must recognize that Laird does not have the faculty to take care of the Cutesies like Annabelle wants."

Morgan waved to Buster. "I'll do it. Thanks for the offer of the loom, but it would be like taking second best."

"We can't continue this charade."

He leaned back on the bench, placed his arm around her and stretched his long, jeaned legs to the spring sun. "You can leave. Invent some excuse."

"Absolutely not.... Neither one of us ... can be certain that Annabelle will ... endow these dolls to us." She said this between his light kisses. "Will you stop that?" she demanded unevenly, trying to catch her breath.

He closed his eyes and leaned closer to take a long, sweet, mind-blasting kiss. "Mmm. Can't. Honeymooning, you know."

Susanah jumped up, releasing her hold on the handle. While Morgan stared at her lazily, she grabbed the handle again. He levered up to his full height, placed his finger beneath her chin and lifted her mouth for another light kiss. "Hold that thought, Loving," he ordered gently. "You're simmering nicely."

Then he entered the post office/dry goods store, leaving her with the dolls in the buggy. Through the window, Susanah saw Morgan bend down to receive Annabelle's pat and kiss on his cheek. "Fiend. Pirate. Fish murderer," Susanah muttered darkly.

From the shadows of the huge, black hood, Lucy, Magnolia, Jessica, Betty, Mary, Elizabeth, Rachael, Opal, Fay and Belle grinned merrily. "Bad Cutesies," Susanah muttered. "Bad dolls."

A shadow crossed her and she looked up to see a western Adonis doffing his wide-brimmed, worn hat at her. As big as Morgan, the man was younger, leaner, and had a friendly twinkle in his blue eyes that she instantly liked. "Well, hello there, little lady," he drawled. "You walkin' Miss Annabelle's dolls? I've taken 'em out a few times myself."

"At the moment, they're well behaved," she returned with a smile.

He grinned boyishly and hooked his thumbs into his front pockets. "You new in town?"

"We're staying at Annabelle's house. Just visiting."

"We?" he questioned with a hopeful grin.

Morgan loomed beside the newcomer. "We," he answered flatly. "We as in married. She's mine."

Susanah stared blankly at this new fierce Morgan, his fingers digging into Annabelle's grocery sacks. She'd heard about the territorial male species, but this was the first time she'd seen one protecting his rights, his woman—which was her. Susanah considered Morgan's grim, locked jaw, the narrowing of his eyes behind his lenses. The two men gauged each other and for a fleeting moment, Susanah knew exactly what gunfighters would have looked like over a hundred years ago on the streets of Pothole.

Annabelle's lovely voice broke the spell. "Buddy, would you mind dropping by Fanny's house and mentioning to her that my bed and breakfast already has two honeymooners? Try to get this into the conversation—they're so pleased that they're coming back and bringing a whole flock of honeymooners and newlyweds. Make sure you tell her that my business is booming.''

Then she peeked inside the buggy, straightened Rachel's bow, placed her hand through the crook of Morgan's waiting arm and said, "Come along, children.''

Chapter Four

Morgan glanced up from sawing a board braced across two sawhorses. Scraps of rotted boards from Annabelle's back porch lay at his feet. Painting the new boards would make an excellent project for Susanah tomorrow. He wiped the sweat away from his forehead and scowled at Susanah, who was lying back in a chaise longue. He didn't trust her cocky look. He'd seen it years ago—just minutes before she had led his mother to where he and Danny Simmons were smoking cigars behind the garage.

The feminine, smug smile beneath Susanah's oversize lenses dug into Morgan's mood like a tick burrowing beneath his skin. When he suggested that she help him repair the broken boards in Annabelle's back porch, she'd come along too easily to plant canna bulbs. Morgan noted the uneven row of freshly covered cannas. They had been planted in the same kamikaze style that marked her driving skills. He changed his mind about Susanah painting the repaired porch. The new coat of paint needed to be applied evenly, skillfully, carefully. Those techniques were unknown to S. E. Loving. Even her untutored lovemaking had a leashed kamikaze touch— A quick mental image of S. E. Loving's honey brown eyes flowing over him with the same delight she demonstrated for a new acquisition stopped his breath. When Susanah's daydream image dived onto his prone and aroused body, Morgan took a long, steadying breath. He turned over that idea just once and decided to place it carefully aside.

His experience seemed lacking. He considered the women seductively slinking through his memory— When compared to S. E. Loving and her sweet, shocked responses, the women in his past seemed like robots. He'd found himself scanning Susanah's backside while she'd planted those cannas and wondered about carrying her off into the pines nearby.

Morgan scowled and committed himself to short, hard sawing jerks. He'd started thinking about lingering in S. E. Loving's suspected kamikaze-style lovemaking technique. Buddy was not a candidate for Susanah's sweet, soft kisses.

Now she tapped her sneaker to a tune coming from her earphones. Periodically she changed cassettes in her hand-held player. She hadn't been out of his sight for a moment.

He hadn't slept last night, and yesterday's episode of Buddy's bird-dogging Susanah had scraped already raw nerves.

He narrowed his eyes as her fingers tapped her jeans-clad thigh. It was a long, slender thigh, with silky soft skin. He knew because it had stayed the night cradled between his.

The woman who spent the night in his arms was exactly the kind of woman he didn't want. The marrying kind. The mommy kind. The loving kind who made him want to forsake The West Was a Man Society. The woman who would excite him beyond any other female and slide under his careful control. Yet each kiss they shared—for Annabelle's benefit—had a little hungry whang to it. As if Susanah wasn't quite certain how to hold her own in a full, body-alert kiss, but that at any moment she wouldn't be able to keep from jerking his mouth to hers and igniting them both. He put that on his keeping-up-the-pressure list—one hungry, hot kiss coming up.

While she had responded nicely on Alice's front seat, she really hadn't released whatever she was holding back. Morgan grimly wanted that secret. He mentally balanced the "whatever" Susanah was hiding against acquiring the Cutesies, and decided that the "whatever" won.

Buster cruised by slowly for the fifth time, peering from the patrol car at Morgan, who waved and forced a blithe grin. Morgan settled back into his thoughts and wondered resentfully, at his age and experience, why he treasured Susanah's soft, untutored kisses and why he desperately needed to know her secrets.

Obviously she wanted the Cutesies and would stop at nothing to get them—that wasn't a secret. Something else roamed behind those honey-colored eyes and though he didn't understand why, it was essential for Morgan to experience.

Only the need to protect a sweet, old-fashioned girl had stopped his primitive urge to make love to her this morning. He couldn't cope with that guilt any easier than conning Annabelle, which had begun to nag at him. Deceit wasn't a skill he employed. His systematic technique usually laid out the pluses for a donation to the museum; however, one of the pluses now was sleeping next to Susanah every night.

While mentally he congratulated himself on his high integrity, his body ached unrelentingly.

He'd always known they would clash someday...had counted on scooping away an acquisition that S. E. Loving lusted for with every ounce of her greedy soul. Morgan's fingers ached around the saw handle and he stared at his whitened knuckles. He wanted to be S. E. Loving's acquisition, the object of her coo's and stroking, loving fingers. He wanted to be the reason her honey-colored eyes lit up or darkened, and the reason she blushed wildly.

Morgan sawed as if his life depended on completing the porch. Susanah's blushes enchanted him, undid his control, and he was too old and comfortable in his ways to find that S. E. Loving could unnerve him.

If he had to respect another woman as a competitor, he was almost glad it was S. E. Loving. Her skills were top-notch. He'd never made love to a competitor or a woman whom he sensed would stick to him the way Susanah's freshly painted lawn chair had when he was twenty-five.

He shrugged mentally. Rose petals and down-filled sleeping bags and S. E. Loving—the thought boggled his mind. Susanah intrigued him as a woman interested in the same need to share unique western finds with the public... to let them experience the nuance of yesteryear. In museum circles, her reputation equaled his—that is, until the acquisition of the Foster loom. S. E. Loving was not and never had been a dull woman; he had thoroughly enjoyed every skirmish with her. She piqued his skills—

S. E. Loving was *exactly* the woman he didn't want near him, he repeated, uneasily noting the soft thrust of her breasts as she squirmed a bit. He pressed his lips together. Leave it to Loving to serve him that last bit of mental *and* sensual excitement at a time when he thought he had experienced everything—that all his life's cogs were neatly in place.

Morgan shook his head and punished the board with the old rusty saw. He could blame his intense need to experience S.E. Loving on his lack of bed-mates for several years.

The drop of sweat that had been clinging to his forehead slid down his cheek. Or he could admit truthfully that Susanah Elizabeth Loving, slaking revenge on him since Oscar died, interested him more than the Cutesies, the Foster loom, or any other acquisitions.

Susanah studiously tapped her foot to the music she wasn't listening to, and tried to keep her eyes from drifting to Morgan. A drift of sawdust clung to the line of hair veeing down into his jeans' waistband. Cords and muscles rippled beneath darkly tanned skin while he sawed fiercely, as if attacking the boards. His broad shoulders gleamed with sun and sweat.

Sweat. Strange, she hadn't thought of calm, distant Morgan Lightfoot, her archrival, as a man who sweated. Yet he'd had a distinct beading across his forehead last night as he'd loomed over her. His great, hardened body had trembled under his control. His expression was dark, primitive, as though nothing could stop him from having her— A little chill of excitement slid along the back of Susanah's neck.

Susanah badly wanted to make his sensual control slip. She knew the Foster loom had irked him. She knew he wanted revenge. She knew she wanted to experience whatever Morgan was holding back from her.

Concentrating on hammering and sawing, Morgan looked nothing like the slow-moving, oblique, well-dressed-museum-acquisitions director or dean of history who had moved in and out of her life and same professional circles. He had invited her to keep him company while he repaired the broken boards. Rather—it wasn't an invitation, more like a demand. She eyed him warily. Morgan was the only man to ever demand anything of her; he wasn't the kind to be swished away. He stood there—solid, determined, and as eventual as spring daffodils and summer cannas. Between kisses on the stairway, Morgan had whispered, "Loving, I'm not leaving you alone with Annabelle. I want you in my sight. Would you mind coming outside while I fix her porch?"

Since Susanah wanted Annabelle to have a safer porch, she abandoned her plans to lobby for the Jennings Museum. Morgan's little fix-up projects surprised her. For a bookish man, he seemed unusually capable with a saw and hammer. He had repaired the old bed very quickly, his hands gliding over the antique walnut almost reverently. This morning he'd quickly veiled the heated look he sent her across the old bed as they made it.

Susanah frowned, noting that Morgan didn't disdain doing dishes or making beds. Her ill-fated affair had gifted her with all the responsibilities of housekeeping and mothering. For Morgan to share housekeeping chores struck her as unique.

Susanah knew that Morgan would have to shower before he came to Annabelle's fried chicken at the dinner table. When Morgan stepped into that shower, nothing could keep Susanah from Cutesy-

Wootsy talk with Annabelle. The elderly lady tended to nod off in the evenings. Showers and baths had to be taken in the evening because Annabelle's ancient water heater needed to revive before morning breakfast dishes and laundry. Tonight's water for dishes was heating on the back of Annabelle's cookstove to allow for Morgan's shower. Therefore, Annabelle would be available for listening before supper, when Morgan took his shower, and nodding off when Susanah took hers.

Taking her time, Susanah intended to sketch a beautiful reason why Annabelle should donate the dolls to the Jennings Museum. With a private, well-paid staff, Jennings would ensure that the dolls were placed in a unique environment, temperature-controlled, proper lighting, and that their clothing and needs would be tended to carefully. Susanah allowed herself a victorious smile—a doll tea party at four o'clock would make a wonderful attraction at Jennings. Also, Susanah wanted to explain that universities always wanted acquisitions like the dolls, but that most likely they weren't equipped with luxury, temperature-controlled showcases. Wrong lighting could overheat the dolls and ruin their complexions.

While Annabelle knew that Morgan was a history professor at a university, she didn't know his other interests. Susanah could arrange visiting sessions at Jennings. Or bring the dolls home to Annabelle.

Elvis Presley's "Love Me Tender" played on the cassette while the little sweet lady scurried up to Morgan with a glass of ice water. After he drank and grinned that devastating, boyish grin, Annabelle patted his cheek. She waved merrily at Susanah and stood there gazing blissfully back and forth to her honeymooners, her hands clasped over her lacy, starched bodice. Annabelle said something, and Morgan nodded, smiling rakishly. Susanah's foot stopped tapping and she jerked the earphones from her head. Morgan couldn't be trusted; he could be making deals right in front of her. "Annabelle? What did you say?"

"Dinner will be a little early. Fanny is having an open house this evening to announce her bed and breakfast to Pothole. I thought you might want to come with me—" Her face lit up. "I would be so pleased."

When Annabelle quickly hurried back to the house, humming merrily, Morgan hammered the last board into place. He dusted his hands and looked at Susanah, who found herself staring at the flat expanse of his stomach and the way his jeans had eased a bit low. The distant sounds of Elvis came from her earphones, and she thought about how she'd like to love Morgan tender and in other less gentle ways. She was certain he could withstand the rigors of whatever was nagging at her sensually when he was near.

Morgan gently scooped her up into his arms and carried her into the kitchen. "We're taking a bath, Annabelle. Won't be long. We'll be right down," he said as they passed Annabelle in the kitchen. Her eyes lit up and she beamed, doing a little two-step to the tune she had been listening to on her old radio. She two-stepped to the oven and bent to take out beautifully browned, latticed cherry pies.

Susanah snagged the post at the bottom of the stairwell. She jammed her foot against the wall, effectively stopping Morgan's passage upstairs. "We?" she asked between her teeth. "Together?"

"You smell like manure, Loving," he said gently, almost tenderly. "We'll save on use of Annabelle's hot water tank. Are you scared?"

"I'll go first. You can stand outside the door if you want," she stated cautiously as he easily carried her up the stairs to their room. She sensed that warriors long ago carried off the women they wanted in just that same purposeful way.

He kissed the tip of her nose and ordered, "Grab our robes from the back of the door, Loving. I'm not taking any chances that you'll run all the hot water out and leave me with the icy dregs."

"Me?" she asked innocently, suddenly aware that her hands were stroking the broad contours of his shoulders when her fingers weren't toying in the damp hair on his chest. She realized suddenly that her ex-lover had never worked up a sweat over anything, and that included herself. Morgan held her in his arms while she debated her choices. "Okay," she said quietly, blushing with an exquisitely wanton feeling she had never experienced before. Just as she had never experienced bathing with a man. "Just as a water saver."

"I won't look unless you want me to, Susanah Elizabeth," he whispered deeply, unevenly, his eyes darkening behind his lenses.

She inhaled, her throat too tight to answer. She was afraid she might inform Morgan that no man had ever studied her with so much interest, so much delicate care as he did now. She flushed, lifted their robes from the door hook and tried to breathe as Morgan carried her into the tiny bathroom. He placed her gently on the cotton rug, started the shower running to warm it, and bent to unlace her shoes. She braced one hand against the wall while Morgan stripped away her shoes and socks and her jeans. His rough fingers swept across her smooth waist once and she inhaled, excitement throbbing through her. "You can trust me, Susanah," he said quietly as he removed his steamed glasses, and slowly stripped in front of her.

When Morgan stood naked, he lifted off her glasses and placed them on a shelf. The steamy room enclosed her, her breath coming in short little bursts as he loomed over her, powerful and incredibly aroused. She locked her eyes to his shoulders as he placed his hands firmly on her waist and squeezed it gently. "My, it's rather close and hot in here, isn't it?" she tried conversationally.

"Very close. Very hot, Susanah," he agreed gently, tugging at the hem of her T-shirt, then on the elastic waistband of her white cotton briefs. "You can put on your robe and wait. Otherwise, you're overdressed for the occasion."

"Darn," she whispered unevenly, unable to look away from Morgan's dark, quiet stare as the steam swirled around them. "So I am."

The choice was hers. She could step outside the small steamy room and never experience a shower with Morgan.

Or she could grab the moment with two fists, which was more her style when making acquisitions. Susanah closed her eyes and jerked off her T-shirt, exposing her practical bra.

Morgan's expression hardened, his dark eyes flowing over her from the top of her head to her feet, methodically seeking each curve and secret place. She trembled as he inserted one finger into her briefs' waistband and tugged on it gently. The shower water pounded in the stall, and yet Susanah could hear her heart as if every other sound in the universe had stopped. Morgan waited as if the world could spin away and he would still be standing there. He was that kind of man, the "always" kind.

He waited, tall and dark and very hungry, while she eased the briefs from her hips and let them slide to her feet. Morgan slowly raised his hand to ease a strand of her hair away from her hot, damp cheek. Then he plucked gently at the satin bow between her breasts. Susanah reached behind to unsnap her bra and, with an incredibly gentle movement, Morgan eased it from her shoulders. His stare touched her breasts and lower, and she wished wildly that she was still boyishly slender. There was a heaviness to her now, rounding her breasts and hips. She looked away, embarrassed by his slow, devastating stare, her eyes burning with tears of twanging emotions she didn't understand.

Morgan's big rough hand cradled her chin and brought her face up to his. He kissed her gently, that wooing, enchanting brush of his hard mouth against hers. She could have stood forever beneath that cherishing, sweet dreamy touch. Then his eyes crinkled at the corners and he smiled wistfully. "Hello, Susanah Elizabeth."

The deep, rich, pleased sound of his voice wrapped around her like warm velvet.

He drew her into his arms and against the long, hard, aroused length of his body. Tucking her face gently into the cove of his throat and shoulder, Morgan smoothed her back slowly up and down. While she adjusted to the rough, hairy surface of his chest against her bare breasts, Morgan stroked and smoothed as if he had all day, as if nothing mattered but holding her against him. Eventually she discovered that her arms had wrapped around his waist and that her hands were exploring the sliding pads of muscles on his back.

They were swathed in steam and gentle exploration. Gradually, Morgan shuddered, his hands tightening on her waist a heartbeat before he stepped away. Taking the back of her hand to his lips, Morgan kissed it gallantly, his eyes making promises that took away her breath. "In," he whispered gently, urging her into the shower and stepping in behind her with an air of a gentleman courting a lady.

"Oh...oh...." Susanah sucked in her breath as the icy water sluiced down. Morgan's muttered curse mixed with the steam as he quickly soaped her down, turned her around once to rinse as though she were a child. He gripped her waist and lifted her out. Susanah was just tying the sash on her robe when he stepped out of the shower.

Morgan shivered, swirled a towel around himself quickly and jerked on his robe. "Only you," he said quietly between his teeth as though those two words explained everything. Then he opened the bathroom door and stalked to the bedroom.

Susanah had the uneasy feeling she was entering the lair of a mountain lion when she stepped into the bedroom. Morgan shot her a dark, disgusted glance and said, "I did not kill your goldfish, Loving. But I am going to claim the Cutesy-Wootsies. We're going to have to deal with everything in between and after, *because you are driving me to the edge,*" he stated in a quiet roar.

She blinked, fighting back tears. She wanted Morgan holding her and kissing her and—she pushed down the lid on emotions that were too primitive for the acquisitions director and curator of the Jennings Museum. To cover her tremulous mood, she returned primly, "That would be interesting, Lightfoot. Or is it 'Wolf'?"

Morgan stopped jerking up his jeans and stared at her blankly. On her way to the dressing closet, Susanah couldn't resist placing her hand on his chest and pushing. With his jeans around his knees, he landed on his back on the bed.

It creaked and fell to the floor. He looked up at her darkly, then a slow, rakish grin spread across his face. "This should be very interesting, Loving."

After dinner, Morgan had placed Annabelle safely in Alice's back seat and ignored Susanah's warning frown. On the front seat, he'd patted the cushion beside him. It had pleased Morgan immensely that Susanah slid against him. Little battles always added to winning major ones. He was good at that—methodical alignment of tidbits to secure something he really wanted. In Fanny's parlor, Susanah sat by his side, cuddled against him, and let him hold her hand. He liked that soft hand in his, he discovered. Liked hearing the ripple of her laughter when Annabelle merrily chatted away about Henry's escapades and her Cutesy-Wootsies.

Annabelle retired early that night, high on success with her resident honeymooners.

Susanah lay beside Morgan. The baby-powder scent of her bath seeped into his senses. She had been responding nicely to his kisses, especially the last, long one on the front porch while Annabelle peered from the window. "I'm feeling guilty about our deception, Lightfoot," Susanah said at last, turning her head to him.

At the moment, Morgan had to place guilt as secondary in his emotions, though he had experienced it almost immediately after meeting Annabelle. He watched the leaf patterns from the moonlight wiggle on the ceiling and tried to ignore the scent of Susanah's baby powder. She raised up on her elbow to study him. "You must realize that Laird isn't the place for the Cutesies."

"Laird is the perfect place for them. In one year, our museum visitation doubles anything Jennings could do in two. More people would be able to enjoy them."

"More exposure to dust, warm, humid breath, and possible theft. Those dolls have souls. They could be traumatized. Your mind set has never been tender, Lightfoot. How can you prey on poor Annabelle, especially when she sees her beloved Henry in you?"

He turned on his side to her, then braced his head on one hand. She was foraging for an angle to get to him and the idea fascinated Morgan. "'Warm, humid breath'?'' he invited slowly, playing with a silky strand of her hair.

"Think about my offer of borrowing the Foster loom. Perhaps the loom and a few other little considerations. Think about it.'' She eased the strand away from his fingers and lay down. Morgan watched, fascinated, while her breasts rose and fell against the heavy quilt. He remembered the soft thrust of them in the steamy bathroom. Susanah didn't need to stuff folded stockings in her bra any longer.

"So..." she was saying primly, her fists clenching the sheet. "I'm feeling a little restless tonight. I think I'll go for a run.''

Morgan clamped his fingers around her slender wrist. "No. Buster the Human Wall has been dogging our trail. He's the kind with the sixth sense about what's right and what's not. If Annabelle weren't so blithely happy, he'd be breathing down our necks. He's probably already run a check on our license plates and knows we're not married.''

She blinked and turned her head toward him. "You mean, he thinks we're con men?'' she asked incredulously.

Morgan noted that she didn't attempt to remove his hold on her. He stroked the soft inner side of her wrist with his thumb and thought her pulse skipped a beat. "Buster thinks one of us is a con man. He knows you're a woman,'' he returned.

"Oh. Right. That's good." She chewed on that for a while and Morgan placed her hand on his chest. It was the first time he had ever invited a woman to test his heartbeat. In fact, he'd never invited women into his life. They seemed to wind through it and leave and he hadn't regretted the loss. He didn't want Susanah leaving.

Something wary and feminine skimmed across her expression. Her hand closed carefully over his chest and she sucked in her breath. She stroked the hair on his chest just the way he remembered her fondling a kitten that she had loved when she was fourteen and coltish. The years had rounded her body and skinny long legs nicely. He noted the slight creases at the corners of her eyes and wished he'd been there each time she'd frowned or smiled.

A searing ache spread inside him as he thought of the children that might have been—

Susanah frowned slightly, her short nails clawing gently at his chest. Excitement raced through Morgan, wilder than anything he'd known. "I'm not easily acquired, Lightfoot."

"Of course," he managed unevenly, stroking the line of her hip over the quilt.

"I'm not a girl any longer."

"Uh-uh," he whispered through a throat gone dry with passion he tried to control.

"You can't use sex to bargain for the Cutesies," she whispered just as his lips touched hers.

Morgan opened the lids he had closed to better savor Susanah's mouth. "What?" he asked carefully.

"You're looking at me just the way you did Lacy Norton all those years ago. And Betty, and Susan, and who was that floozy you brought home from college and the two of you crawled all over each other in Alice's back seat? Then the whole town gossiped about you and your—what's her name, the ex-wife?—making out on a blanket next to the cemetery. Disgusting.... You must have forgotten, Lightfoot, that I know what you are—I know where you live—I know that you deliberately premeditated Oscar's premature death by flushing him out to sea. I had big plans for that fish. You broke my heart. And I wasn't that happy about your— What's her name? The ex-wife?"

She took a deep breath, stared at him and said stonily, "I will not allow my walls of Jericho to be seduced by a goldfish-killing, Cutesy-grabbing, article-writing, unscrupulous acquisition hunter named Wolf. If it isn't the Cutesies, which I know fully well it is, your attraction for me lies in the fact that you're missing your nightly—" She faltered a bit here, then continued breathlessly, and blushing. "Rendezvous with savage, untamed passions. With lust," she finished dramatically, pointedly.

With that she scrambled out of bed. While the bed crashed to the floor, she jerked off the nightgown that had concealed her jeans and whipped a sweatshirt over her head. Her sneakers flashed whitely as she opened the window and stepped out onto the moonlit porch.

"Kamikaze," Morgan muttered, struggling out of the tangled bedding and up to his feet.

Incensed, Morgan couldn't think of "the ex-wife's" name, either. All he could think about was the woman scampering down the rainspout. Morgan closed his eyes, sighed once, and began drawing on his clothing.

As he stepped out onto the roof and sniffed the lingering scent of baby powder, he wondered distantly how much of him would be well and safe by the time he convinced S. E. Loving to acquire him.

Chapter Five

Susanah sprinted around the block and glanced back over her shoulder. Morgan was gaining on her, displaying an easy, steady long-legged run. She frowned and turned, pushing faster, grateful for the ponytail she'd quickly fashioned while climbing down the roof. At forty-three, Morgan should have been paunchy and out of shape, wheezing and falling flat on his face about two blocks ago. Susanah looked again. While she could sprint, endurance runs had never been her strength. Unfortunately, she suspected that Morgan could run forever.

He caught up with her in front of the post office and turned to run backward as she pushed air into her lungs. His grin taunted her in the moonlight. "Out of shape, Loving? Bit off more than you can chew?"

"That will be the day," she managed. She noted his bare chest and worn, frayed jeans as she surged past him. "Shouldn't you be wearing a shirt?"

"Tore it on the window. It's hanging from Annabelle's rosebushes. She'll probably think you tore it while having your way with me."

"Ha! That will be the day," she returned with more certainty than she believed.

He ran beside her, matching his stride to hers. There was something inevitable about their run that evening, she decided. As though all through their lives they were meant to have this moonlit run through the empty streets of Pothole. "You do this often?" he asked as they rounded another corner.

"When I sit too much. I'm not a health club person. I like freedom . . . air."

"Me, too." Then he reached over and patted her bottom lightly.

"Watch it," she warned without malice, and not wanting to be outdone, reached over to pat his hard bottom. Morgan's chuckle was slow and rich and Susanah felt about fifteen again. She realized that she hadn't seen Morgan laugh or give more than a small movement of his lips in his adult life. "I'm sorry about your divorce, Morgan," she said quietly after a moment.

He ran beside her, big, lethal and solid. The always man. She knew that he'd never hurt her and that he'd never expect her to be a mommy-provider-caregiver.

He cursed as Pothole's only patrol car slid out of the darkened alley between the café and the grocery store. He slid an arm around Susanah's waist and carried her into the shadows behind the bakery's sidewalk sign. Susanah crouched behind the sign with him while Buster's car slid on down the street. She frowned at Morgan, who had just placed the palm of his hand over her head and pushed her down. "Take a note, Lightfoot. I can hide behind signs without your help."

He chuckled again, bent to kiss the side of her neck and nibbled on it while growling teasingly. Chills ran up her spine and she jumped, rubbing her neck. He stood slowly, tugging her ponytail and grinning down at her as though he was a boy with his best girl. The air sailed out of Susanah's lungs as Morgan slowly, inevitably lowered his head to kiss her. "Hello, Susanah Elizabeth," he murmured once more against her lips.

"Hello, Morgan." She met the soft kiss, testing it and him, savoring the taste of time and hunger that brewed between them.

On the way back, she glanced at Morgan running at her side. He had been silent after their kiss, looking down at her from his height, his face harsh in the moonlight. Then he had taken her hand, drawn her palm to his mouth and pressed his lips into the exact center. Morgan was the kind to find the exact center of anything and head directly for it. She had shivered a bit in the moonlight and in the knowledge that Morgan the Wolf was circling her, finding her incredibly sensitive spots and heading straight for them. She'd always been breathless when the movie actors performed that gallant, hand-kissing magic. Morgan was the only man who had reached inside her romantic whimsies and tasted her virgin palm. She carried the kiss in her fist like a gold doubloon, freshly recovered from the sea.

They reached the trees across the street from Annabelle's house and Morgan cursed, glancing behind them. He grabbed her arm, drew her to the huge tree with new leaves, and ordered, "Up."

Susanah was lifted easily to the first large branch and Morgan heaved himself up beside her. They sat there, legs dangling while Buster's patrol car slid by Annabelle's. He stopped in front of the house.

"It's midnight. Shouldn't Buster be in his lair?" Susanah mumbled, the chill seeping into her sweatshirt and jeans. Morgan's arm drew her close, protectively, as if he'd fight anyone who harmed her. When he shivered once, Susanah hesitated, then reached her arms around him. When he lifted that cocky, left eyebrow, she sighed. "It's the least I can do, Lightfoot. Don't make more of it than it is."

He studied the patrol car, laid his chin in her hair and held her against him. His fingertips smoothed the outer perimeter of her breast, the caress distracting her as much as Morgan's deep frown. "Sheila didn't want the baby," he said quietly.

His fingers slid along Susanah's breast, slowly, gently possessing the softness. He kissed her forehead, nuzzling her hair, his tone deep, sad and whimsical. "My son would have been just seventeen. Maybe sitting on a tree limb with his best girl, hiding from the local sheriff, just like I am with you." Then he kissed Susanah's lips lightly. "But then he wasn't really my son, though I wanted him. I married her anyway. And then one day, a month after our wedding, he wasn't a baby," he said unevenly, closing his eyes. "Sheila decided she didn't want children. She packed and left in one day. I hear she's happy."

"Oh, Morgan. Did you love her very much?" Susanah asked quietly, hugging him closer.

"Fast and hot. I thought we had it all, that love would grow out of what we had. Looking back now, I see love wasn't possible," he answered with a sad smile. "I thought she'd settle down with a marriage license in her hand. I was cocky enough back then to think that anything was possible with a baby coming. Other people have started happy marriages—lives together—with much less," he said quietly. "We'd been married three weeks when she lost the baby. When she walked out of the clinic, the man who fathered the baby was waiting.... As easy as that."

Susanah closed her eyes and rocked him gently. "Don't get mushy, Loving," he muttered grimly. "I've never told anyone that bit of history. Chalk it up to sitting on a tree limb with a woman who thinks I'm a fish murderer."

Susanah pushed Oscar's belly-up mysterious death back into the past for the time. "I'd never hit a guy when he's down," she whispered gently, then for the first time, reached up to pull his head down to hers. She kissed him with all the sweet ache in her heart.

The kiss slanted and changed. Hungry tremors ran through her, and Morgan's big rough hand slid up under her sweatshirt to smooth her back. The long, slow caresses claimed, eased and soothed—almost. When Susanah drew back slowly, she whispered, "Your glasses are steamed, Lightfoot."

"You're a hot woman, Loving," he returned gently, kissing her just once more before swinging to the ground.

When he held his arms up for her, Susanah hesitated, watched his harsh, taut expression and gently allowed herself to fall to earth. His "hot woman" statement did wonders for an ego that had long ago been smashed by taunts of "bookworm" and "cold fish." He grunted a bit, staggered once, and carried her toward Annabelle's house across the street.

Susanah looked at him, locked her arms around his neck and snuggled to him. "You carried me just like this when I was nineteen and you were twenty-four. I'd hurt my ankle doing the limbo rock. Or was it the mashed potato?"

"You were something then, Loving. All long legs and long blond hair. Your short-shorts caused mine to shrink. I barely delivered you to your parents without tossing you into the bushes."

"Lightfoot! I was injured. You wouldn't sink so low."

"Wouldn't I? The only thing that kept me on the straight and narrow path back then was knowing that I'd forfeit my mother's apple pie if something happened to you." He placed her on her feet near the mangled rainspout. "They're not making them like they used to," he said, lifting it with his toe. "This is a fine mess you've gotten us into."

"You're such a baby," she returned, patting him on that hard bottom—one she suspected she would like to grab firmly with both hands while— Susanah pushed that thought back with the rest she'd been hoarding since they'd crossed the street. While she could fight Morgan on business and career issues, snatching really good finds from his grasp with sheer joy, she wasn't certain about returning his melt-down kisses. She had a quick image of fusion or combustion. At their ages, the thought was frightening. Most of the fusion and combustion should be eased during their younger years. Still...steaming up Morgan's glasses was exciting and tantalizing and exotic. She tugged a ladder from Annabelle's bushes, propped it against the house and dusted her hands. "You first."

"Huh. Not likely. You've had a look in your eye all day, Loving. I wouldn't trust you not to run for Buster and plead kidnapping long enough to get at Annabelle and the Cutesies.... Up."

Fifteen minutes later Susanah emerged from the tiny closet where she had changed into her nightgown for a second time. This time without retaining her jeans and shoes. From the shadows of the fallen bed, Morgan watched her cross the room. She sensed his eyes following her, tracing the voluminous flannel gown. She stepped over him to ease beneath the sheets. "My, that was refreshing," she whispered after a time, very conscious of the way he was watching her.

"Did it ever occur to you, Loving, that the scent of baby powder has been found to drive grown men over the line?"

"Nah. We're middle-aged—too old for that stuff, Lightfoot. Too set in our ways—" Her last words were muffled against his mouth.

She moved into his arms as if she'd always lain at his side. Morgan reached to draw her thigh between his and she nuzzled the crisp hair on his chest. She slid off into sleep with the sense of coming home.

Susanah jerked herself away from the frightening dream. The last shreds of it clung to her and she closed her eyes, recalling the nightmare. Morgan had held the Cutesies in his arms. He gave her a peck on the lips and grinned rakishly, his steamed glasses askew. "Thanks, Loving. These little gems—and last night—will make up for the Foster Loom and whatever."

She closed her eyes and settled down to listen to the slow thump-thump of Morgan's heart. Then she lifted over him, looking down. He had a smug smile on his lips as though he'd just gotten everything he'd ever wanted in life. The cherry off the top of her sundae, the chunk of butter out of the center of the mashed potatoes, the Foster Loom and the— Susanah frowned. He wasn't running away with the Cutesies. She nudged Morgan's shoulder. "Morgan," she whispered slowly, while his lips lifted into a broad grin. "Oh, Morgan," she singsonged gently.

"Mmm?" he answered, still asleep.

She waited a moment, testing him. Then ever so softly, she asked, "Morgan, dear. If you had the chance, would you take the Cutesies from poor little sweet Susanah?"

He snuggled to the pillow, sighed and murmured something about "getting Loving where I want her" in his sleep.

Susanah leaned closer. "Morgan...if you had the chance, would you grab the Cutesies and run with them?" she asked more insistently.

"Uh-huh. Get everything I want," he murmured slowly before he turned over, taking all the blankets with him.

The next morning, Annabelle looked up from whipping pancake batter. She tilted her head to one side and listened to the whump-whump sounds coming from the upstairs bedroom. Susanah placed butter and warmed blueberry syrup on the table and hoped Morgan didn't hurt himself. Tying him to the bed was a necessity. One, to prove that she could meet him on any level and two, to get a few moments alone with Annabelle. While her need to experience Morgan ran piercingly deep, she was dedicated to the acquisition of the Cutesies. Then too, if Morgan knew he could distract her by a few sweet kisses and tidbits of romantic gallantry, she'd never be able to hold her own with him. "Ah... Annabelle, what were you saying about the Cutesies?" she prompted as the whump-whumps continued.

Annabelle poured the batter into a huge, ancient, black cast-iron griddle. "That I'm so glad that you and Morgan are here. The Cutesies love excitement and you two certainly are scamps—the both of you. I thought I heard footsteps on the roof again last night."

She cleared her throat while the bed creaked noisily and the whumps continued. "Ah... dear...shouldn't you check on Morgan? He's probably dreaming about—you know men dream about their ladyloves. You could wake him with a kiss," she suggested sweetly, her eyes sparkling.

"Oh, heavens, no. I wouldn't think of waking Morgan while he's thrashing around like that. He was captured by gorillas once and became the spark of a lady gorilla's eye. The experience sometimes causes him nightmares and I've found that leaving him alone lets him work out his frustration."

Annabelle hummed and swung her spatula to the beat. Susanah took a deep breath and continued her suit for the Cutesies. "I may have to leave before Morgan fully wakes. He knows that I must be getting back. He's had a bad night and I think he'll fall back asleep after he escapes the lady gorilla. If you think that the Cutesies would be happy with custom-controlled heat and cooling, with beautiful new clothing and lots of people to chat with, I'd be happy to start dressing them for the journey now. They can sit up in the back seat of my car—I have a thick flannel quilt all ready—and they can watch the scenery until I take them to their new home. Morgan can get the rest he needs and I'll have the exhibit all set up before he comes home.''

When Annabelle continued humming, Susanah offered, "Or you could sign an agreement that allows my museum to show them off—a care and receipt sort of thing—'

Annabelle eased the edge of the spatula under a bubble covered pancake, checking it. "You know, dear, I've been worried about this museum thing. The Cutesies are used to people sleeping near them. They are used to home living, more specifically living in a house with people moving around them. They aren't that young anymore, and changing lifestyles is difficult."

Was the floor dropping away beneath Susanah's feet? She had a quick image of hanging by her fingertips from a high cliff as Annabelle continued. "I wouldn't want to submit them to any unnecessary trials. I've been thinking how nice it would be if they lived in your home. With Morgan to protect them. They were so happy when Henry was here and I think they'd like having a man around again."

Susanah willed herself not to speak. The issue was too fragile and required careful thought. Her fingertips hurt, clawing for a secure hold on her mental cliff. She swallowed tightly, pushing away the panic. She opened her mouth, then closed it. She cleared her throat. "Annabelle, don't you think—"

Heavy footsteps sounded on the stairway. There was a crash of wood, a dark male curse and the steady, ominous tramp of footsteps toward the kitchen. "Susanah Elizabeth?" Morgan's quiet roar demanded an answer.

"He's done that vaulting over the end of the stair railing, just like my Henry used to do when he was a bit miffed." Annabelle sighed dreamily and whipped her batter. "It was so romantic back then—so heart thrilling to have my husband come storming through the house. Oh, we had our tiffs, but making up—" Annabelle frowned slightly, then began humming again as Susanah eased into the pantry and closed the door behind her.

Morgan jerked it open a second later. Dressed in his boxer shorts and nothing else, he stepped into the small room. "Oh, hello," Susanah managed breathlessly, scooping a jar of peaches from the shelf. "Ah... Annabelle thought peaches might be—"

Morgan bumped his head against a low shelf, cursed darkly, and grabbed her wrist, drawing her out into the kitchen. He smiled briefly at Annabelle in passing and continued drawing Susanah out the front door. She noted the broken railing as they passed. The image of Morgan, dark with temper, vaulting over the old railing caused her to grin. He stood on the porch, his hands on his hips, and glowered down at her. "You tied me to the bed, Loving. Explain yourself."

His hair stood out at angles. White down feathers caught in the thick strands, clung to one dark earlobe and dusted his shoulders. They clung to his stubble-covered jaw and tangled in the hair on his chest. He looked so derailed, so unlike the cool professor she had known and circled for years, that Susanah burst out laughing. "You think this is funny?" Morgan said in that peculiar quiet roar.

"It's equality," she answered, smothering a new round of giggles. "You tied me to the bed."

His glower at her deepened. "That was different," he stated in an outraged tone. "I see now that you'll stop at nothing to get those dolls." Feathers fluttered rhythmically along his jaw as if he were gritting his back teeth. "You didn't tie one ankle, as I did, Loving," he returned. "You wrapped the clothesline around me and the bed. About two hundred times."

"I was never good at knots, Lightfoot." She looked past him to the newcomer at the bottom of the porch steps. "Oh, hello, Sheriff."

"We've got a law against indecency here, Mr. Lightfoot," Buster said between thin lips. He glanced at Morgan's discarded, torn T-shirt dangling from the rosebushes, picked it up like an important bit of criminal evidence and handed it to Morgan. The sheriff scanned the broken rainspout, the ladder leaning against the roof and turned Annabelle's antique door knocker.

The tiny, perky lady appeared instantly. She scurried between Buster and Morgan and smiled. Not sweetly, her eyes twinkling as they usually did, but more like a hen defending her chick. Both men towered two feet or more over her, yet she planted herself firmly in front of Morgan. Buster looked sheepish, then frowned as he looked inside the house to the broken stair railing. "Problems, Annabelle?"

"Go along now, Morgan...Susanah," Annabelle ordered firmly, plucking a feather from his chest. "Morgan is fixing up the house a bit and Susanah is helping him. I'm afraid things are a bit untidy."

Buster's beady eyes narrowed. "This guy is wearing nothing but feathers and shorts, Annabelle," he insisted doggedly. "It's seven o'clock in the morning."

She shrugged her thin shoulder. "Honeymooners, the scamps," she said, as if the word explained everything. "Go along now, Buster. Everything is just fine. Shoo."

Annabelle glanced at Morgan and Susanah, who were unwilling to leave her to Buster's threatening presence. The little lady's small firm hand pointed to the door. "In. Where you're safe."

Morgan hesitated and looked from the small, defiant woman up to Buster's dark scowl. "I can handle Buster," she said confidently, turning to the sheriff. "You should take off your hat on porches as well as in houses, Buster. It's only good manners."

"They're not married, Annabelle," Buster growled, his heavy jowls settling deep into his shoulders as he removed his hat. "Their car license plates check out to one Morgan Lightfoot and one Susanah Elizabeth Loving."

"Heavens, Buster. You are living in the last century, aren't you?" Annabelle asked haughtily. "Women nowadays can choose to keep their names. Sometimes it suits their career. At any rate, if you wouldn't keep pestering them, they may decide to have a another wedding here—at my bed and breakfast. Honeymooners are scarce as hen's teeth around here, especially ones that might want to have my Cutesies as bridesmaids. Both these children love my Cutesies. I'm going to name the honeymoon suite 'Loving,' after Susanah, and if you tell Fanny of my plans or say one word that could annoy my guests, you...will...never...be...elected again," she said fearlessly. "*I* will run against you. And if *I* run for sheriff, so will Fanny. She's competitive by nature, poor thing."

Buster shivered, fear darting in his small eyes. Morgan blew a feather away from his top lip, raised his eyebrows, and glanced at Susanah. She placed her hand through the crook in his offered arm. They stepped into the living room, quietly closing the door behind them and leaving Annabelle on the battlefield. Buster's hulking shadow slipped through the oval glass door window.

"I have never hidden behind a woman's skirts," Morgan muttered, glaring down at Susanah. A feather lost its mooring in his hair and fluttered down to land on his nose. He blew it away as Susanah backed away a step.

"Oh, look. Buster is arresting Annabelle," she said, pointing at the silhouette of the enormous sheriff and the tiny woman shaking her finger in his face. Morgan frowned threateningly, then jerked open the door. In that instant Susanah leapt over the broken railing and ran up the stairs. She reached their room, turned the key in the lock and leaned against the door, trying to catch her breath.

The running footsteps taking the stairs two at a time never sounded. She waited, then braced a glass against the wood door, placed her ear against it and listened. Silence.

Susanah breathed easier. If Annabelle and Morgan shared dressing the Cutesies and Morgan ate the delicious breakfast waiting for her, his temper would be dulled. Susanah smiled to herself, dusted her hands and, for the first time, surveyed the fallen bed and the room filled with feathers. She sneezed once, then her eyes widened as Morgan jerked up the window, stepped inside and closed it.

He looked thoroughly disgusted and menacing.

She began laughing.

"You," Morgan said darkly, his rigid anger slipping a bit as Susanah held her ribs and doubled over with laughter. She spotted the battered pillow that had come apart in his bid for freedom, grabbed it and started slugging him with it. "This isn't dignified, Loving," Morgan stated, grabbing the pillow to jerk her toward him. While she pulled back, he bent, snatched the good pillow and buffeted her with it.

She stopped pulling, blinked and blew away a new froth of feathers. "You hit me," she said warily. "You actually hit me, Lightfoot," she repeated, this time in an incensed tone. Then the laughter that had been gathering in Morgan escaped. When he laughed aloud, Susanah launched herself at him.

The thrust of her body unbalanced him and he went down on the fallen bed, taking her with him. "Wild woman," he taunted with a grin.

"You'll never get the Cutesies," she warned fiercely, straddling him with her jeans-clad legs. She pushed at his shoulders, pinning him to the feathers and the tangled rosebud sheets. She refused to relay her middle-of-the-night interviewing secrets.

Morgan grinned, moving his shoulders slightly to feel her fingers dig into them. His hands spanned her thighs and he smoothed them while she glared down at him. His gaze slid to her quickly rising and falling breasts, noting the buds that thrust at her T-shirt after a few seconds. Susanah followed his intent gaze, her eyes widened and then she crossed her arms in front of her bosom. Morgan noted with satisfaction the slow blush rising from her throat and the sudden awareness of his arousal beneath her spread thighs. "We're *both* getting the Cutesies. Now come here," he urged unevenly, sliding his hands to her hips, then up to her back.

She resisted at first, eyeing him warily. "You should be frightened, Morgan," she said finally, allowing him to ease her down on top of him. "I've never felt so strongly about revenging my honor with another man."

"Mmm," he agreed, wallowing in the scent of baby powder and Susanah's unique femininity. No other woman smelled like her. "So, go ahead. Revenge away."

The honey brown eyes darkened as he took away her glasses and his, placing them by the bed. He hoped he would be repeating the same gesture for the rest of his life. With the same woman. "Okay. Fine," she returned breathlessly. "Then you'll really be frightened."

"My heart is palpitating with fright now. Lead on, Loving."

"I doubt that you could withstand my beastly urges, Lightfoot. I frighten men. Scare them off—"

"Scare away."

"Then I will," she threatened, lowering her mouth to his.

"You're very soft, Loving," he whispered moments later when she lay naked and shy against him. The rosebud sheet was clutched up to her chin. He smoothed the softness that was her breast, sliding to the thrusting jut of her hip and then cupping the sheet between her thighs.

"You're very skillful, Lightfoot. You undressed me while I was kissing you senseless," she whispered unevenly. "It's daylight," she added in a sudden breathless statement.

"So it is," he whispered, wishing back all the years he'd been apart from S. E. Loving.

"I'll get you for this," she threatened, blowing away a feather that tickled her cheek.

He stroked away another from her breast. "I hope so."

"You're still wearing your shorts," she said, her cheeks flushing again as she glanced down to his immediate problem. Then her eyes jerked back to his. "I won't be your floozy, Lightfoot. Not another notch on your well-worn bedpost."

"There aren't that many notches." He lifted her hand to his lips and kissed the exact, soft center of it, inhaling the baby powder with delight. "You're a primitive, savage, pagan sorceress, Loving. An animal.''

She blushed deeper and he stroked her hot cheek with his fingertip. ''I've never really been able to release my...tensions before, Lightfoot. Congratulations. You seemed to hold up admirably.''

''We didn't do anything, Loving,'' he reminded her with a kiss. He could go on wallowing in feathers, rosebuds and baby powder forever, he decided. ''But I wanted to.''

She bit her lip, searching his eyes, and shivered delicately. ''The situation is critical. You know that, don't you?''

''Mmm. Critical,'' he agreed, watching her forage through her thoughts. ''But don't ever think,'' he added softly, slowly, ''that you're going to ignite like this with another man. Because as your pseudo-husband, I've got dibs.''

''This will never work,'' she whispered unevenly, her eyes wide with discovery.

''It's perfect, Loving. Trust me.''

''You're a romantic sort of old-fashioned guy under all that Mr. Macho Cool, aren't you, Lightfoot?'' Susanah asked warily.

He frowned slightly, considering her remark. ''Well...I don't have your kamikaze technique, but I get there in a methodical sort of fashion.''

When she laughed outright, Morgan grinned.

Epilogue

"A June wedding. A June bride. The first in Pothole's bed-and-breakfast history." After the Lightfoot's wedding reception, Annabelle sighed dreamily, then wiped away a tear from her eye with a lacy handkerchief. "Henry would have been so proud of my business skills. When you two finish your honeymoon next week, a nice couple has asked me to arrange their wedding in my parlor. They want to honeymoon with me, of course. The Cutesies are just glowing from all the excitement. I'm glad they're staying with me until your home is ready. I would have missed them so, though I know that you two will take excellent care of them later."

Annabelle beamed up at Morgan, the always man, who looked extremely desirable in his western-cut wedding suit. He carried a tray of emptied punch cups and cake dishes to the kitchen. Then Annabelle raised on tiptoe to hug Susanah. "Sweet. So sweet. Thank you," she whispered, drawing away and scanning Susanah's frothy old-fashioned bridal gown and veil, which Morgan had insisted she wear. "Your Morgan is a romantic. He'll be like that all your lives," Annabelle said, picking up her purse and overnight bag. "Now I've warned Buster that you'll be honeymooning by yourselves for tonight. I'm staying at Fanny's. Buster will watch over you."

Morgan entered the parlor, slid his arm around Susanah's waist and eased her against him. As always, Morgan's love and gentle strength and a sense of forever enveloped Susanah. "Thank you, Annabelle. We'll watch the Cutesies."

"I've told them to behave, the scamps."

Morgan and Susanah watched Annabelle get into Buster's patrol car, then turned to each other. He breathed unevenly, jerked off his jacket and tie, and flipped open his shirt buttons. He lifted his challenging left eyebrow and looked down at Susanah. "Well, Loving?"

"Lightfoot, to you," she corrected as he pulled down the shades and locked the door.

Half an hour later, Morgan lay under Susanah, his heartbeat slowing beneath her cheek. She smoothed the hair on his chest, a little ashamed at releasing her pent-up desires. Her new husband hadn't seemed to mind, though he had muttered something about a slow, steady approach to making love when he caught his breath. He'd blown away a fold of bridal veil tangled around them, then added the strangest comment about a late model Buick running over Alice.

Morgan had treated her very carefully during their courtship, wooing her with bouquets and picnics and sharing his heart with her. He was everything she'd ever wanted as a friend, as a lover. Then there was that bit of a rake lurking in him, the challenging tilt to his head when he was on the scent of a new acquisition that might interest her. She thought about the old house they planned to restore and stock with "finds." The Cutesies would have their own place in a parlor much like Annabelle's. Morgan had gone to extreme lengths to determine the stability of the rain guttering. The climbing rose trellis reminded her of a sturdy ladder.

Now lying on the newly fallen mattress, enclosed by the antique, walnut four-poster bed, she loved him more than ever.

"I love you, Susanah Elizabeth," he whispered unevenly, his mind flowing with hers. He blew away a bud of Annabelle's Lily of the Valley that still clung to her hair.

"And I love you," she returned, lifting up to tuck a Lily of the Valley stalk above Morgan's ear. She read eternity in his dark eyes, her always man.

After a long, slow, sweet kiss, Morgan whispered huskily, "I don't know if I can repeat this experience next month at your mother's house."

"Morgan, sweetheart, baby," she returned unevenly, blushing as she thought of how she had just ignited beneath Morgan's gentle lovemaking. She hadn't been gentle once she'd discovered that he wasn't that fragile and could withstand her passions. Morgan had risen to the occasion, responding magnificently. "Your mother is planning to bake apple pies."

He kissed her forehead. "They'll expect us to stay with them. You can get excited when you're going in for a kamikaze landing. The purrs could keep them awake."

"This was my first chance to experience you, Lightfoot. You've been very proper," she reminded him with a blush.

"Mmm," he murmured, turning her beneath him. "I'm a safe kind of guy. I wanted to know I had you fully in my lair before pouncing."

She adjusted another sprig of Lily of the Valley over his other ear and studied the dashing effect. His eyes darkened when his hand caressed her breast. She shivered, realizing how deeply this man loved her... how deeply she loved him. The sense of forever ran through her, as inevitable as spring and Annabelle's daffodils. "Hmm. Don't worry about staying with your parents on our next wedding night. There's always Alice."

The next June, Morgan watched Susanah work through her paperwork for a new acquisition. He enjoyed the quick slash-slash of her pen, the sound of papers jerked impatiently aside. Sitting at her desk, she glanced at him and he knew that he was due for another kamikaze session of lovemaking. She tapped the correct measure of food into a new Oscar's fishbowl and eyed Morgan warningly. He grinned and nuzzled their daughter, who had just burped satisfactorily on his shoulder.

Elizabeth Lynn arrived exactly nine months from the night Susanah and he spent in Alice's front seat.

The Cutesies cuddled together in front of their doll house, waiting to return to Annabelle's for a visit. Morgan studied them while he rocked his daughter. The dolls seemed extremely happy with the new activity in the house. In fact, they had seemed right at home the minute they were introduced to the parlor. They sympathized with Susanah when she began to waddle and hadn't minded Morgan's distraction during the last days before the baby's birth. They had listened to his fears, his joys in the gentlest of ways.

He blew them a night-night kiss and found Susanah looking at him strangely. No doubt, sometime in the night she would try one of those sneaky little interviews when she thought he was sleeping. Morgan blew her a kiss. Those interviews delighted him; wonderful things happened while he led her on.

Annabelle was waiting to see the Cutesies and the baby, and in the morning—Morgan met Susanah's steamy gaze and his grin widened. In the morning, if he was able, they would pack the Cutesies, Oscar and Elizabeth in Alice and go to Pothole. A small trailer attached to Alice's rear bumper would provide more room.

He savored the thought of making the pilgrimage that had begun the previous spring.

He caught the scents of daffodils in fresh spring air, baby powder, rosebuds, and love. "Pretty nice way to spend a lifetime," he murmured against Elizabeth's soft baby curls.

"Hmm?" Susanah asked softly, her eyes shining with love.

"I love you, S.E."

"Ditto, Lightfoot."

* * * * *

SPRING

Daffodils. Robins. March winds lifting kites high into the clear blue sky. Little girls wearing brand-new Easter dresses. All these things are caught in the scent of spring. It's a time when we begin anew, anticipate what the year will bring. There's a special energy swirling through spring air, zipping into hearts and lifting them high, just like those March winds carrying kites. Since my birthday is in April, it's my favorite spring month. I do a bit of gardening, a bit of housecleaning and a whole lot of enjoying life, big bouquets of daffodils, riding my bicycle, and occasionally that kite-flying caper. I hope you enjoy Lightfoot and Loving's story, because it bears that scent of spring and the surprise that lovers can discover at any age—if the heart is willing. To spring, April and new beginnings. Enjoy.

Cait

OUT OF THE DARK

Pepper Adams

Chapter One

Hallie Stewart climbed the stepladder with a sticky strip of wallpaper in her hands. She groaned when she attempted to align the floral pattern; it didn't match. She shouldn't make such stupid mistakes, as an amateur decorator she'd hung wallpaper many times. But not, she reminded herself, with three bored children underfoot. The little darlings were driving her crazy.

Only an hour ago, she'd issued them an ultimatum disguised as a choice: go outside and play in the sunshine or suffer a fate worse than death. Said fate to be determined later by one very desperate mother. They'd sulked out, none too happy about the forced exile.

It had been a month since they'd left Dallas, and the kids still hadn't adjusted. To them, the move to Jacinta was comparable to being marooned on a desert island without cable TV. According to ten-year-old Mark, it was a "dumb hick place," forever doomed to ignominy because it boasted neither video arcade nor McDonald's.

But it was exactly what Hallie was looking for. After fifteen years in urban Dallas, she welcomed the slower pace and security of the sleepy little town.

No one had ever been mugged in Jacinta, and the last murder had occurred in 1912—when local ranchers had lynched a cattle thief. It was a safe environment for children, and the rambling eighty-year-old, two-story Victorian farmhouse she'd bought was the culmination of a dream.

For years, she and Jim had saved to get their kids out of the city. They'd planned to buy an old place with character and turn it into a bed and breakfast. Renovated to showcase Hallie's design talents, it would bring in decorating commissions to supplement Jim's job as a smalltown lawman. It was a good plan.

But Jim was gone now and it was up to Hallie to make the dream a reality. A patrolman with the Dallas police force, he'd been gunned down by a motorist he'd stopped for speeding. Shattered by the mindless violence, it had taken Hallie three years to get herself and her finances together. When they'd finally left the city, she'd heaved a sigh of relief heard all the way to the state line.

The children's protests had been just as loud. City kids, they didn't know what to do with themselves in the country. But they'd come around—if they survived all the family togetherness.

Hallie had recut the strip of paper and was smoothing it into place when her dusty herd stampeded into the guest room where she was working. They all shouted at once and her youngest, six-year-old Katie, was crying.

"What's going on?" Hallie demanded in her sternest mom voice. After another spate of incomprehensible babble, she added, "One at a time, if you don't mind? Mark, what's this all about?"

"We saw a demon in Donahue's living room," he explained matter-of-factly. "These big babies got scared when the window broke. They ran all the way home."

"Did not," eight-year-old Andy and his sister replied in unison, their breathlessness giving lie to their denial.

"Did so." Mark liked having the last word.

Hallie gave the wallpaper a final swipe. "I can't believe you guys went over there. I've told you a dozen times to leave that poor man alone."

"He is not a man," Mark proclaimed in a hokey Hungarian accent. "He is vun of de living dead."

"And he has a big, ugly dog." Katie sniffed.

Mark rolled his eyes. "It's not a dog, it's a familiar. It guards the coffin during the day and makes sure no one bugs the vampire. Jeez, everybody knows that." An avid reader, he was the resident expert on all things that went bump in the night.

Hallie sent her eldest a quelling glance. "I want to know who broke the window."

"The dog . . . I mean, the familiar did," Andy offered.

"We were peeking in and the hairy thing jumped up and the window broke," Katie summarized in her typically succinct manner.

"It wouldn't have happened if you three hadn't disobeyed me."

"Mark's right, Mom." Andy's eyes widened behind his red-framed glasses. "Donahue is a vampire. There was a scary-looking creature just sittin' in his living room. There's ooky things all over the place and there's a big box in the corner."

"That's his coffin," Mark insisted. "He sleeps in it during the day and only comes out at night to suck the blood of innocent victims." He hissed at his sister and bared imaginary fangs.

"Mom-mee!" Katie brushed a blond curl out of her eyes. "I don't wanna get my blood sucked."

"That's enough! You're all in big trouble this time." Hallie was furious that they'd disobeyed specific orders to stay away from Donahue's place. The man was a recluse and somewhat of a local enigma. According to rumor, he never left his house during the day, and had only been seen at night. He had no visible means of support, never had visitors, and didn't shop in Jacinta for food or anything else.

The children's fertile minds had put two and two together and come up with 666. It didn't help that Mark covertly read *Dracula* to them as a bedtime story. Or that their superstitious live-in believed the tall tales herself. Petrita Gomez's room reeked of garlic, and crosses adorned every wall. Even though the woman was part of the problem, Hallie couldn't let her go. She needed Pete's help with the kids and she had an embarrassing weakness for her *chili rellenos.*

The local plumber was the only one in town who'd actually seen the inside of Donahue's house. He'd been called out after midnight and had been well paid for the trip. He, too, claimed it was a spooky place, dark and full of shadows. Of course, it had regular pipes like any other house.

He couldn't say much about the mystery man himself. Donahue had lurked in the shadows of the candlelit kitchen, a storm having played havoc with the electricity. The plumber had fixed the broken pipe by flashlight.

"Why did you go over there, when you had orders not to?" Hallie's sharp gaze pierced the three young miscreants.

"To check out Donahue, of course." Mark's reasonable tone irritated his mother. "How many chances do ordinary kids get to see a vampire's coffin close up?"

Andy and Katie nodded in mute agreement, but they did not seem as enthusiastic about monster hunting as their brother.

Hallie closed her eyes and counted to ten. "Okay, troops, listen up. The following is a Mommy Pronouncement. *There are no such things as vampires.* Vampires are imaginary. Period."

"Not according to Bram Stoker and Jonathan Dark," Mark put in. After finishing the classic, he'd turned to contemporary tales written by popular horror novelists. Hallie encouraged her children to read and tried not to censor their books, but she might have to reconsider that policy.

"Do you know the difference between fiction and nonfiction?" she asked her eldest. Leaving his friends had been hardest on Mark, and she tried to be sympathetic.

"Yeah, why?"

"When you check Jonathan Dark books out of the library, in what section do you find them? Fiction or nonfiction?"

"Fiction," he mumbled.

"I rest my case, end of discussion. Now go wash up." She called into the kitchen, "Pete, fix these little monsters some lunch before I throw them all in the dungeon."

"We don't have a dungeon," Mark pointed out.

"A minor detail. Now, scoot!"

Over enchiladas, Hallie announced, "I've decided you three owe Mr. Donahue an apology. We'll have to go over and pay for that window."

"Not!" Mark was adamant. "Now that I know what he is, I'm not going over there and get turned into one of the undead."

"Me, neither," said Andy.

Katie's lower lip trembled. "Can little girls be undeads?"

"Nah," said Mark. "Vampires eat runts like you."

"Mark Stewart, that is quite enough! The fact that he never comes out in the daytime does not make him a vampire. Maybe he has a medical condition. Some people are allergic to sunlight, you know."

Pete crossed herself. "Or maybe he turns himself into a bat at night and eats bugs," she said in heavily accented English.

"Or maybe his real name isn't Jake Donahue, at all," Mark said brightly. "Maybe it's Count Gargoyle."

"Or maybe he sleeps in his coffin all day on a bed of dirt from Transylvania," contributed Andy.

Katie said nothing. For several days she'd worn a garlic necklace of Pete's construction, and refused to open her windows at night despite the June heat.

Hallie banged her fork down and stood. "That does it! If you won't go over there and apologize for breaking that window and making pests of yourselves, I'll have to do it for you."

Her announcement caused general alarm. "No, Señora Hallie." Pete clutched the crucifix around her neck. "You must not go to that evil place."

"Don't go, Mom," begged Andy. "We promise we won't even look in his direction again. We'll make our beds every day and wash all the dishes. Won't we, Mark?"

"Speak for yourself, dweeb." Turning to Hallie, Mark said, "Don't do it. It's hard enough being the new kid in town without having a mom who's a creature of the night.''

"Don't get your blood sucked, Mommy," Katie cried.

Despite promises to give up their investigation of Donahue, Hallie didn't believe them for a moment. Children were always fascinated by the forbidden and they wouldn't be able to stay away. Now that their imaginations were stirred, her home would be in a constant uproar. She'd never get any work done if she didn't resolve the vampire issue once and for all.

She was already behind on the renovations. The electrical and plumbing repairs had been more extensive than she'd expected, and she'd had to pay for them out of her savings. That's why she was doing the papering, painting and minor repairs herself. At this rate, she'd never be ready for autumn guests, and she'd be lucky if she didn't run out of funds before the work was finished.

Seeing their concern, Hallie dropped the subject. She'd go talk to Donahue after they went to bed. Maybe he'd agree to meet them in the daytime, thus permanently disproving the vampire theory and restoring peace. The kids would be leaving for church camp in two weeks. Hopefully, they'd forget all about Count Donahue while they were gone. Since Pete was going to Mexico for a family wedding at the same time, Hallie anticipated two weeks of uninterrupted work time.

Tired by their day's adventure, the children settled down just after dusk. The night was pleasant and the moon was full, so Hallie decided to walk the mile or so to Donahue's house. She hadn't had much time for aerobic exercise lately.

On the way over, she rehearsed what she would say to her mysterious neighbor. First, she'd apologize for her children's behavior and explain their overactive imaginations. Then she'd graciously offer to pay for the damage. She had a gift for winning people over and once she established rapport with the man, she'd hit him with her request.

Demons and coffins in the living room! It was so silly, it was almost funny. Donahue was probably a nice old man who collected taxidermy specimens or something.

When she arrived, Hallie had second thoughts about her mission. Who knew a log cabin could look so foreboding? Clouds temporarily obscured the moon and the untended bushes and trees around the house added to the eerie darkness. The only light was a weird green glow leaking from a side window. She felt an icy prickle of dread inspired by her children's wild tales, and clutched the crucifix Pete had insistently draped around her neck.

Nocturnal visits to the homes of strangers definitely fell into the bad idea category. Donahue was no blood-sucking vampire, but he could certainly be a pervert of some kind. Why else would he sleep all day and skulk around in the dark of night? She stood on the porch, trying to decide what to do.

Deep in the recesses of the house, a dog howled balefully. Hallie jumped; the gloom and silence must be getting to her. She should leave. He probably wasn't home, anyway. At this hour minions of the night were out preying on innocents, weren't they? Chastising herself for behaving like the heroine in a gothic novel, Hallie turned to go.

Just then the heavy door creaked open on unused hinges and a voice from deep in the shadows demanded, "What do you want?"

She was so startled by the sound of that creaking and by the tone of that voice that she said the first thing that came to mind, "I hear you have a coffin in your living room."

Jake Donahue was as startled as his uneasy visitor. Klute had let him know someone was outside, but hadn't expected the prowler to be an attractive young woman. The clouds drifted and the moonlight revealed a trim figure in baggy denim shorts and pink T-shirt. Her shoulder-length hair was ash brown and her delicately sculpted features were set in a worried frown.

"I asked you a question," he repeated gruffly.

"And a very rude one, at that." Hallie couldn't see the man's face, he stood well back in the shadows. He hadn't switched on a light or in any way tried to make her feel welcome.

"If you're with the 'please' and 'thank you' patrol, consider me warned." Jake wasn't accustomed to making small talk and it showed.

Hallie's frown turned into determination. "I'd like to speak to you, Mr. Donahue. You are Jake Donahue, aren't you?"

"Yeah. Who are you?"

"I'm your neighbor, Hallie Stewart. My family and I moved into the old Cantwell place last month."

"Pleased to meet you." He sounded anything but pleased as he eased the door shut a little farther.

"I understand my children were nosing around over here today and broke a window. I'd like to pay for it."

"No need. Your kids didn't break it, my dog did. Good night, Mrs. Stewart."

"Go ahead, slam the door in my face," she challenged.

Donahue stepped out into the moonlight and Hallie finally got a good look at him. He certainly wasn't old and he didn't appear to be the type who engaged in taxidermy. He was over six feet tall and well-built. His dark hair needed trimming and the stubble he sported was at least a three days' accumulation. His black shirt and jeans were seriously rumpled, as though he'd slept in them more than once. His fashion statement, if he was trying to make one, was of the grunge persuasion.

His eyes were wary behind thin, metal-framed spectacles, his white teeth straight and un-fanglike. She could rule out vampire, but pervert was still a possibility.

"What do you want, Mrs. Stewart?" His voice was sharp and edged with weariness.

Hallie stated her business before she could chicken out. "I'd like you to come to my house for lunch tomorrow."

The invitation took Jake by surprise. The locals had long since given up trying to include him in social activities. "No, thank you. Good night."

"Are you always this rude?" Now Hallie's voice was demanding.

"Only to strangers who come snooping around uninvited."

"I am not snooping! I'm trying to be neighborly," she said indignantly.

"Don't trouble yourself, Mrs. Stewart. I have no need for your hospitality."

His unrelenting gruffness irritated her. It didn't cost extra to be civil. She wanted to turn around and walk off. But she needed this man's cooperation if she was to rid her children of their fascination with vampires. And something, some uncertain note in his otherwise brittle manner, told her Jake Donahue needed someone, too.

"You're not a very nice man," she observed.

"That's right, I'm not. Now, for the last time, good night!' Jake was surprised to find one of the woman's small-size tennis shoes wedged in the door.

"I still need to talk to you," she insisted.

She was persistent, he'd give her that. His first reaction was to take her advice and shut the door in her face, but something about her intrigued him. "Make it quick. I'm busy."

Doing what? Hallie wondered what his business was. Behind him, the house was dark and silent except for the rustling of the dog. Or bats. It could be bats.

"My kids think you're a vampire and that you sleep in a coffin in your living room."

Vampire, huh? An unexpected smile softened the hard line of Jake's lips. In a town the size of Jacinta, gossip and speculation was a major form of entertainment and he knew he was the subject of a strange assortment of rumors. He'd heard some of the more colorful ones from the voluble plumber. A: He was with the witness protection program. B: He was a disfigured burn victim. C: He was a burned-out covert operative. D: All of the above. His personal favorite involved a mob hitman hiding from his associates. He had to hand it to the lady. Vampire beat hitman, any day.

"What do you think?" His tone betrayed none of his amusement.

"I think you're a crotchety, antisocial hermit with paranoid delusions and possible agoraphobia.

Which I'm willing to overlook if you'll come and meet my kids in the daytime to prove to them that you're a mere mortal, however maladjusted you may be."

"You're kinda crotchety yourself," he said with a wry smile. She was also pretty, like a steel butterfly who only looked soft on the outside.

"I can be when the occasion demands." Hallie smiled back. That brief flash of humor had transformed Donahue. His eyes, once suspicious and secretive, sparkled with intelligence. His lips, which she'd thought grim and uncompromising, curved sensuously. He was darkly handsome, and she was disarmed by the unwanted attraction she felt for him.

"So? What do you say?" she prompted.

"I can't help you. I sleep during the day." Jake preferred to work at night, even when that work was going badly. The darkness and silence, which usually inspired him, also kept daytime types away. Ordinarily.

"On a bed of soil from Transylvania?"

"Actually, it's a waterbed, if you must know."

"Bad back?"

"Something like that."

Hallie felt encouraged. They had actually engaged in what could almost be called a conversation and he hadn't ordered her off his property or brandished a chainsaw. She glanced at the lone twig chair on the porch longingly. "Mind if I sit down? I've been hanging wallpaper all day, and I'm beat."

Before Jake could object, the woman appropriated his chair. His chair. The chair no one else ever sat in. Who did she think she was, barging in, making herself at home? Given little choice, he followed and perched on the porch railing nearby.

"Look, Mr. Donahue, I realize you don't know me and you could care less about my problems, but I need your help."

She yelped when the front door creaked open and a large, dark form slipped onto the porch. Then she realized it was a dog. *The* dog. Katie had been right, it was big and ugly. It thrust a damp muzzle into her lap, and she had no choice but to stroke the large, scruffy head.

"What kind of dog would you say this is?" Her skeptical tone said she was unconvinced of its canine origins.

"Part Irish wolfhound, part Rhodesian Ridgeback. The rest is anyone's guess. Don't be afraid of Klute. She looks scary, but she's a big sissy. Most dogs bark at intruders, Klute cries." He leaned over and ruffled the dog's fur affectionately.

The man was an animal lover. That was encouraging. "My son thinks she's a familiar. Do you know what that means?"

"Yes, I do. I hope she didn't frighten your kids too much."

"They'll survive. But I may not. This vampire thing is making me crazy. Andy said he saw a coffin in your living room."

"Actually, it's in my office. You and your husband should teach your children the concept of trespassing, Mrs. Stewart."

So he did have a coffin? He was strange, but she didn't think he was that strange. "I'm a widow and I'm doing the best I can. Except for money set aside for the children's educations, I've sunk every penny into the Jacinta Inn. I've been working day and night to get it ready."

Strangely enough, Jake was relieved to learn she wasn't married, though he didn't know why her marital status should concern him. "The what?"

"The Jacinta Inn. That's what I plan to call the Cantwell place. I'm renovating it as a bed-and-breakfast establishment."

"You must be a masochist," he said sarcastically. "That place is a dump."

"You're telling me." Encouraged, she recounted some of her more horrifying electrical problems. "If Jonathan Dark wanted to write a really scary book, he'd write one about remodeling."

"Jonathan Dark?" His eyes grew suspicious again.

"You know, the horror novelist? It's his fault my kids are so spooked. I may have to ban his books from the house to keep Mark from frightening his brother and sister."

"Pretty bad, huh?"

"Petrita, that's my cook, hides crosses all over the house and genuflects whenever your name is mentioned. My daughter Katie wears a huge garlic lei, even to bed. She's no joy to be around, if you know what I mean."

This time Jake laughed, and the release felt good. He hadn't laughed in a long time.

His laughter caught Hallie unaware. Rich and masculine, it was totally unexpected. But the sound of it made her inexplicably glad. "Look, if you can't manage lunch, just come over tomorrow and let Pete and the kids see your reflection in a mirror. Eat a piece of garlic, kiss a crucifix, and you're outta there. What do you say?"

"You know a lot about vampires," he observed.

She shrugged. "Mark's the expert. Jonathan Dark taught him everything he knows. And stop changing the subject."

Jake wavered. He felt Hallie's warmth and enthusiasm in ways he'd long since thought lost to him. For five long years he hadn't allowed himself to be charmed by anyone. Now, within fifteen short minutes, the pert Widow Stewart had done just that.

She looked at him questioningly. "Will you do it?"

"Is Petrita a good cook?" Jake had grown tired of microwave dinners.

Hallie smelled triumph in the air and went for the kill. "Her *chili relleños* are to die for."

Jake knew he should refuse. Five years of social withdrawal made it hard for him to say yes. The power of Hallie Stewart's appealing personality made it even harder to say no. Now he knew why moths and flames had become such a cliché.

Sensing a mistake in the making, he asked, "What time do you want me?"

Chapter Two

The vampire luncheon, as the kids called it, promised to be a dark and stormy affair. When Hallie broke the news to them at breakfast the next morning, all three were violently opposed to meeting a real live ghoul face-to-face.

Katie looked as if she'd just been informed that there was no Santa Claus. Her eyes filled and two fat tears rolled slowly down her cheeks and plopped into her cereal bowl.

"Don't you love us anymore, Mommy?" she asked incredulously.

"Of course, I love you, sweetheart. Very much. That's why it's important that you learn, once and for all, there's no such thing as vampires. Once you've met Mr. Donahue, you'll see that he's just a...a...regular man. It's for your own good."

Mark rolled his eyes at his brother. "Ever notice how grown-ups always say that just before they do something bad to you?"

Andy nodded and his glasses slipped down his nose. "That's what she said when we moved here."

"You all seem to forget that you voted 'yes' to this move." Hallie was proud that she and her children were a team. She tried to give them a voice in the major decisions affecting them.

"But we didn't know about *him* when we voted," Katie wailed.

"Yeah," Andy agreed. "We didn't know there'd be a vampire living down the road."

"He's not a vampire," Hallie insisted. "He's just a man. And his name is Mr. Donahue."

Mark's glare was mutinous as he crossed his arms over his chest. "I vote we call and cancel the whole thing."

"Yeah," Katie and Andy cried together.

"It's too late for that," Hallie said firmly. "He's coming and that's the end of it."

"What if I'm not hungry at lunchtime?" Katie wanted to know.

Hallie gave her a stern look. "Then you may sit quietly at the table and watch the rest of us eat."

Katie hung her head, but not so far that her mother couldn't see her pouty bottom lip.

Andy was silent. He pushed his glasses up on his nose, a sure sign he'd have more to say later.

Mark took a mouthful of cereal; he was never too upset to go off his feed. "What are we gonna have for lunch? Eye of newt and bat wing stew?"

"We're having homemade soup and tuna salad sandwiches." Hallie hoped Donahue wouldn't be too disappointed about the *chili relleños,* but Petrita had refused to come out of her room, much less cook for him.

Mark laughed and jabbed his brother with an elbow. "It doesn't matter what we have. He won't eat it."

"Right!" Andy agreed excitedly. "Vampires don't eat real food, they just suck blood."

"Okay." Hallie smiled smugly. "There's your proof! When Mr. Donahue eats the tuna sandwiches, you'll know he's not a vampire."

As lunchtime drew near, Hallie chided her kids to be on their best behavior. Which was pointless. Katie refused to remove her garlic necklace. Mark and Andy were much too noisy for company.

To top it off, the roiling clouds that had hung low in the vast Texas skies all morning had finally obliterated the sunshine and burst their seams. The rainstorm was a regular frog washer and showed no signs of letting up. Maybe that's why their guest was late.

Or maybe he'd changed his mind about coming and hadn't bothered to call. After all, he wasn't famous for courtesy.

Katie skipped into the kitchen where Hallie was preparing the food. "Wanna play dolls, Mommy?"

"I have to finish making lunch, sweetie. How about a rain check?" she suggested as she spread slices of bread with generous portions of tuna salad.

Katie grinned expectantly. "It's raining now."

"That means that I'll play with you later," Hallie explained. "It's past lunchtime. Go wash up and tell the boys to do the same."

"We did already. Can I eat a sandwich in my room?"

"No, we're all having lunch together in the dining room with our guest. And everyone had better use good manners." Hallie lifted the lid from the soup pot. The savory beef, vegetables and barley had been simmering all morning and was ready to serve. She poured the soup into the warmed tureen.

Carrying the food into the dining room, she gave the table a final check. It was five minutes past the time she'd told Donahue lunch would be served. The table was set, the food was ready, and her children were filled with anxiety. Where was he?

"I've got to be nuts," Jake grumbled to himself as he trudged through the pouring rain to the Stewart house. What had seemed like a good idea last night seemed merely stupid today. He had better things to do on a dark and stormy Monday afternoon. Doing lunch, especially with a potentially nosy neighbor, was not his style.

He and Klute had started out in plenty of time. Then the thunder cut loose and the dog had whimpered and whined until he'd had to turn around and take her home. Guests were supposed to bring the hostess flowers, not a big, drippy dog who would surely shake herself all over the living room. He knew he was late, but wasn't alarmed about it. Since his self-imposed exile, he'd given up living his life by a clock. Schedules were just one of the things he'd come to Jacinta to forget.

For the past five years he had worked when he felt like it, ate when he was hungry, and slept when he was too tired to do anything else. He answered to no one but himself. It was a great way to live.

So, why was he interrupting his life today? Why was he tramping through mud and rain to eat a lunch he didn't want? He was no good samaritan. Why had he agreed to help Hallie Stewart rid her nosy kids of their misguided notions?

He hated to admit it, but the simple truth was, he was attracted to the young widow. Strongly attracted. Last night, when he'd gazed into Hallie's hazel eyes, he'd felt stirrings of desire. During the course of their conversation, he'd found himself wondering what it would be like to touch her, to kiss her. To take her into his arms and have his way with her. Then, hot on the heels of that disturbing thought, came the surprising urge to protect her. From himself. Five years of celibacy could do strange things to a man.

No doubt it was the result of testosterone overload, he decided as he trudged around to the back door of Hallie's house. As much as he disliked the idea, it was true. He'd risked getting struck by lightning and gambled his anonymity to have lunch with an attractive woman. Men were such pitiful creatures.

Jake paused on the back porch to shake off some of the rainwater. Through the window, he watched Hallie bend over the open oven door and peer inside. She straightened and brushed back a stray lock of hair. Her face was flushed from the heat and she was even prettier than he remembered. Soaked or not, Jake was suddenly glad he'd come. And he was glad all over again that Hallie Stewart was a widow.

When he knocked, her three kids skidded into the kitchen to peer anxiously at the door, as though expecting the spawn of Satan to walk through it. What kind of mother let her children read Jonathan Dark's books? They weren't meant for young, impressionable minds. Attractive as Hallie Stewart was, those kids reminded Jake that he wasn't interested in getting involved with anybody's family. He'd eat the garlic and make tracks.

It didn't turn out to be that easy. In fact, Jake had never been so uncomfortable in his life. It had little to do with the fact that his jeans were wet, his feet were cold, or that the paint-spattered T-shirt Hallie had insisted he wear while she dried his shirt was several sizes too small.

It was mostly the three sets of frightened blue eyes that stared at him from their various positions around the table. The Stewart children acted as if they expected him to bare his teeth and bite them at any moment.

Hallie looked around and sighed. This wasn't the ice-breaking event she'd planned. The storm outside raged on, the thunder and lightning lending an ominous mood to the gathering. No one was getting acquainted—she was the only one doing any talking.

Jake was quiet, too quiet, and her children weren't their usual, exuberant selves. Normally that wouldn't be a bad thing, but for once she wished they'd say something. Instead they just sat there—staring at the man like a tree full of young owls.

She was no better. She had to force her own gaze away from him. Not because she was afraid, but because she was so surprised by the transformation in his appearance. Last night he'd seemed rumpled and grumpy and formidable. Today he was clean-shaven and his wet hair was finger-combed straight back from his high, intelligent forehead. His dark eyes, which had been wary last night, now seemed to plead for divine intervention to get him through the meal.

She tried not to stare, but she couldn't help noticing how the too small shirt stretched across his chest and shoulders. His muscles were firm and well-defined, but not overdeveloped. She'd never wear that shirt again without recalling his powerful virility. Jake's physical strength was in sharp contrast to the emotional vulnerability she sensed in him, and that contrast made him even more intriguing.

"I hope you like tuna sandwiches and vegetable soup, Mr. Donahue," Hallie said as she passed him a steaming bowl.

"Thank you." Jake tried to be gracious, but vegetable soup was way down on his list. He hadn't eaten tuna in years out of loyalty to the hapless dolphins of the world.

"I understand the annual Jacinta rodeo is next month." Hallie hoped she could start the conversational ball rolling. "Is it as much fun as we've heard?"

Jake looked at his food because when he looked up, there were all those eyes watching him. "Nothing's ever as much fun as you think it'll be."

So much for the old conversational ball. Hallie glanced at her middle son and watched him push his glasses up the bridge of his nose. His I-told-you-so look said it all.

She tried again. "Have you always lived in Jacinta?"

"No." Jake hated talking about himself, so he didn't elaborate. Hallie looked at him expectantly, so he added, "I'm from Chicago."

She could see that if they were ever going to learn anything about Jake Donahue, it was up to her. "We're from Dallas. Jim and I always wanted to move to a place like this and raise the children in the country."

Suddenly the departed husband was also at the table. Jake hadn't expected that. "I see."

"Our daddy was killed in the line of duty," Andy put in.

"I'm sorry to hear that." Jake was suddenly even more uncomfortable.

"Dad was a good cop," Mark said. "A hero."

"What's a hero?" Katie asked.

"Someone admired for his achievement and noble qualities," Hallie put in.

"Is it a good thing to be?" her daughter wanted to know.

"Yes," Hallie said. "Now eat your soup before it gets cold." She noticed that Jake wasn't eating. "Is your food all right?"

He looked up and saw the challenge glittering in Mark's eyes.

"It's great soup," the boy said. "Go ahead, try some." The unspoken "if you dare" hung between them.

Jake knew the kids were testing him. He took a bite, chewed, then swallowed. It wasn't as bad as the canned fare he was used to, but it was still vegetable soup. When he glanced up, everyone was looking at him, apparently waiting for his response.

"It's fine," he said impatiently. Why had he agreed to come here? He should have taken a cold shower instead.

Hallie turned to Mark and raised an eyebrow. Her oldest son shrugged noncommittally. "One bite of soup does not a mortal make," he whispered out of the corner of his mouth.

Katie clutched her garlic necklace with one hand and asked Jake, "Why do you have a coffin in your house?"

"Katie!" Hallie admonished.

"Mom, you said we should get to know him." Mark took up for his sister. "Since he's not talking much, somebody had to ask."

Jake had spent the past five years staying away from people, especially children. Although they had been fairly quiet so far, he suspected that subdued was not the Stewart kids' normal behavior pattern. There was too much mischief in their eyes.

Jake decided to answer the rude question. "The coffin was a gift from a friend."

Mark folded his arms across his thin chest. "This friend isn't by any chance a royal count of Transylvania, is he?"

Andy had just taken a bite of soup and nearly lost it when he got tickled by his brother's silly question. "Yeah, maybe it was from good ol' Count Dracula himself."

"That's enough, boys." Hallie's voice was quiet and serious. She didn't like to discipline her children in front of others. It was embarrassing for everyone. But this line of talk needed squelching immediately.

"Mr. Donahue was kind enough to meet you in an effort to allay your fears. He is our guest and I won't stand for rude behavior."

The two boys hung their heads and muttered apologies. They deserved the scolding, Jake thought, but he couldn't help feeling a bit contrite, especially when Katie's bottom lip trembled. He hoped she didn't cry, he wasn't up to a bout of tears.

"My friend is not of royal lineage. Her name is Suzy Stein and she lives in New York City."

Hallie smiled but her heart wasn't in it. So his friend was a female. That raised other questions, but none she could ask until she knew him better. Her daughter felt differently.

Katie wrinkled her nose. "I don't think I'd like her anymore if she sent me one of those. Is she still your friend?"

"Yes," Jake said. Though theirs was primarily a business relationship, Suzy was about the only friend he had these days. Aside from his parents, he'd managed to alienate everyone else when he'd left Chicago and stopped answering letters and phone calls. Suzy had refused to be put off. She'd pushed and bullied him until he'd agreed to keep their line of communication open. It had paid off for both of them.

The macabre gift had been the product of her dark sense of humor. "Yes, Katie. She gave it to me as a joke."

Katie frowned. "I don't think it's very funny."

Hallie frowned, too, she didn't like the expression on Jake's face when he talked about Suzy Stein.

274 Out of the Dark

The woman was evidently important to him, and for some unknown reason that bothered her.

Jake shrugged. There was nothing he could say to the child's remark without revealing more than he wanted.

Toying with her pungent necklace, she asked, "Do you ever sleep in it?"

Jake looked at her solemnly. Holding up his right hand, he said, "No. I swear I've never even considered doing that."

Katie's relief was evident. The boys were still suspicious, and he couldn't resist teasing them a little. "If you'd looked more closely, you'd have noticed that it's much too short for me."

"See, Mom," Andy replied smugly. "The only reason he doesn't sleep in it is because it's too short. I've been watching and he's only eaten one bite of his soup."

Mark glanced at the untouched sandwich on Jake's plate. "If you're not going to eat that, I'll—"

Hallie interrupted her son, whose stomach was a bottomless pit. "Mark, there are more sandwiches in the refrigerator. Would you get them, please?"

As he left the room, Katie asked, "Don't you like real food?"

"Yes, I do. I like tuna, but I don't eat it because—"

"I agree with your stand, Mr. Donahue," Hallie interrupted his explanation. Her daughter was a picky eater and she didn't want him to give Katie a reason not to eat something she loved. "That's why I only buy politically correct brands."

"In that case—" Jake picked up his sandwich and took a bite. He looked surprised. "It's delicious."

After taking another sandwich for himself, Mark held out the platter for Jake. "Want another one?"

"Thanks. I was so busy this morning I forgot to eat breakfast. I just realized how hungry I am."

Hallie was sorely tempted to ask him just what it was that he did for a living, but he'd probably tell her it was none of her business. He wasn't as cool and aloof as she'd expected him to be after their encounter last night. But neither was he warm and forthcoming. He certainly had her curiosity aroused. That wasn't the only thing he aroused in her, but she pushed those thoughts to the back of her mind.

Her purpose in inviting him here was to prove to her children that he was not a vampire and it appeared that her plan might work. The boys were impressed when he ate two sandwiches and a double helping of dessert, a banana cream pudding with browned meringue. They asked to be excused, obviously in a hurry to discuss this latest development in private.

Katie lingered. She sidled up to her mother. "May I take Pete a sandwich?"

Hallie nodded and waited until Katie left. "Petrita is very superstitious. She's the one who made those smelly necklaces for the children. She locked herself in her bedroom when she heard you were coming and refused to cook. I'm sorry about not having those *chili rellenos* I mentioned.''

''Just so she doesn't put some kind of hex on me,'' Jake said with a grin.

''So far, her defense against you has been in the form of prayers and rosaries.'' Hallie stood. ''Come on, I'll give you a tour of our soon-to-be bed-and-breakfast inn.''

''Is there much demand around here for a place like this?'' Jake never thought much about the rest of the world.

''It's actually an ideal location. We're not that far from San Antonio and its attractions,'' Hallie said enthusiastically. ''A lot of people like to avoid big hotels and stay in quaint places like this when they travel.''

Jake surveyed the inn in progress. Quaint wasn't the word he would have used, but it had possibilities. There was still a lot of work to be done. ''Do you ever worry about opening up your home to strangers?'' His sudden concern for her welfare surprised him.

''I know how to protect myself, I'm a cop's widow. People who choose bed and breakfasts usually aren't the dangerous type.''

As she was showing him the downstairs rooms, Jake noticed a stack of library books on the hall table. Most of them were by Jonathan Dark. No wonder Hallie's kids had such wild ideas.

Hallie was telling him about further remodeling plans when a particularly loud roll of thunder vibrated the floor beneath their feet. The boys were crashing down the stairs.

"Maybe we should turn on the TV weather show," Mark suggested.

"It's gettin' dark outside," Andy said from the window. "And the wind is blowing so hard, it's bending the trees over."

"*¡Señora! ¡Señora!*" Pete called as she came running down the stairs with Katie in her arms. Both of them were wet and they had little pieces of plaster in their hair. "The roof, she cave in on me and Katie."

"Oh, no. Are you hurt? Is Katie all right?" Hallie rushed toward them.

Pete shook her head. "We are only wet. The bed, she is wet, too. Everything is *muy* wet."

Jake saw Hallie's frustrated expression and took action. "Boys, run in the kitchen and get the largest pot you can find and bring it upstairs. Pete, you and Katie get dried off. Hallie can show me the damage."

Hallie led the way to Pete's bedroom, dreading what she would find. "Mr. Costas was supposed to start on the roof last week, but he never showed up. I've called him every day but he keeps telling me not to worry, that it will hold until he gets here."

She pushed open the door with a moan of dismay, and Jake stepped inside to survey the damage. "It's not so bad." He patted Hallie's shoulder in an awkward attempt to comfort her, but the feel of her warm skin only reminded him of his earlier thoughts. Those also involved comfort—mainly his own.

Little currents of awareness raced through Hallie when Jake touched her. Out of nowhere came desire, sudden and surprising. For an instant she wanted more from him than a casual pat. She wanted to be enfolded in his arms, drawing assurance from his strength. It had been a long time since she'd had someone to share her problems with.

Quelling her disturbing thoughts, Hallie stepped away from Jake. She noticed the plaster on the bed, and the dripping hole in the ceiling, which was slightly larger than a watermelon.

Jake turned to Hallie. "I'll need some heavy plastic to secure over the hole in the roof, and a hammer and nails."

It felt good to leave the decisions to Jake, to allow someone else to handle the crisis. She'd always been self-sufficient, but it was nice to share the worry—even if it was with a virtual stranger. Still, she couldn't allow him to go out in the storm to take care of her problem. "I can't ask you to—"

Jake interrupted her. "You didn't ask. I offered."

Mark came racing down the hall with a large plastic tub that Hallie used to wet strips of wallpaper. "Pete said this would be big enough unless we spring another leak."

Jake pushed the bed toward the wall, then took the tub from Mark and placed it beneath the hole. When Pete and the rest of the children peered into the room, he set them to cleaning up the mess.

Jake took Hallie's elbow as they left the room. "You can show me where you keep the tools."

Again, she experienced the jolting awareness of his touch. Not once in three long years had a man's nearness affected her as Jake Donahue's did. If such casual contact could stir her like this, what would a more intimate one do?

"The tools are in the barn," she said when they reached the kitchen. "That's where Mr. Costas stored the roofing supplies. I'm sure you'll find everything you need out there."

Jake removed his glasses and dropped them into her hand. Pushing the door open against the wind, he said, "Take care of these, and stay inside."

Wordlessly, she took a large-size slicker from a peg near the back door and handed it to him. She stared after him as he raced through the rain. Who was this stranger? Why did he have such a powerful effect on her?

When he reached the barn, Jake wrested the door open and stepped in out of the weather. He shook water from his hair and when he turned to close the door, Hallie was there, leaning against it. She was out of breath, and her heaving chest drew his gaze.

She'd held a slicker over her head, but her white shirt was soaked. Through the wet material, he could clearly see the lacy imprint of her bra and the hard tips of her breasts beneath it. His heart thundered as he imagined his hands cradling their weight, his lips tasting the rain on her skin. Had it been so long that the mere thought of a woman's body could make him ache like this?

His eyes lifted and met Hallie's. She knew what he was thinking. Furthermore, she didn't disapprove or she wouldn't be here. Without thinking, he took a step toward her, then stopped to remind himself that he couldn't act on his impulses. Hallie Stewart was not a woman who would tolerate being tumbled in the hay in her own barn.

Still, he couldn't bring himself to turn away from her. Nor could he get that thought out of his mind. There was something in the way she looked at him that said she might consider it.

Chapter Three

Hallie's heartbeat quickened as Jake's gaze traveled slowly up her body, and desire ran through her as sweet and thick as honey. She'd seen passion in a man's eyes before, but for the first time since her husband's death, she felt it within herself. She had thought those feelings were lost to her forever, and yet Jake had awakened them with a single, longing look.

One minute they were standing apart, trying to make sense of the mysterious need they shared. Then without a word, they came together, her arms wrapping willingly around his neck as his lips found hers. He pressed her body tightly against his and her breasts strained against his chest. His tongue slipped inside her mouth, tentatively at first, and then with an ardor that filled her with desire.

His hands explored her shoulders and back, then slipped down and came to rest in the pockets of her denim jeans. He massaged her bottom and pulled her so close that she felt the power of his arousal between them.

His demanding lips continued to caress hers and one of his hands strayed upward into her hair. A small moan escaped her and her head fell back in pleasure. Hallie was totally immersed in the moment, in the heat of his mouth upon hers, in the touch of his urgent, exploring hands on her body. When the hand in her hair slid down her neck to capture her aching breast, she melted against him.

Jake couldn't get close enough to Hallie. From the first moment he touched her, his body wanted more. Her mouth was sweet and hot and tasted faintly of banana. She smelled of rain and flowers and her wet blouse was cooling to his hot flesh. They were as close as two fully clothed bodies could be, and yet it wasn't enough.

As he massaged her breast, he heard a little whimper from deep in her throat. She wanted him as much as he wanted her and that made him feel powerful and humble at the same time. His body grew uncomfortably hard, and he knew it wouldn't be long before he passed the point of no return. It was time to make a decision.

As he pulled her arms from around his neck, he thought of all the reasons for his choice. This wasn't the time or the place. They didn't know each other at all. He hadn't remained celibate for five years just to give in to a moment of weakness. Nor was he the kind of man who took advantage of a woman's needs. With iron resolve, he stepped back, away from Hallie, and forced his gaze to a spot beyond her shoulder.

When he finally spoke, his voice was hoarse. "I'm sorry. I shouldn't have done that."

Hallie was shaken by the enormity of her feelings and his apology took her totally by surprise. She sensed his inner turmoil and wondered at its cause. "Is there someone else?"

"No," he said, running a hand through his damp hair.

"There's no significant other in my life, either. There hasn't been anyone since my husband died. So, if you're concerned about…well…my past, you needn't be."

He laughed and the sound was bitter. "I never gave that a thought." Which was ironic, since fear of a disease was one of the reasons he'd chosen celibacy in the first place.

What had he been thinking of? Jake Donahue was full of secrets and didn't seem willing to confide them. Not to her, anyway. She'd hoped he would take her into his arms again, but the moment had passed. She said with false lightness, "It was no big deal."

"Look, Hallie, I don't want the complications a relationship would bring into my life. I was perfectly happy with the way things were."

Was? Were? He probably didn't realize that he'd used the past tense. Hallie smiled for real. If he thought he could ignore the heat that sizzled between them, he was kidding himself. But there was something to be said for self-delusion. She should try it sometime.

"I understand. It was a momentary lapse on both our parts. It certainly doesn't have to happen again if we don't want it to."

Jake was obviously relieved. "Good. I'm glad you see it that way. Let's forget it ever happened."

Fat chance, she thought, but she nodded, anyway. He'd been on the verge of making love to her and she was none too sure she could have stopped him. Or that she would have wanted to.

He took a deep breath. "You should have stayed inside like I asked."

She couldn't admit that she'd been drawn to him by the powerful force of his sensuality, so she came up with another excuse. "I thought the least I could do was to show you where things are."

"You needn't have bothered. I would have found everything. I know what I'm doing." He glanced around and, spotting the ladder in the corner, walked toward the shelves beside it. Keeping his back to her, he crammed some nails into the pocket of his jeans.

"I know a little about carpentry and have even patched a few roofs in my day," he told her.

"Well, then, I'll just go back to the house and let you get on with it." She started for the door but stopped and turned back for one quick look, and caught him watching her. "Be careful you don't fall, Jake."

"I'll do that." He wondered if she was referring to the roof.

Hallie made a running dash to the house. The cold, pelting rain cooled her off and pounded some sense into her. She should be grateful that Jake had been honorable enough to put an end to the madness that had almost overwhelmed her. A less scrupulous man would have taken her right there in the barn. Her face flamed with embarrassment. It might have been temporary insanity. She had practically attacked the poor man. How could she have thrown herself so wantonly at a perfect stranger? She needed to get a rein on her runaway emotions before she saw him again.

She didn't think he was as unaffected by their encounter as he would have her believe. He was trying to act as if that remarkable kiss had never happened. And the worst part of it was, she didn't know whether to be glad or sad.

As Jake worked atop the roof, he welcomed the cool sting of the rain and the mind-clearing wind. It gave him plenty of time to think about what had almost transpired in the barn. He liked what he knew of Hallie Stewart, and he wanted her. That was a dangerous combination.

Celibacy was as much a state of mind as it was of body, and that kiss had reminded him just how much he missed having sex. But he'd found out long ago that sex without love only left him feeling empty inside. And at this point in his life, love was out of the question. Love equaled trust, and he wasn't ready to trust anyone with his heart or his secrets.

When he finished patching the roof from the outside, he went into the house to find out how he could gain access into the attic. Pete explained that the *señora* was taking a shower, and reluctantly told him the ladder was in a hall closet upstairs.

Once he reached the damaged area, he mopped up the water so he could tell if his patching job would hold until the roof was professionally repaired. When he was satisfied there were no other potential trouble spots, he anchored a piece of plastic over the gaping hole in the ceiling.

When he climbed down the ladder, Hallie was waiting for him. "Thanks. You didn't have to do what you did."

"It was nothing. I'm glad I could repay you for lunch."

"You don't owe me anything, Jake," she said softly, and he wondered if she was still talking about the repairs.

He turned his gaze away. He couldn't look at her without remembering how she had surrendered to his kiss. "Glad to do it."

"I left some of Jim's things for you in the bathroom, and there are fresh towels on the rack." She pointed to a door across the hall. "I'll take you home when you get dry."

"I'm fine. I can walk, it isn't far."

"No, I insist," she said stubbornly. If he thought he could slip in and out of her life this easily, he was mistaken. She was determined to learn more about him. In one lifetime, a woman didn't run across that many men who could turn her knees to butter.

"When you're dressed, come down to the kitchen, I'll make a pot of coffee," she said over her shoulder.

Hallie barely glanced up from her plans spread on the kitchen table when Jake entered the room. He took the mug she handed him, sipped, and glanced over her shoulder.

"Plans for the outside trim?"

"Yes, but I may have to put it off for a while." She kept her eyes glued to the papers in front of her. "As a carpenter, what's your professional opinion?"

"I never said I was a professional. I've had some experience, is all."

"So what do you think?"

She seemed genuinely interested in his opinion. He looked over her shoulder at the plans. "I noticed this place a long time ago. The trim was probably replaced twenty or thirty years ago, but it's out of sync with the style of the house. Victorian style, with turned corbels and spindles, would be more attractive." He sat down in the empty chair beside her and pointed. "If I were doing the work, I'd use

scalloping there. And gable decorations there. Go
for the gingerbread effect.''

Hallie had discussed that with the contractor
who'd drawn up the remodeling plans, but she had
an idea and she wanted to hear what Jake had to say
before she could put her plan in action. "It wouldn't
look too fussy?''

"Not if it's done right.'' Jake was intrigued by the
project, it had been a long time since he'd known the
satisfaction of taking a board and creating a thing
of beauty. "The trim makes a house.''

Hallie looked over the plans again and sighed. "I
think you're right. It's a shame I have to put it off.''
She folded the papers with a good deal of resignation. "But the plumbing and rewiring blew a big
hole in my budget. I have enough to buy the supplies, but unless I dip into the kids' college funds, I
can't afford to pay union scale for the services of a
professional carpenter.''

Jake shrugged, feeling the web of attraction
tightening around him. God, she smelled good.
"Maybe if you advertised, you could get someone
willing to work for less.''

"Do you think so?'' she asked doubtfully.

"Maybe.'' Jake looked at her intently. "It's a very
tempting piece of work.'' His voice was low, sug-
gesting that the work wasn't the only thing that was
tempting. "If I weren't so rusty, I might offer to do
it for nothing.''

"Wonderful!" Hallie couldn't believe her good fortune. "But I insist on paying you something. Is five hundred dollars reasonable?"

"It's a generous offer, but I haven't done this kind of work in years," he protested. "I can't guarantee the results."

Hallie was aware that she was probably taking advantage of the man. But she wanted to get to know him, and what better way than to employ him? Maybe he could use the money; everyone said he had no visible means of support. If left alone, Jake would continue to hole up in that cabin of his and she'd never see him again. If he came to her house every day, she could work on him. Maybe even find out what had driven him to withdraw from the world.

"It's probably like riding a bicycle, it'll come back to you," she suggested. "And I'll throw in two meals a day. No more tuna sandwiches. Pete's a great cook."

Jake wasn't sure how he'd gotten into this mess, but now that he had, he kind of liked the idea. Maybe working with his hands for a while was just what he needed. His work hadn't been going well lately and he needed something to force him out of the proverbial rut. "I've heard that promise before."

"But that was before she met you. And I haven't heard even one reference to *diablo* since you patched up the roof over her bed. I think she'll come around.''

Jake wondered what kind of condition his tools were in. He hadn't used them for a very long time. And he'd have to get used to working all day and sleeping at night, like normal people did. Maybe that wouldn't be so bad. He'd been living in the dark too long. Suzy kept telling him that, and so did his parents.

Hallie could see he was mulling it over, and worried that he'd come up with too many reasons why he shouldn't. Impulsively she held out her hand. ''Shall we shake on it?''

Jake took her hand in a brief handshake, but even those few seconds were long enough to send dangerous arrows of awareness zinging through him. He quickly reminded himself that he had agreed to do the work because of its potentially cathartic nature. It had been years, but he still recalled the feeling of renewal he'd always experienced upon completion of a building project.

But that had been before things had started to go wrong. Would it have the same effect now?

Stepping back a pace, he dropped his hand to his side and asked, ''When do you want me to start?''

''Weather permitting, how about tomorrow?'' Hallie was as eager to begin the exterior remodeling as she was to begin her association with Jake, even if it would be on a professional basis.

"You don't fool around, do you?" he asked with an engaging grin. For some reason he felt happier than he had in a long time.

"Not when I want something as much as I want this." She returned his smile.

Chapter Four

The next day Hallie got out her wallpaper supplies after breakfast. She tried to work, but spent most of the morning wandering from window to door, expecting Jake to appear at any moment. Lunchtime came and went before he drove the fully loaded Silverado into the driveway. He climbed out, and his big dog bounded out after him. In the daylight, Klute didn't look so much fearsome as she did klutzy.

Jake felt a lurch of excitement as he watched Hallie come out of the house to greet him. She looked pleased to see him, like maybe she hadn't really expected him to show. Today her hair was plaited into a braid that bounced as she walked, and silver hoops in her ears caught the sun. She wore jeans and her blue shirt was knotted at the waist. She looked too damn good.

Was it only yesterday that he'd last seen her? It seemed longer. Her smile touched him with sunshine and he was glad Hallie Stewart had come into his life. Jake knew it didn't make sense, but in the next moment he was suddenly angry with her for making him feel things again. Things he didn't want to feel.

"I was beginning to think you weren't coming," she said quietly.

"I told you I'd be here," he replied sharply. Her smile faltered and he immediately regretted his tone. He had no one but himself to blame for allowing her to get under his skin. He leaned down to pull out the red flags stapled to the longest boards.

"It's a thirty-minute drive to and from San Antonio, you know," he said by way of apology. "I had to wait for the guy at the lumber yard to cut the boards. Then I had them order the millwork from a place in Quinlan. I stayed within the budget you gave me, is that all right?"

"Of course," she agreed, feeling foolish for having doubted him. "A carpenter can't work without wood. I should have thought of that." When Jake was around, she couldn't think about anything rationally.

He noticed the pink tinge to her cheeks and wondered what had caused it. Were her thoughts as wicked as his own? Probably not. To keep his hands occupied, he brushed at some lingering sawdust, but he was thinking of the heated kiss they'd shared in the barn. His hand slowed its movement down the length of the wood as he vividly recalled the smoothness of her skin and the way their bodies had molded to each other.

"It's soft as silk, Hallie."

She was so mesmerized by the low sensual timbre of his voice and the way his hand lovingly stroked the bare wood that she could almost imagine it was her skin he caressed. He rekindled all the sensations she'd felt when he'd held her body against his. She ran her finger along the outer edge of the boards.

"Strong and hard," she said softly. Their gazes met and Hallie recognized the hungry look in his eyes. Propriety be damned. She would have taken the first step toward him, but Mark and Andy chose that moment to race outside. The boys slid to a stop just before plowing into the rear of Jake's truck.

Andy pushed his glasses back up the bridge of his nose. "What's going on?"

Jake brushed his hands on the seat of his jeans. "We were just admiring the wood I'm going to use to replace the trim on your house."

Mark looked from the lumber to the house, then back again. "I think I like the old stuff better, even if it is all rotten. It's got designs and stuff, this is just plain ol' boards."

Jake chuckled, partly because the remark amused him and partly because he was relieved the children had intervened before he could make a fool of himself. "These 'plain ol' boards' will have designs and stuff when I get through adding the millwork."

"No kidding?" Mark asked. "Will they have little holes and spokes and thingys?"

"That's the plan." Jake pulled his new work gloves from his back pocket and put them on. He scooped up an armload of lumber and started off toward the barn.

"I'll help unload," Hallie said.

He stopped in his tracks. There was no way he would let her haul wood and under no circumstances did he want to be alone with her in that barn again.

"No need," he said over his shoulder. "You have plenty of work to do, I'll get this."

"Can we help?" Andy called out to him.

Jake tore his gaze from Hallie and looked down at the two expectant little faces. He felt a sharp twist of pain in his gut. He hadn't considered that this job would mean getting close to Hallie's children. He couldn't allow that to happen. "No, you'd just be in the way. Why don't you boys play with Klute?"

Hallie saw the look of disappointment on her sons' faces before they turned away. Jake's words hadn't been sharp, but they'd cut just the same.

She wondered why he was so uneasy around her children. "I'll try to keep them out of your way," she said pointedly.

"Yeah, thanks." His response was gruffer than it needed to be, and Jake wanted to explain why he couldn't allow her kids into his life. He wanted to, but he didn't.

Hallie watched him disappear into the barn. He'd told her he wasn't interested in the complications a relationship would bring. She should be glad he was able to maintain some emotional distance between himself and her family. So why wasn't she happy?

Maybe it was because she was a package deal. Love me, love my kids. Love? That was premature. Hallie shook her head in disbelief and went back to her wallpapering. She didn't know Jake Donahue well enough to even consider that, but she couldn't deny the possibility definitely existed.

When the wood was unloaded, Jake set up his saws in the barn. His job was made easier because the previous owner had built a long worktable against a side wall, and installed a convenient number of electrical outlets. He went right to work.

An hour later Mark and Andy drifted out to the barn on the pretext of finding a ball. Jake and the boys mutually ignored one another for several minutes. Then they sidled over to the worktable to inspect his progress. Mark folded his arms and rested his chin on top of them. "You sure got a lot of tools."

"Mmm-hmm." Jake didn't want to encourage the boys' curiosity. "Don't you guys have anything better to do?"

"Nope," Andy said. "What's that called?"

"A jigsaw."

"Like a puzzle?"

"Not exactly. Is that your mom calling you?"

"Nope."

His father was a carpenter, and as a child Jake had been fascinated by the things in his workshop.

When he recalled the patient way his father had answered his many questions, he felt guilty for being so taciturn. But that had been different, he told himself. He wasn't Mark's and Andy's father. Still, their friendly little faces chastised him.

Several more minutes passed. The boys said nothing, watching intently as he tried to work. He could stand it no longer. "Do you boys know the difference between tools and toys?"

Andy took off his glasses and attempted to wipe the smudges with the tail of his shirt. "Sure, we do. We're not babies."

"Mom says we'll always be her babies, but that's just the way mothers talk," Mark said sagely.

"Dad called us his little men," put in his brother.

"Andy, you're such a dweeb," Mark said with a sigh.

"Well, he did," Andy replied defensively. "I remember."

Jake didn't like being reminded of their fatherless state. It made him feel even guiltier for not wanting to befriend them. "Then you both know that you do not touch tools without permission from the owner."

"Well, sure," Mark replied.

"These are your tools, and we can't touch them unless you tell us to. Right?" Andy asked.

Jake nodded. "Right."

They were clearly disappointed. Mark said, "We want to help."

Jake sighed. "You can, but only when I say so."

"Mom said not to bug you," Andy said with a grin. "If we promise not to bug you too bad, can we kind of hang around with you while you're working?"

"Yeah," Mark agreed. "That way we'll be handy in case you need us. Okay?"

Jake couldn't think of any situation that might require the assistance of two overeager little boys, but if he told them that, it would only hurt their feelings. He wasn't overjoyed to have them underfoot, but he didn't want to deliberately hurt them, either.

Actually, they would make good chaperons when he had to be in Hallie's company. There would be no more kissing interludes in the barn. He could hardly give in to his baser instincts with impressionable children nearby.

"Okay," he agreed somewhat hesitantly. "But you just watch."

"Yessir!" The boys followed him around like grateful puppies, careful not to touch his tools or get in his way. They chattered too much, in Jake's opinion, but their eager talk was a good way for him to find out more about their mother. By the time they stopped for the day and went in to dinner, he had learned that Hallie enjoyed reading mystery novels, that she had a weakness for double-fudge brownies, and that she didn't believe in spanking children.

This time Pete did cook, and the food was delicious as promised. After finishing the *arroz con pollo,* Jake complimented the cook. "I'd forgotten what real food tastes like. This is really good, Pete."

Hallie smiled when the older woman blushed and dropped a coy curtsy. In no time, Jake had won over the suspicious housekeeper. Even though he was still a bit aloof with them, Mark and Andy were already his devoted fans. She hoped her own feelings were not so obvious. Only little Katie still kept her distance.

The rest of the week passed smoothly. Jake became accustomed to his new schedule and found that he actually looked forward to spending each day with the Stewarts. The adjustment from antisocial to social hadn't been as difficult as he'd expected it to be. He'd gone without human companionship for so long, that after a taste of it, he craved it like a man who had been denied food.

He was still afraid to be alone with Hallie, and was careful to keep their relationship on a purely business basis. It was enough to know that she was nearby and that he was entitled to sit across the table from her twice a day.

She seemed willing to accept his terms and didn't venture out to the barn unless she had at least one child in tow. When they talked, it was about the project or other things of general interest. She didn't ask him any personal questions, and for that he was grateful.

By the end of the first week, he had even come to appreciate Mark's and Andy's company. The boys admitted, somewhat sheepishly, that it had been dumb for them to think he was a vampire. When they brought up the subject of the strange things they thought they'd seen in his cabin, he always changed the subject.

The boys were quick studies; when Jake asked for a one-by-four, they knew exactly which pile to go to. They learned the difference between a mallet and a hammer, and a sixpenny and a finishing nail.

Although similar in looks, each boy had his own personality. Andy was quiet, calm, and possessed a dry sense of humor. Mark was more vocal, always moving, and his humor was of the slapstick variety. Katie seldom came to the barn, so Jake didn't see much of her except at mealtimes. The little girl was still suspicious of him, but by the end of the week, was no longer wearing her garlic necklace. Jake considered that progress.

Hallie seemed to be keeping her distance, as well, a fact that should have pleased him, but didn't. He kept remembering how he'd felt when he'd held her in his arms, how warm and sweet her lips had been. He could still hear her little sigh of surrender, even in his sleep. He'd been foolish to think he could go back to the blissful state of unfeeling limbo in which he'd existed for the past five years. As painful as the loneliness had been, it was nothing compared to the pain of not touching Hallie.

He was exhausted when he returned to his quiet house each night, but he still had trouble sleeping. He kept thinking about Hallie and what his feelings for her might mean. He didn't want to have those feelings. He didn't want to consider how meeting her had changed his life. Working for her meant he had to arrive at her house every morning at a reasonable hour, not whenever he felt like it. He ate at regular mealtimes now, not just when he was hungry.

But it was more than that. It meant living in the sunlight instead of the darkness. Of constantly thinking of others, considering their feelings. It was terrible. But it wasn't all bad.

He knew he had come to care too much for Hallie. If not for caring, he would have taken what she'd freely offered him that first day in the barn. Caring about her was the only thing that kept him from pursuing her openly. He didn't want to hurt again. But most of all, he didn't want to hurt Hallie.

Many times, he considered quitting, so that he could go back to the days when he'd thought of no one except himself. Things had been so much simpler then. He'd been happy with his life. Happy? That wasn't exactly true. He'd been gratified. Like a monk who wore a hair shirt to repent, Jake felt better when he suffered.

The darkness had once provided solitude and time to remember his mistakes. Dwelling on those mistakes had often brought unpleasant dreams. Now, all the darkness provided was emptiness. The thoughts that kept him awake these days didn't induce nightmares, they were the stuff of fantasies. Fantasies of laughing with Hallie, of making love with her, and living happily ever after.

But like morning fog, those fantasies disappeared with the sun. Jake knew from experience there was no such thing as happily ever after. He'd tempted fate once before with his contentment and fate had decided he didn't deserve even that.

The next morning, when Jake arrived at Hallie's, he grabbed a hammer and went straight to the listing old gazebo. His thoughts had kept him up again last night, and he felt like doing something destructive. Today would be the perfect time to knock down the rotted trelliswork and replace it with the new lattice panels he'd bought in San Antonio.

When Jake stalked into the gazebo the last thing he'd expected to find was Katie and her doll sitting on a small quilt on the floor. She looked up at him, her big blue eyes wide with surprise and a hint of fear.

"Hi, Katie," he said softly. It bothered him to think the child was frightened of him. "Can I come in?"

Katie shrugged her tiny shoulders. "I guess so."

Jake leaned against the doorway. "What are you doing out here alone?"

"I'm not alone," she insisted as she held up a bedraggled doll by one arm. "Shorty came with me."

Jake reached over and shook the doll's free hand. "Well, good morning, Shorty. I'm Jake and I'm very pleased to meet you."

Katie giggled and it warmed him to know that he'd made her laugh.

"Shorty's glad to meet you, too." She propped the doll against the wall, then set another tiny cup and saucer on the blanket. "She wants to know if you'd like to join us for a cup of tea?"

"Well, I really should get started with my work," Jake said.

Katie's eyes lost some of their sparkle. "Mark and Andy don't like tea, either."

It wasn't his concern that this child was lonesome and needed attention, and it wasn't his job to see that she got it. So why did he feel compelled to drink imaginary tea? He sat on the floor and crossed his legs. "I guess I have time for one cup."

Katie grinned at him again as she pretended to pour tea from the miniature pot. In a formal, grown-up tone of voice, she asked, "Would you like sugar or cream?"

"Yes, thank you," he said, imitating her formality as he held the cup toward her.

Katie giggled again. "Which one? Sugar or cream?"

"Why, both, of course," he replied in a broad British accent. "Doesn't everyone?"

Katie measured out the condiments with glee. "I don't know. I've never served tea to one of Mommy's boyfriends before."

If the tea hadn't been imaginary, Jake would have choked on it. Was that how these children thought of him? As Hallie's boyfriend? If so, what had given them such an impression?

Katie held up a little plate. "Would you like a cookie?"

Jake didn't answer, he couldn't trust himself to speak yet. Not when he wanted so badly to ask about those other "boyfriends." He recovered enough to take one of the make-believe cookies.

"We never even got to meet Mommy's boyfriends before. Did we, Shorty?" Katie turned back to Jake. "Mommy went out on dates three whole times. Mark and Andy said we'd probably get a new daddy, but we never did."

"How do you feel about that?"

"I liked having a daddy, so did Mark and Andy. We told Mommy it was okay with us, but she said she didn't want another daddy. She said she had us kids and didn't need nothing else." Katie offered Jake another cookie.

"Thank you."

"Aunt Karen told Mommy that she was ol'fashion and needed to loosen up with her dates. Mommy said dating was a lot of horse poo."

Jake felt as guilty as if he'd been listening in on a private conversation, as Katie had evidently done.

"Aunt Karen said Mommy better get another man before she lost her looks and Mommy would be sorry when it was too late. When will that be?"

"What?" he asked.

"When will it be too late for Mommy?"

"Never," he said softly. But he could tell by the child's eyes that she needed more reassurance. "You don't need to worry, Katie. Your mother is a beautiful woman and she always will be. She could have her pick of men."

"Whew!" Katie wiped a hand across her forehead. "I'm sure glad to hear that. When Aunt Karen called Mommy this morning, I thought her time was up."

Jake grinned and glanced at his watch. "I need to get to work."

"Shorty's glad you came to our tea party," Katie said. "She likes you a lot."

"Thanks for inviting me, Shorty." Jake nodded to the doll before standing. "I enjoyed it."

"Promise?" she asked as she gathered the corners of the quilt, making a hobo sack of her toys.

"Promise." Jake put a hand over his heart. "I can honestly say this was the very best tea party I've ever attended." He didn't bother telling her it was the *only* one.

"I'm gonna ask Pete to help me make some real cookies for the next one," she said over her shoulder as she left the gazebo. "You're invited."

Hallie intercepted her sons as they toted the rotted trellises into the barn and sent them inside to clean up for lunch. She knew she could have called out to Jake, but she strolled toward the gazebo, anyway. When she was just a few feet away, she stopped. Shading her eyes with one hand, she stood there, enjoying the sight of him, watching him work.

The day was hot and he'd taken off his shirt. His skin, which had been pale at the beginning of the job, had been tanned by daily exposure to the sun. It was slick with perspiration and the muscles rippled in his back as he pulled at a particularly stubborn nail with his claw hammer. When she began to fantasize about running her hands over those broad shoulders, she moved closer and called out to him.

"Jake?"

He stilled, but didn't turn around. "Yeah?"

"Lunch is ready."

He placed the hammer on the stepladder and came toward her. "So am I."

Were they really talking about food? Hallie wondered when he reached her side. He didn't touch her, but her pulse quickened as if he had.

"I finished hanging the paper in the dining room this morning," she said in a voice that sounded too breathless. "I'm famished."

"I know the feeling." Jake stopped at the truck and took his shirt from the tailgate where he'd left it. As he slipped the T-shirt over his head, he noticed Hallie's gaze on his chest and stopped.

Knowing she'd been caught in the act of ogling, Hallie decided it was time to confront Jake about the subject they'd both been tiptoeing around all week. She hopped up on the open tailgate and sat down. "I think we should talk about our feelings."

He pulled his arms through the sleeves and tugged the shirt down. He tried not to notice her long, tanned legs dangling enticingly nearby. "Feelings?"

"Yes." She folded her hands in her lap. "It shouldn't come as any great surprise that I'm extremely attracted to you."

Jake took a deep breath. "You don't hold anything back, do you?"

Hallie had hoped that once she'd admitted her weakness, he'd reciprocate in kind. "I learned a long time ago that it isn't healthy and it resolves nothing. It's better to get feelings out into the open where they can be dealt with."

Jake dropped his gaze and said nothing.

She swallowed nervously and asked, "Is it my imagination, or are you attracted to me?"

He glanced at the house and wished Pete or one of the children would step out and call them inside. There was never an interruption available when you needed one. "Very much."

She hadn't realized she was holding her breath until she let it go. "Then what's the problem? Why won't you at least try to get acquainted? Aren't you curious about me, at all?"

"I came here to work, not to analyze my feelings. I'm out of here." Jake was suddenly angry with her for starting this conversation, and mad at himself for being put in a position where he'd have to deal with emotions. He stalked around the truck, yanked open the door, grabbed his glasses from the visor and jammed them on. He jumped into the truck and reached to turn on the ignition.

But when he glanced into the rearview mirror to make sure Hallie was out of the way, he saw her still sitting there, a mutinous look on her face. She wasn't going to let him run away. He got out and strode back to her. "I know all I need to know about you."

"Like what?" she challenged.

"I know that you're not the type for a short fling, and I'm not interested in anything more. Is that the kind of open honesty you want to hear?"

Hallie glared back at him. "Last week you said you weren't interested in a physical relationship."

"I've been celibate for five years," he said through gritted teeth, "not dead."

She hadn't intended to make him angry, but at this point any emotion was better than none. "And you're willing to sacrifice those five years for a short-term relationship with me?"

Jake didn't need to think it over, he'd thought of nothing else since the day he'd met her. "Yes."

She looked into his eyes and knew that he told the truth. "Why?" she asked softly.

"I've never wanted anyone as much as I want you," he replied.

"But," she prompted.

"I don't want any entanglements. I like being on my own. I'm not the kind of man you need, Hallie."

"I see."

He stuffed his hands into his pockets. "No. You don't understand at all."

"So explain it to me."

"I can't. So what happens now?"

"Nothing?" She shrugged. "I don't know."

"I could leave and never come back," he suggested halfheartedly because it was the last thing he wanted to do. "That might be best for both of us."

She suspected his feelings ran deeper than he was willing to admit, especially if he was worried about his single status. She wouldn't give up on him yet.

She jumped down from the tailgate and dusted the seat of her shorts. "You can run and hide like a coward if you want, but I'd appreciate it if you'd finish the job first. A deal's a deal."

"It may not be wise."

"But it's cost-effective," she said pointedly. "I can't afford to hire anyone else, Jake. I need you. If you're not willing to be anything else, can we just be friends?''

"We could try," he agreed. "I should finish up here in a couple of weeks and then everything can go back to the way it was."

Hallie nodded. But in her heart she knew that nothing would ever be the same again, no matter how it ended.

Chapter Five

The third week of June was a time of goodbyes. On Saturday, Hallie and the kids put Pete on a bus to Nuevo Laredo, Mexico. Her niece's wedding would be a week-long affair and, since the children would be gone to camp, Pete planned to stay an additional week visiting relatives and friends.

On Monday, Hallie drove the kids and their odd assortment of baggage to St. Mary's Church to catch the bus to Camp Ko-Ma-Kee. They'd planned the trip for weeks, and were well prepared for leave-taking. At least, the kids were. Hallie felt a stab of maternal concern when she kissed her babies good-bye and told them to have a good time.

Of course, they would have a good time. They'd make new friends, toast marshmallows, swim, hike and ride horses. She was the one being left behind. Needing quiet time to work, she'd looked forward to this moment for weeks. Now that it was here, she wasn't sure she wanted to be alone, day after day, with Jake.

Since she'd confronted him with her feelings, their attraction had taken on a life of its own, taunting them with their desire, making itself impossible to ignore. It was only a matter of time and opportunity until they crossed the line, and Hallie worried about what would happen when they did.

When she got home, Jake was up on the ladder, nailing the newly delivered millwork over the porch. He waved briefly as she got out of the car and turned back to his work. She stood in the yard for several minutes, admiring his graceful movements and the confident way he wielded tools. He was good with his hands and sure of his body. Before she could stop the thought, she wondered how that confidence would enhance his lovemaking.

As usual, he'd stripped to the waist and she noticed that his skin had continued to darken in the sun since he'd begun spending so much time outside. His smooth muscles had the firm, well-defined look associated with weight training. Still no fashion plate, he wore low-riding jeans with holes in the knees and a baseball cap emblazoned with the San Antonio Spurs' logo.

So far, she'd found much to like about Jake Donahue, despite the fact that he obviously felt no need to endear himself to her, or anyone else. After two weeks he was still an unknown quantity. Close-mouthed as ever, he hadn't discussed his past with her, he hadn't told her what he was doing in Jacinta, nor had he felt compelled to explain the unusual hours he had kept before coming to work for her.

His reticence invited speculation, but Hallie respected his need for privacy and hadn't asked unwelcome questions. She wanted him to want to talk to her, for she sensed that he needed very much to open up to someone. That was the only way he could begin to throw down the wall he'd built around himself.

She didn't know what tragedy had driven him to shut himself away from the world, but whatever it was, it was his alone until he chose to share it with her.

Until then, she had to be patient. She'd offered him friendship, and she would give him both time and space, for he was not a man to be crowded. Not physically, and certainly not emotionally. Jake was like a wounded animal who had once loved and trusted people, only to be betrayed by them. Now he was suspicious and wary, doubting her sincerity and motives, always taking two steps backward for every tentative step he took toward her.

Hallie didn't know the source of Jake's pain, but she understood it. She'd felt an overwhelming sense of hopelessness when Jim died. She'd wanted to give up, to turn her back on a world that was no longer worthy, much as Jake had done. For months following the shooting, she'd been apathetic, barely able to get through the days. The nights had been even worse. When she thought of life without Jim, it didn't seem worth living.

But she hadn't given up. The children had saved her from herself. Their love and need and the promise of many tomorrows had pulled her through. Because of them, she'd given life a second chance.

Hallie suspected that Jake needed a reason to get off the self-destructive path he'd set for himself. He needed someone to help him exorcise the demons that haunted his past and prevented him from facing the future with hope, for no one could do that alone. She didn't know if she could be that reason, but she wanted to help him. Jake had so much to offer, if only he weren't afraid to give.

Hallie smiled sadly when she realized that memories of Jim no longer made her cry. So, it was true that time healed all wounds. She would always cherish the time she'd had with her husband, but memories, even those tucked away in a special place in her heart, weren't enough to sustain her forever. She could love again, and she knew with mounting certainty that she could love Jake. If she could bring him out of the shadows for good.

"Hey, mister! Are you ready for an iced tea break?" she called up to him.

"In a few minutes. I want to finish this section." Jake felt driven to work for Hallie. Not only was he helping her, doing something for her that no one else could, but it was a way to be near her and maintain his distance at the same time.

"It's looking good up there, Jake, you're doing a wonderful job."

Embarrassed by the compliment, he said nothing, but beamed a wide grin down at her. It was funny how much better he felt now that she was home. He liked knowing she was nearby. He liked the way she hummed off-key when she worked, and the way she mumbled mild expletives when she made mistakes. He'd never heard a grown woman utter the phrase "Oh, horse poo!" so charmingly. So far he hadn't found much about Hallie he didn't like.

With Pete and the kids gone, he'd have to be extra careful to keep those feelings to himself. It had been a long time since he'd gotten close to a woman and he was afraid of what might happen if he let himself care too much for this one. He told himself the attraction was purely physical. After all, he'd ignored his needs for years and Hallie was a very desirable woman. But he wasn't convinced. There was something special about her that had nothing to do with the ache in his body.

Hallie counted Jake's grin a blessing. How many more would it take before he dropped his guard enough to let her be his friend? Being patient with him was the right thing to do, but that didn't make the waiting any easier.

Stopping to pet Klute, who was napping in the shade on the porch, she went inside and prepared a tray of iced tea and cookies. Calling to Jake, she carried the tray to the newly refurbished gazebo in the backyard. He and the boys had finished painting it a few days ago and it gleamed white and inviting, a place of respite from the sun. She sat in one of the rustic cedar chairs and was sipping tea when he came around the side of the house.

She watched him over her glass, appreciating the up-close view of his smooth chest and well-developed body as he stopped at the hose and doused his head with water. When he shook his dark hair, a million crystal drops of water sparkled in the sun. He slipped on a chambray shirt, which he didn't bother to button.

"We can start painting outside tomorrow," he said after downing half a glass of iced tea. "Shouldn't take more than three or four days to finish it."

"Great," she said with an attempt at enthusiasm.

He glanced at her with a raised brow. "What's the matter, mama hen, you missing the chicks already?"

She laughed self-consciously. "It's silly. For weeks I've wanted them to go so they could make new friends and have a good time. Now all I can think about is how quiet it's going to be around here without them."

Jake smiled. "Yeah. Terrible, isn't it?"

"I won't know what to do with myself. For the first time since Mark was born, I won't have to wake up in the middle of the night to check on them."

"You still do that?"

"I know it's unnecessary, but it's a habit. I can't go back to sleep until I've gone to their rooms, touched their faces and felt their warm breath. Life is so uncertain, I suppose it's a way to reassure myself that we've all made it through another day."

"It seems a little obsessive, if you ask me," he said as he finished his tea and poured himself another glassful.

She smiled. "You don't have children, so you don't know what it's like to feel responsible for helpless lives."

The tea tumbler slipped out of Jake's hand and shattered on the wood floor of the gazebo. "I'm sorry," he said, his voice gruffer than it should be.

Hallie saw a flash of pain in his face. Surely he wasn't that concerned about a broken glass? "Don't worry about it," she said lightly. "The good stuff is packed away until the kids leave home."

He put the shards of glass on the tray and jumped to his feet. "I need to get back to work. You're not paying me to sit around and drop dishes."

Hallie stood and touched his shoulder. "What is it, Jake? Did I say something wrong?"

He flinched away from her touch. He couldn't let himself respond to the comfort she offered; it could prove addictive. He paused, torn between wanting to pull her into his arms and tell her the whole terrible story, and knowing that he couldn't. She was a loving and dedicated mother. What would she think of him if she knew the truth?

"No," he said brusquely. "I have to get busy, that's all."

By word and deed, he made it clear he didn't want her company and went back to work. Hallie had seen the need in his eyes and was frustrated that he turned away whenever he found himself vulnerable. Would he ever learn to trust her? Or was it himself he didn't trust?

That afternoon as she painted the trim in one of the guest rooms, she replayed the scene in the gazebo over in her mind. She knew intuitively that it held a clue to Jake's past. What had she said just before he dropped the glass? Something about him not being a parent. Was that it? Did he have a child somewhere?

The thought that Jake might have a wife and family, a whole other life, shook Hallie. Had he abandoned them? Was he the kind of man who could walk away from responsibility? She didn't think so, but there was so much she didn't know about this stranger she'd come to care for.

She didn't know how to get through to him, but maybe she'd have a chance tonight. With the house all to themselves, he might be more willing to talk about his personal life. They had to make conversation over dinner, and she could always point it in that direction. If he told her it was none of her business, which was certainly possible, she would have to accept yet another rejection.

However, she was determined to discuss their attraction and what they should do about it. It wouldn't be denied much longer.

They worked separately until after five o'clock. Hallie was cleaning her brushes when she sensed someone watching her. She turned and found Jake leaning against the doorjamb, his shirt slung over his shoulder. His dark eyes were intense and she felt their heat from across the room. She swallowed hard and tucked a lock of errant hair back under her bandanna.

"It looks good," he said simply, and she assumed he meant the room.

"Thanks to you, the place might actually be ready for guests by September. It'll be nice to have some money coming in for a change."

"I'm finished for the day. Do you need any help in here?" Jake felt awkward, like an inexperienced teenager. Why was he always so tongue-tied around Hallie? He made his living manipulating words.

"Why don't you start a fire in the grill? I can never get the darn thing just right. The steaks are in the fridge."

"I thought I'd go on home," he said. "With the kids gone, there's no need for you to go to the trouble of cooking for me."

Dammit! Didn't he know she enjoyed doing things for him? "It's no trouble. The steaks are already thawed. If you don't stay, we'll have to feed them to Klute."

Jake knew he should go. How could he spend the evening alone with Hallie and not touch her? How could he eat food she prepared for him when every time he looked at her he got a knot in his throat? Even now, he had to hang on to the door frame to keep from going to her. He wanted to hold her and feel her softness in his arms. He wanted to kiss her and hear her soft sigh of surrender as he removed her clothing and touched her body.

He wanted to make love to her, and the wanting was an ache he couldn't live with much longer.

Hallie knew Jake didn't want to leave any more than she wanted him to. He was being stubborn again, only this time he was fighting himself. She was a witness to his internal battle, for it was waged primarily on his face.

"Look, meals were part of our deal," she reminded him. "If you don't stay for dinner, I'll have to increase your salary and you know darn well I can't afford that. By not eating my steak, you are actually undermining my whole financial future and that of my innocent children."

Jake laughed. "All right. You win. I'll start the fire."

During dinner, they talked mostly about the progress they'd made on the renovations. Jake agilely deflected Hallie's attempts to discuss anything more personal. After stacking their dishes in the sink, they took their wineglasses out to the gazebo, where they sat on opposite ends of the cushioned settee.

The night was hot, but a light breeze made it bearable. Cicadas hummed in the grass and fireflies made their low-wattage presence known in the meadow behind the house. The air was heavy with the sweet fragrance of the wild roses rambling along the fence.

"You've never asked me about my husband," Hallie said into the silence.

"I didn't think it was any of my business." Jake desperately wanted to know about the man Hallie had loved, yet he was afraid to ask about the fallen hero, lest he not measure up to that man's deeds.

"Would you like to know now, Jake?"

"Do you want to tell me?"

Hallie smiled. "You have a real problem with commitment, don't you?"

He ignored her observation, which was particularly astute. "I should go home. We have a lot of work ahead of us tomorrow," he said as he stood to leave.

"Not so fast, sporty." She hooked her finger in his belt loop and pulled him back down beside her. "I respect your right to mind your own business. I also respect your right to tell me to mind mine.'

"I sense an unspoken 'but' in there somewhere."

"*But,*" she emphasized, "I don't know why we can't be friends."

"I thought we were," he said quietly.

"Friends share things about themselves, Jake. They even share secrets. What they don't do is skulk around like the Phantom of the Opera."

"I'm a private person," he said by way of explanation.

"And an expert at understatement, I might add."

He looked away, but his curiosity finally got the best of him. "Tell me how he died, Hallie."

It wasn't much, but it was a start. Maybe he could learn to relate to others—one tiny step at a time. By sharing something of her life, he might be encouraged to share something of his.

"Jim was a patrolman for six years. He'd passed the test and earned a promotion to vice detective. It meant a raise in pay, which meant we could put more money in our 'escape' fund. On his last night on patrol, an hour before he was to go off duty, he stopped a van for running a stop sign. The driver was a burglar and the van was full of stolen goods. He shot and killed Jim to avoid arrest."

Jake covered her hands with his own. "I'm sorry, Hallie." He didn't know what else to say. How could anyone understand such senseless violence?

"The man was a petty thief who panicked and became a cop killer. He was convicted and sent to prison. Jim's friends on the force and in the D.A.'s office saw to that."

"It must have been terrible for you and the kids."

"It was a nightmare. I confess I didn't handle it very well. I was so lost, I didn't want to go on."

"You must have loved him very much." Jake felt her pain and it was like reopening an old wound that had festered for years.

"Yes. When he died, I wanted to turn my back on society. A world where such things could happen didn't deserve a second chance."

Her words echoed his own feelings and he wondered if she knew how close she had gotten to the truth. "But you didn't."

"No." She told him how the children had made it possible for her to keep going. "I needed professional help to cope with my loss. The counselor taught me about the stages of grief and eased me through them. Only then was I ready to start living again. Everything happens for a reason, Jake. Even if we never learn what that reason is."

He wanted to ask her if she could ever love anyone else the way she'd loved Jim Stewart. Instead he lifted her hand to his lips and kissed it gently. "I'm sorry such a thing had to happen to you, Hallie."

She moved close and cupped his face in her hands. The light in the gazebo was dim, but she could see the sheen of unshed tears in his eyes.

"Something bad happened to you, too, didn't it, Jake?"

"Yes."

"I'm a good listener. Do you want to talk about it?"

"I don't think I can." His throat was so tight, he could scarcely breathe.

She pulled his head down on her breast and stroked his hair back from his forehead. She leaned close and kissed him there, much as she would kiss a child who was in pain. "It's all right, Jake. I'll be here if you change your mind. That's what friends are for."

His heart pounded in his chest until he thought it would burst. God, what kind of beautiful woman was this? Why did he deserve to be the beneficiary of her special brand of compassion?

"Do you know how wonderful you are?" he asked her, his eyes on her lips.

"Show me, Jake. Show me how wonderful it could be between us."

He groaned, the ache in his body had become as acute as the pain in his heart. "Are you sure?"

Her answer was to kiss his cheek gently before reaching down to unbutton his shirt. Spreading the edges open, she flattened her palm on his chest. His skin was hot and quivered beneath her hand. "I want this, Jake. More than I've ever wanted anything."

Fighting the web of growing arousal, he tried to speak but she put her fingertips to his lips. "Don't talk now. There'll be time for that later. After."

In moments, they had undressed one another and spread the settee cushions on the floor of the gazebo. They knelt, facing each other, kissing and touching, not feverishly and with pent-up need, but with tenderness and wonder. She gave him a quivering, tentative touch.

"I haven't been with a man since Jim died," she whispered.

"It's been a long time for me, too." Slowly, he eased her back on the cushions and lay down beside her. One hand slid across her stomach to the swell of her hip. "I don't want to hurry this."

Hallie shivered as desire for Jake pounded through her. She moaned as his lips traveled to her breasts and his hands caressed and gentled her. She felt the brush of masculine hair on her skin as he kissed her face, her chest, her abdomen. Incredibly, he knew exactly where to touch her to free the passion she'd held in check for so long.

His own ardor was touchingly restrained as he stroked her, building the fire that only he could extinguish. His mouth found hers and he kissed her deeply, intent on maximizing her pleasure. She moaned softly in anticipation, exalting in the male strength and beauty of him.

Jake shuddered when Hallie took him in her hands. Her touch was light, yet firm, and he felt his desire quicken. His heart pounded as he kissed her and felt her answering need. He lowered his body onto hers and heard her whispered "Yes" as she welcomed him into her body.

Hallie reveled in the delicious weight of him. She stroked the muscles of his back and her hands slid down to cup firm buttocks. His skin was hot, feverish with desire and need. And yet he moved languidly, setting a teasingly slow tempo that belied the frantic pounding of his heart against hers. Raising himself up on his elbows, he clasped her hands in his. The long strokes quickened as he lost control, and she was thrilled by the magnitude of her own desire.

There was just enough moonlight for Jake to see Hallie's sweet face. Her head tossed wantonly from side to side and she matched his pace, her warm body sheathing him and exerting its own erotic pressure. Her hands squeezed his and she bucked beneath him as the ecstasy mounted and the world disappeared. He kissed her again, hard and passionately, and she writhed as her impatience grew to explosive proportions.

Suddenly he was beneath her, his arms spread-eagled at his sides. Intent in her pleasure, she took him deep within her and leaned forward to explore his face and neck with her tongue. His deep growl of arousal heightened her own and she felt him tremble. She knew a powerful sensuality as she found the tempo that bound their bodies together.

His slow movements sent her to even higher levels of ecstasy. The night closed around her and she was consumed by ultimate pleasure. The fire spread to her heart. She cried out when she found release and experienced a flood of uncontrollable joy.

Jake had stopped thinking long moments before. Hallie's fulfillment excited him and the feeling was much more than sexual desire. A golden wave of passion and love flowed between them, and he rolled atop her again. The dormant sexuality of her body had been awakened and her breath came in long, surrendering moans. The moment went on and on because he was reluctant to let it end.

Again, Hallie felt passion rise in her as the turbulence of Jake's lovemaking engulfed her. Their bodies found exquisite harmony and she was pulled to the pinnacle again. Together, they found an awesome, shuddering ecstasy that left them weak and tremulous, shaken by what they had just discovered. Their bodies melted together and the world was filled with hope.

Chapter Six

Jake and Hallie made love again in the moonlight. Their joining was hungrier and even more passionate the second time. Afterward, they gathered up their clothing and went inside to Hallie's bed where they snuggled and held each other, silent, lest words break the spell of magic that surrounded them.

Succumbing to the numbed sleep of satisfied lovers, they dozed, only to awaken later to a gentle rain. A cool breeze blew through the screens at the open windows, riffling the white muslin curtains and guttering the flame of the candle on the nightstand.

"It's raining," Jake pointed out unnecessarily.

"Yes, it is," Hallie agreed.

"I'd better not try to go home just yet." The comment was also unnecessary. He had no intention of leaving Hallie's bed for a very long time.

She opened her arms to him. When he nestled his head on her breast, she held him close and kissed his hair. "You just try to leave me, Donahue."

"I wouldn't dream of it." His lips touched her nipple with tantalizing possessiveness. "In fact, I can't think of any place I'd rather be."

"What happened out there in that gazebo was really quite remarkable." Her words were whispered and full of wonder. She'd never expected to experience that kind of love again. It had taken her completely by surprise.

"In a word, stupendous," he drawled lazily.

"I don't know about you, but the earth moved for me," she confided in a teasing tone.

"Nine on the Richter scale," he agreed.

"At least. Maybe ten."

"Possibly. What I don't understand, is how we held out so long," he said with mock amazement.

"I think it happened pretty fast. We've only known each other a couple of weeks," she pointed out. It was incredible, but in such a short time Jake had become so important to her that Hallie couldn't imagine life without him. She shivered at the thought, and pretended she was cold.

He pulled her into his arms and kissed her soundly. Now that she was his, he never wanted to lose her. "I feel I've known you forever, Hallie."

She stiffened inadvertently and Jake sensed her withdrawal. "What is it? Did I say something wrong?"

After a few moments she said quietly, "Physically, we've been as close as two people can be. But I don't feel that I really know you at all, Jake."

He tightened his hold on her. He'd known this moment would come sooner or later, but he'd hoped it would be later. Now that it had arrived, he'd have to face it. He couldn't continue to take her good grace for granted, it was time he opened up. He just didn't know how to begin.

"What do you want to know?" he asked, trying to hide the weariness in his tone.

Hallie sat up in bed and pulled the sheet up to cover her nakedness. She wrapped her arms around her knees and looked at him with what she hoped was an encouraging smile. "For starters, I'd like to know who you are."

He stretched out on his back, clasped his hands behind his head, and stared at the ceiling. "You know that already. My name is Jacob William Donahue."

She looked out the window and watched the rain running off the eaves. "A name doesn't tell me who you are, Jake."

He sighed. "There's nothing remarkable. I grew up in Illinois. I have an older brother in Pennsylvania. My parents are retired and still live in Chicago. I was an okay student and didn't play sports in high school. I worked my way through college, helping out in my dad's carpentry business. I eventually earned a relatively useless degree in English literature. Since then, I've never actually held a regular nine-to-five job, so by some people's standards, I guess you could call me a bum."

"Those are statistics, Jake. Interesting enough, but not enlightening. If you don't want to talk to me, just say so and I'll try to understand."

"I want to tell you everything, Hallie. Confession is supposed to be good for the soul. I just don't know where to start. I've kept to myself so long that the words won't come."

She reached out and touched him. There was a flood of emotion behind the dam he'd built. She was a bit frightened of what might happen when that flood tide was freed, but she had to take the chance. If she and Jake were to have any kind of future together, he had to stop denying the past.

"Tell me about your child," she said gently.

His eyes widened in surprise and his heart thudded in his chest. "How do you know I had a child?"

"Things you've said, things you haven't. I've seen you watching my kids with a look so sad it broke my heart. It finally occurred to me that you were gruff and distant with them at first, because you were afraid of getting close for some reason. Was I right?"

He nodded and commended her observational skills. "You're a very perceptive woman."

"I really am a good listener. Can't you tell me what happened?"

"He died. My son died five years ago." His voice caught in his throat and he could say no more until he'd cleared it.

Hallie took him into her arms as she would a lost child. She stroked his hair and murmured reassurances. She'd guessed that Jake had suffered, but she hadn't realized its full extent. "What was his name?"

Jake hadn't spoken it aloud for many years and wasn't sure he could now. Just thinking about his little boy caused his chest to tighten with pain.

"Corey," he whispered at last. "I was in the delivery room when he was born and I thought he was the most beautiful baby I'd ever seen. He was pinch-faced and red, and didn't have a hair on his head. But he was my son and I loved him at once."

"I know that feeling," she said quietly. "It never goes away. No matter what." Hallie wanted Jake to talk about his son. She suspected that he'd never worked through the acceptance stage of his grief and she'd learned that until that happened, the grieving wasn't over.

The dam broke and years of silence gave way to sweet memories. Jake realized that he wanted to tell Hallie about Corey. "He was such a joy, perfect in every way. Slept when he should, never had colic. Perfect. He was so good and sweet that he made it easy to be a good parent. My wife Becky went back to work a few weeks after he was born, and since I worked at home, I got to stay with Corey. It didn't seem fair to her, but she was content with the arrangement, and by that time I was totally in love with him."

He paused in his narrative and Hallie waited patiently for him to begin again. She felt a mounting sense of dread that something terrible had happened to Jake's perfect little son and wasn't sure she wanted to hear the rest of the story. But she knew Jake had to tell it.

"When he was six months old, we found out that Corey had a congenital heart defect. The thought of surgery terrified us, but he clearly needed it. It was just that he was so tiny and the operation so delicate. But he was a tough little guy, a real fighter. He survived, and, in time, began to thrive again. We were filled with hope. The doctors said the prognosis for a complete recovery was good, and I allowed myself to start thinking about the future again. We'd been given a second chance and I believed that I would yet see my son grown to manhood. For a while everything was fine."

Jake paused again, recalling memories that were too painful to examine alone. Only with Hallie's strength and support could he face them now. "He crawled and walked on time. He started talking. His first word was Da-Da." He laughed. "You should have seen me that day. I called Becky at work and told her. She said it was an accidental pairing of consonants and vowels, but I didn't believe her. Corey had called me Da-Da and life was wonderful.

"We celebrated his second birthday with a big party and lots of presents. I got the whole thing on videotape. It was a milestone, you see. It had been over a year since the surgery and he was well. A few weeks later, Corey became ill. His repaired heart started to fail and he deteriorated rapidly."

"Oh, Jake! I'm sorry." Hallie hugged him to her. As a mother, she felt some of the anguish he must have known at the time. She ached with the cruel injustice of a child's suffering.

"He got sicker and sicker. The doctors told us he needed another operation, but they couldn't guarantee the results. they gave him less than a fifty-fifty chance for survival this time. It was the hardest decision I ever had to make, but I thought we should go through with the surgery. It was his only chance."

"I understand. It was the right choice."

"Becky was against it. She said Corey had suffered enough. She believed his little body was too weak to undergo the eight-hour operation. We had a terrible row. Our child was dying and we were screaming at each other in the corridor. I'm not proud of that."

Hallie reached out to Jake, but he moved away from her and sat on the edge of the bed, his head in his hands. "She didn't think the risk was worth the slim chance that he'd get better. If our son was meant to die, she wanted him to die at peace and without pain. She was only thinking of Corey.

"I couldn't accept that we might lose him, so I pushed for the surgery. I guess I was thinking of myself and how empty life would be without him. Our disagreement caused a rift between us. As Corey's condition worsened, our battle intensified and the rift became a chasm." He looked at her over his shoulder, his eyes full of torment.

"Why do people turn away when they need each other most?"

Hallie sat beside him and draped her arm around him. "I don't know, Jake. When bad things happen, we sometimes turn our pain and guilt on the ones we love. Maybe it's a way of protecting ourselves from feelings too terrible to live with."

He cleared his throat. "When Corey developed respiratory problems, he was rushed to the pediatric intensive care unit. Watching that little boy suffer was more that I could bear and I made all kinds of deals with God. If only He'd let Corey live. I couldn't bring myself to leave the hospital, and one day when Becky went home to rest, I talked to the doctor and gave permission for the surgery."

There was so much self-loathing in Jake's words, Hallie wasn't sure she could hear the rest of the story without crying. "Go on."

"He died on the operating table. I'll never forgive myself."

She embraced him. "Oh, Jake. It wasn't your fault. You made the only decision you could have made under the circumstances. You mustn't keep blaming yourself for what happened."

"Becky did. She couldn't blame God, so she blamed me. She said I killed him, me and my selfishness. I thought she'd lose her mind with grief. Things were never the same between us."

"What happened?"

"We buried our son and were divorced a few months later."

Hallie rocked Jake in her arms and cried for him because he refused to give in to his own tears. She thought of her three children, healthy and whole, and felt blessed. She knew how devastated Jake had been. Time had done little to ease the raw pain he carried in his heart.

"Thank you for telling me, Jake," she whispered. "I know how hard it was for you to dredge up such painful memories. You loved Corey very much, and you were a good father. As small as he was, I'm sure he knew just how much you loved him."

Jake was quiet for a long time. He lay in Hallie's arms and drew strength from her acceptance. She didn't blame him and she didn't think him the monster Becky had accused him of being.

Eventually the rain dwindled down to a steady drip. Talking to Hallie hadn't been as hard as he'd expected. Maybe it was time to tell her the rest.

"There's more you should know about me, Hallie." He moved out of her arms and leaned back against the headboard of her brass bed.

"I'm listening."

"A week after Corey's funeral, I sold my first novel. I'd been writing and struggling for years. I sold enough articles to keep things going, but what I really wanted to do was write fiction. When it finally happened, I was so heartbroken I didn't even care."

"You're a writer?" Hallie asked incredulously. "But I thought—"

"I never said I was a carpenter. That's just something I did to earn money for college and help out my dad."

"You're a writer," she repeated. "That's why you worked at night and slept during the day."

"At first I adopted that schedule to avoid curious neighbors, but it became a habit and I started doing my best work at night. I guess darkness inspires me. I stayed away from Jacinta because I didn't want to talk to people. I shop at a twenty-four-hour supermarket in San Antonio where no one asks questions. No one around here knows who I really am."

She pulled back and looked at him suspiciously. "And who are you? Really?"

"I'm Jonathan Dark. Or at least, Jonathan Dark is me."

Hallie was stunned into speechlessness. Jake Donahue's alter ego was Jonathan Dark? The novelist that critics called the Master of Darkness? It was hard to believe.

"Say something, Hallie," he urged.

"I don't know what to say." On reflection, she decided that it wasn't so unbelievable, after all. Jake's compelling novels were a natural extension of his reclusive life-style and deep melancholia. She'd read some of them and knew that Jonathan Dark did not write run-of-the-mill horror stories. His books were frightening because they were expertly crafted and provided a disturbing insight into the human condition. Winding through all of them was the dark thread of ineffable loss.

Now that she knew what had happened to him, she surmised that he wrote for catharsis. Jake Donahue peopled his tales with minions of the night and other dark creatures in an effort to exorcise the demons of guilt and shame that haunted him.

"I think I understand why you agreed to meet the kids in the first place," she said. "You felt responsible, in some way, for their fascination with vampires."

He nodded. "You said Mark learned it all from Jonathan Dark."

"What I don't understand is why you agreed to work for me. You're a bestselling author whose books have been made into successful movies. You don't need the money."

He shrugged. "I never planned to take your money. My writing wasn't going well and I thought physical labor would help the block. And there's another reason. I like doing things for you. It makes me feel useful. I haven't felt needed and useful in a long time. Not only that, but it was nice to eat someone's cooking besides my own for a change."

"You turned your life upside down and worked like a dog for food? I find that hard to believe."

"I did it for you, Hallie. I've cared about you since that first night you showed up on my porch. You're an incredible woman." He brushed the hair away from her face and kissed her cheek.

"You're pretty amazing yourself. I know why you shunned the limelight, Jake. But your books are bestsellers. How did you manage to avoid it?"

"It started with my first sale. I was still grieving and wanted no part of publicity. I made sure my publishing contract included a clause keeping my true identity a secret. My publishers and Suzy went along with it."

"Suzy?"

"My agent. I know you thought she was an old girlfriend, but she's old enough to be my mother and just about the only friend I had left before you came along."

She smiled, touched by his words. "The mystique didn't hurt your career—it enhanced it."

"People love to speculate about who the real Jonathan Dark might be. I think it's funny that such literary luminaries as Gore Vidal and Norman Mailer have been singled out as possible culprits. I'm not so sure they're amused."

"Why didn't you tell me about Jonathan Dark before?"

He grimaced. "It's not something you discuss at a first meeting. 'Oh, by the way, I scare people for a living.' I'd gotten into the habit of keeping myself a secret, so it was easy to maintain the pretense. But I never lied about it.''

She thought back. No, he'd never lied. He'd evaded, sidestepped, backpedaled and circumlocuted. But he'd never lied. She ran her fingers through her hair. ''Gosh, this is going to take some getting used to. I've never slept with a literary giant before.''

''You said you wanted to know me better,'' he reminded her.

''I did say that, didn't I?'' She sat cross-legged on the bed and faced him. The sheet she'd used as a covering dropped away unnoticed. ''Do you have any more secrets I should know about?''

He reached out and tested the weight of her breasts with his hands. Electric desire filled him and he desperately needed reassurance that the lovemaking they'd shared hadn't been clouded by his confessions.

''Well, I do have some kinky sexual preferences that you might be interested in,'' he teased.

She pretended to be shocked. ''Oo-oh, tell me more, oh, Master of Darkness.'' She ducked under the sheet. ''Never mind, don't tell me,'' she murmured as she found him again. ''Show me.''

Chapter Seven

The moment Jake opened the door, Hallie stepped up to him and placed her hands on his chest. "I know you're working and I'm not staying. I just came over to kiss you good night."

He moved closer, smiling down at her. Their eyes met and he felt a flame ignite in his brain to spread liquid fire to every nerve in his body. In the week since they'd first made love, he'd become so sensitized to her touch that his flesh reacted instantly with need.

"It will be a good night, now that you're here," he said.

Hallie should have stayed home. Jake had left her house right after dinner, claiming an approaching deadline that had been ignored too long. She should have stayed away, but she couldn't.

She reached up to touch his face, her thumb moving slowly across his cheek, then across his lips. The feel of him sent urgent messages to her body. "I know you cherish your solitude, and I promised myself I wouldn't invade—"

"Hush, I'm glad you're here." His words were almost a groan as he clasped her neck and urgently brought her lips to his. It felt as if he'd been waiting for this moment forever, and he gave himself over to the pure pleasure of kissing her. As crazy as it seemed, he felt that only in her touch, her lips, her lovemaking, could he find himself and recreate a whole man from the broken pieces.

Hallie was shaken by the intensity of his kiss, and every doubt in her mind slipped away. There was no future, no past, no problems to resolve. There was only Jake's mouth upon hers, only his tongue seeking hers, and the rapid beat of his heart beneath her hand. There was only Jake.

A rough sigh escaped him and he deepened the kiss. He kissed her like a man starved, starved for love, starved for her. Hallie felt the emotion, the desperate hunger, and she responded to his need by arching her body into his, giving him the closeness he pleaded for.

Tearing himself away long enough to lift her into his arms, and looking deeply into her eyes, he said, "Will you stay with me tonight?"

Hallie wrapped her arms around his shoulders and buried her face in his neck. "What about your deadline?"

"There's always tomorrow."

"In that case, I might be persuaded. But I'm not sleeping in any darn coffin."

He laughed and was reminded that it was something he'd done a lot of lately. He'd been happy since he'd confessed the past to Hallie. A dark weight had been lifted and he felt more secure than he had ever hoped to feel in a relationship.

"No problem," he teased. "I have a real live bedroom, just like regular people."

"Show me."

He carried her into the bedroom and flicked a switch by the door. The lamp beside the bed came on, bathing the room with a muted glow. He turned his back to the bed and, still holding her tightly, fell onto it. It undulated beneath them.

She giggled and turned on her side to face him. Her voice was filled with mock surprise as she drawled, "Why, Mr. Donahue, what a big ol', fancy waterbed you have!"

"All the better to make love on, my dear," he said with a big grin that spoiled his leer.

Hallie put out one hand to thwart his move toward her. "Oo-oh, Mr. Donahue, what lovely teeth you have."

"All the better to bite your neck, my dear." He grabbed her and gently raked his teeth over her neck.

"I came in here with the big bad wolf," she said, laughing, trying to wriggle out from beneath him. "And I end up with a vampire. Are vampires ticklish, Jake?"

"Stop. Stop." He laughed against her neck when her fingers found their mark.

When she didn't stop, he tickled her in retaliation. One minute they were laughing joyfully and wrestling around on the bed, the next they were kissing passionately and tearing at each other's clothing. When the last barrier was removed and tossed aside, Hallie pushed him onto his back and they made wild, sweet love until the wee hours of the morning.

Hallie was pinned beneath the weight of Jake's arm across her chest. She'd worked up an incredible thirst, but each time she tried to move away, he tightened his hold.

Finally she whispered, "Are you asleep, Jake?"

"No," he whispered back. He didn't tell her that he'd been lying there, basking in the afterglow.

"All that exercise made me thirsty."

"In that case, let's go get you a drink of water and I'll show you how handy I can be in the kitchen."

Hallie stopped gathering up her clothes and watched him saunter toward the door in all his manly splendor. "Aren't you going to put something on?"

"You'd only have to undress me again later," he said with a wink. He walked over to the bureau and opened the drawer. "But if you insist." Pulling out a pair of sweat shorts, he made a big production of putting them on. "Will these preserve your modesty, Little Red Riding Hood?"

"Behave yourself." She laughed and threw her bra at him.

Jake held it up as if he were examining it. "I take back the 'little' part."

"Be good and help me find my clothes, Jake. I refuse to go roaming around your house in my birthday suit."

"Too bad," he said sadly. "It's such a spiffy little suit, too." Hallie's glare prompted him to offer her something to wear. "I think I have a robe in the closet."

"Is this what you're talking about?" Hallie pulled out a short, silky kimono.

"Yeah, that's it. It's got a tie belt so you should be able to keep it on."

She slipped it on and tied the sash, and noticed that it barely covered her thighs. "This is too short to be a robe, it must be a smoking jacket."

"Yeah, Suzy Stein sent it to me the first time one of my books hit the bestseller list."

"I didn't know agents did that sort of thing," Hallie observed.

"Suzy is more than an agent," he said thoughtfully. "I went to school with her son. I was the first client she ever signed who was unpublished. She's the one who kept after me to keep writing when my life fell apart. She sort of forced me to be successful in spite of myself."

"I'm glad she did."

Jake didn't want to talk about the past, it would only cast a shadow on the brightness Hallie had brought into his life. "How about a snack?" he suggested. "We need to keep up our energy, you know."

Between impromptu kisses, Jake and Hallie fed each other a snack of cheese and crackers. When they'd finished, he suggested they go back to bed.

"Are you really, really sleepy?" she asked.

He grinned. "Not very. What do you have in mind?"

"I've never known anyone kinky enough to have a coffin and I was hoping you'd show it to me."

"It really isn't all that kinky." Jake sighed. "I'll show you, but I'm afraid you're going to be awfully disappointed."

He led her into the room he used as an office and switched on the overhead light. "This is where I work."

Laden bookshelves lined the wall behind an oak desk that held a computer, printer and scattered papers. Three oak file cabinets stood nearby. On the other side of the room, two red leather armchairs flanked what appeared to be a coffin.

"Yikes," Hallie gasped, and clutched his arm. In one of the chairs sat a very lifelike vampire, his fangs bared in a menacing smile.

"That's just Drac. One of my fans is a doll-maker and he sent it to my publisher, who forwarded it on to me."

"That's what the kids saw when they peeped in your window."

"Yeah. I'm sorry it frightened them."

"You should keep him in the coffin," she suggested.

"Can't." He hummed dramatically as he slowly lifted the lid.

When she saw what was inside, she laughed. "A bar!" she exclaimed.

"I don't know why people think they have to give me weird things. Just because I write scary books, doesn't mean I have a warped mind."

"They just don't know you," she said as she placed a kiss on his chin. "Why didn't you tell me it was a bar?"

"The first time you asked, I decided to let you worry about it for a while. And it never came up again until tonight."

"I love it."

He gestured at the life-size doll. "What about Drac?"

Hallie wrinkled her nose and shook her head.

"I felt the same way at first," Jake said. "But after a while he kind of grows on you and you'll wonder how you ever got along without him."

"I see," she said softly as their gazes caught once more. "To know him is to love him."

He nodded. "Yeah, something like that."

She glanced around the room. "Where's all your memorabilia, Jake?"

"My what?"

"Your awards. Plaques, you know. You're a bestselling, award-winning author. Most of your books have been turned into movies. But there's nothing in here to show the world what you've accomplished. I don't even see a scrapbook."

He shrugged. "All that stuff is packed away somewhere."

"Why?" she asked incredulously. "Aren't you proud of your work?"

"It's not as if I won a Nobel prize or anything."

"But you entertain people, millions of people. You should be proud of that."

"I used to dream about being published and what it would mean for my family. Then all of a sudden, I didn't have a family anymore. Now, I just enjoy the writing part of it, I never wanted any fame."

"Maybe it's easier for you to face life when you're lost in the fantasy world of Jonathan Dark. You don't like to be reminded of who you are."

Her observations made him uncomfortable. "I don't want to waste time dwelling on the past. When I'm with you, I can think of better things to do." With one deft move, he sat down in the unoccupied chair, pulled her onto his lap, slowly untying the belt at her waist.

"What are you doing?"

"Research," he said huskily, lowering his head to kiss her breasts.

"The lights are on," she purred.

"So?" he managed to say between nibbles.

"What about Drac?"

"Let him get his own girl," he said, his words no more than a growl.

Chapter Eight

For the rest of the week, until time for the children and Pete to return, Jake and Hallie spent every possible moment together. Mr. Costas finally came to replace the roof, and while he was there, he and his two-man crew shored up the sagging front porch. When Jake finished putting up the millwork and trim, he and Hallie spent several days scraping and painting the exterior, even though that project had not been part of their original deal.

On the Friday before the children were to return on Sunday, Jake and Hallie stood outside admiring their handiwork.

"It's amazing, that's what it is." Hallie couldn't believe the transformation in the old house. Now, instead of looking forlorn and empty, it appeared welcoming and warm. The trim was painted a gleaming white, the exterior walls a pale saffron, a shade that was picked up in darker tones by the sunflowers blooming in the meadow behind the house. Jake had repaired the broken swing he'd found in the barn, and it now occupied one end of the wraparound porch.

Hallie had put down white gravel on the walkway leading to the house and planted bright marigolds along the borders. Lace curtains, sewed by Hallie's sister Karen and shipped from Dallas, fluttered at the windows.

"It's a very fine inn," Jake agreed.

"If I were a tourist, I'd want to stay here," she said. "Wouldn't you?"

"Of course. The proprietor is so cute."

She punched him playfully on the arm. "I never could have done it without you, Jake. Thank you for all your hard work."

"It was my pleasure." He grinned wickedly. "In more ways than one."

"Won't the kids be surprised when they get home? I don't think they ever really shared my vision for this place."

He appeared to study the exterior. "Something's missing."

"What?" Hallie was alarmed. As far as she could tell, everything was perfect.

"Wait here." He loped toward the barn and returned a few minutes later with something large wrapped in canvas. "Close your eyes," he instructed.

Hallie did so and heard the rustling of the canvas covering.

"You can open them now."

Tears immediately welled up in her eyes. Jake had made a colorful sign, proclaiming The Jacinta Inn in bold green letters. Bright, graphic sunflowers adorned the border.

"Do you like it?" he asked.

"I love it."

Her heartfelt words were enough for Jake. He felt an overwhelming sense of pride that he had helped Hallie create something that meant so much to her. It had been a long time since he'd accomplished anything that made him feel so good.

They chose a spot near the entrance and Jake gave Hallie the honor of driving the supporting stake into the ground.

"This makes the dream a reality," she said wistfully. "There were times when I didn't think it would really happen."

"Your first guests will make it a reality," he pointed out.

"True. But now that the basic painting and papering is finished inside, I can start decorating. That's the fun part. Karen has been scouting estate sales and antique malls for me and has accumulated a garageful of stuff. I can't wait to get started."

They walked back to the house, hand in hand. "I have something else for you," he told her. He went to his truck and returned with a cardboard box.

"Jake, you've done enough already."

"Open it."

When she did, she found a beautiful set of cream-colored vellum stationery, imprinted with The Jacinta Inn letterhead and adorned with a stylistic sunflower. In neat script letters were the words, Hallie Stewart, Proprietor.

"I took it upon myself to create a logo for the inn. I hope you don't mind," he said.

"Mind? It's beautiful." She hugged his neck and kissed him soundly.

"I think we've earned a vacation," he told her. "Why don't we pack some things and go into San Antonio? We can stay at the Menger Hotel, walk on the riverwalk, and drink margaritas. Can I tempt you?"

He could always do that. "What about your deadline?"

"No problem, in fact, I've been inspired lately." He grinned. "Maybe it's the company I've been keeping. I'll have plenty of time to finish the book when Pete and the kids get home."

"What about Klute?"

"We'll only be gone twenty-four hours. She can manage if I put out enough food."

Within an hour they were on their way to San Antonio. They were lucky enough to get a room at the historic Menger Hotel, which was just across the street from the Alamo. They enjoyed a cajun seafood dinner at the Bayous restaurant and later strolled along the romantic riverwalk. Then they returned to their quaint Victorian-style room and made love in the four-poster until nearly dawn.

The next day they toured the Alamo and visited the shops and galleries of La Villita and El Mercado. Later, they rode the river barge for a different view of the sights. After enjoying a Tex-Mex dinner, they drove home, determined to return soon and bring the children, who would love the Fiesta Texas theme park and Sea World.

When Hallie met the children's bus on Sunday, she found a dusty, suntanned trio, eager to share their adventures with her. They chattered all the way home, vying for her attention. They had all made new friends, most of whom lived in nearby Jacinta. Hallie was happy for her children, and knew that they'd come a long way toward adjusting to their new home.

When Hallie turned the station wagon into the driveway, there was a moment of silence that was soon punctuated by shrieks.

"Gosh, Mom. What'd you do to the place?" Mark asked.

"Mommy, it's so pretty," Katie put in. "Just like a flower."

Andy pushed his glasses up. "Is this really the same house?"

"One and the same," Hallie declared. "Well, guys, what do you think?" She parked and the children jumped out of the car.

Mark stared up at the house. "Jake was right. It has curlicues and thingys, just like he said it would."

"Look, Shorty." Katie held up her doll. "We can have another tea party in the bazebo since we learned to make cookies at camp."

"Is it neat on the inside, too?" asked Andy.

"It will be soon. No more paint fumes and sawdust. Now that you guys are back, you can help decorate your rooms."

The kids let out a collective yippee and charged up the front steps.

Hallie and the children didn't see much of Jake for the next few days. He was busy finishing a manuscript that was due in his publisher's office soon. Klute, always hungry for attention, wandered over from time to time to play with the children and beg handouts from Pete, who had returned the day after the children.

Hallie's sister and brother-in-law, Karen and Steve Scott, arrived one day with a rented truck full of antiques and Victorian accessories. Jake dropped by to help them unload and stayed for lunch. After the

Scotts departed for Dallas, he asked Hallie if she could delay her decorating long enough to take in the Jacinta rodeo with him.

"The kids really want to go, you know."

Hallie looked up from a box containing crochet-trimmed linens. "Well, I don't know. I really need to unpack these crates."

"Please, Mom," her children chanted as they danced around the box. "We've never been to a real rodeo before."

"I finished the book and I need to celebrate," Jake put in.

"Is that how you usually mark such an auspicious occasion?" she asked.

"No. I usually just open a can of hash. But I'm willing to make an exception this time."

Hallie realized what it meant for Jake to "go public." He'd never felt a part of the community before and had shied away from local events. Maybe this was his way of showing her that he was finally ready to start the long journey back into the mainstream.

"I'd love to go," she said with a smile.

The children were enthralled by the rodeo. They sat in the stands and ate hot dogs and cotton candy and drank homemade lemonade. They watched the local cowboys, who were mostly high school kids and ranch hands, wrestle steers and ride bucking broncs. After the barrel-racing event, Katie was convinced she needed a pony of her own.

Midway through the evening, the rodeo announcer proclaimed there would be a greased pig contest for all children between the ages of six and twelve. When Jake suggested that the Stewart kids participate, they were doubtful.

"What is a greased pig, anyway?" asked Mark.

"They take a little piglet and rub him down with shortening and let him loose in the arena. Then the kids get in there and try to catch him. It can get pretty exciting."

"What happens if you catch the pig?" practical Andy wanted to know.

"You get a prize," Jake informed them. "Are you game?"

"Nah, it sounds dumb," Mark said. "Who wants a greasy old pig?"

Just then a small pinto pony was led into the arena. The announcer's voice boomed out of the speakers. "This year the prize in the greased pig contest will be a pony donated by Mr. Clem Travers of the Circle T Ranch. All you little buckaroos better get down to the staging area and get your numbers if you want a chance at this here pony."

Katie's eyes widened. "Really? You get a pony if you catch the pig?"

"That's what the man said," Jake told her.

"It isn't as easy as you think, Katie," Hallie put in. "That little pig will be scared and he won't want you to catch him. Besides, there'll be lots of bigger kids after him, too."

The little blonde pushed her curls out of her eyes. "I'm gonna go for it," she announced.

Her brothers looked at each other, and before Hallie could respond, they were off and running. Jake laughed and followed them down to the area to get their numbers.

A few minutes later a group of milling children, with cardboard numbers pinned to their backs, stood in the center of the arena. Hallie picked out her three and noticed that their earlier bravado turned into uncertainty when a small white pig dashed into their midst.

Pandemonium broke loose as the children gave chase to the startled young animal. It dashed this way and that, with twenty children in hot pursuit. Someone grabbed it, but the slippery creature got away and the chase was on again. Some of the bigger boys had obviously worked out a plan and managed to pin the pig in between them. When they closed in for the catch, the animal squealed and darted between their legs, landing smack-dab in the middle of a group of little kids who were mostly trying to pick their mothers out of the crowd.

In the confusion, Hallie saw Katie fall to the ground, landing soundly on her bottom. She looked up to protest the rough treatment and saw the frightened piglet running toward her. Hallie laughed as Katie flung her small arms around the animal and hung on for dear life. It was hard to tell which was more surprised by the capture—the pig or the little girl.

A buzzer sounded at that moment and the contest was over. Katie just sat there, her arms full of squealing piglet, her face smeared with dirt, and wreathed in smiles.

"Katie's asleep. I'll carry her," Jake offered as he scooped the child into his arms. She stirred and wrapped her arms around his neck. An unexpected lump formed there as he recalled other days and the feel of other small arms. "Mark and Andy are barely awake, can you manage them?"

"Sure, we do this all the time." Hallie smiled as she led her sleepy sons upstairs. For a man who hadn't wanted to get involved, Jake was doing a good job of it. While he carried Katie into her room, Hallie ushered the boys into theirs.

"No bath tonight, boys," she said as she crossed the room to their bureau.

"What about the pig grease?" muttered Andy.

"I'll get your pajamas, you two get undressed and get washed up in the lavatory," she instructed as she slid open a drawer.

Jake chuckled from the doorway. "I think it's too late."

Hallie turned. Mark and Andy were sprawled on their beds—grubby hands and faces, shoes and all—sound asleep. "I can't let them sleep like that. I'll have to wipe them off with a wet cloth and change their clothes."

"That won't wake them?" he asked.

"No, they're all sound sleepers," she said, untying Andy's sneakers.

"I'll do that," he volunteered. "You take care of Katie. She woke up just long enough to ask me if she really won the pony. She made me promise to take her to get it tomorrow."

"I never thought she would actually win. Whatever will we do with a pony?" Hallie asked in exasperation.

"It can't eat much more than Klute," he teased.

"You really showed the kids a good time tonight, Jake. Thank you."

He took her hand in his. "How could I not want to do things for such great kids, especially when I'm crazy about their mother?"

She touched his cheek with her other hand. She loved him so much it hurt. Maybe because neither of them had ever mentioned the word love. Oh, he'd made teasing comments about being crazy about her, and he'd shown his feelings in many ways. But he'd never actually told her he loved her. She wanted that.

It might be too late to save herself from a broken heart if their affair ended, but she had a responsibility to protect her kids from pain. They had gotten far too attached to Jake, and she believed that he shared their feelings.

"We need to talk, Jake."

"Yes," he agreed, kissing her nose. "As soon as we get these little cowboys tucked into bed."

Jake was waiting for Hallie downstairs when she finished with Katie. He would prefer to take her away for another romantic weekend and do his proposing over a candlelit dinner. But he was resourceful, he'd just have to make do. He patted the cushion next to him when she entered the living room. But when she sat down, she left a good deal of space between them.

"Is something wrong?" he asked, scooting closer and hooking his arm over the cushion behind her back.

"I don't know how to say what I have to say."

Jake frowned. Had he just assumed she felt the same as he? "Just say it."

"I'm worried about the kids," she began. "They like you too much."

"Are you saying I'm a bad influence on them?"

"Of course not," she reassured. "The opposite, really. You've been a wonderful influence on them, especially the boys. They really look up to you."

"How can that be bad?" Irritated, Jake pushed his glasses up on his nose. "I think it's good that the kids and I like each other. Especially if I'm going to be their father."

"Their father?" Hallie was stunned by his unexpected announcement. She was also irritated that he'd never seen fit to discuss his feelings with her. Had he ever once proclaimed his undying love for her? No. And she'd dreamed of it so many times.

"I must be getting hard of hearing, I guess I missed your proposal." She hadn't meant to sound so churlish.

"Now, Hallie, there's no reason to argue, I—"

"Wait a minute. When we started seeing each other, you told me you weren't available for anything more than a fling. What's really sad is that I was so crazy about you, I was willing to settle for that."

"The rules changed."

"And you forgot to tell me." She couldn't conceal her temper. Why was she mad, when this was what she'd wanted all along?

Jake had planned to ask her to marry him to-night, but things had gone wrong. He'd made a mess of it. He made a conscious effort to lower his voice and tell her what was in his heart. "I told you about Corey, things I've never told anyone else. I told you everything."

"Not quite everything, it seems." She sighed. "You never said you loved me."

"I'm sorry," he said softly. "I was getting around to that."

"When?"

"Tonight."

"Really?"

"Yes, really, Hallie. I screwed it all up."

"You really do love me?"

"Yes." Jake took her hands in his.

"I love you, too," she whispered.

He touched his forehead to hers. "I don't think I've ever been so glad to hear anything in my life. I want to spend the rest of my life with you. Will you marry me, Hallie?"

Joy overcame irritation. "Yes, Jake. Oh, yes."

He wanted to shout his joy, but remembered the children were asleep upstairs. "Does this mean you're not mad at me anymore?"

"I was never really mad. You just caught me off guard, is all." She frowned thoughtfully. "Are you sure you're ready to leave the past behind?"

"Yes," he said softly. "Your love gave me the strength to do that. Let's get married quick. I want to be with you every minute. I want to go to bed with you in my arms every night and wake up with you every morning. I can't wait much longer."

His mouth captured hers and he was filled with a need greater than any he'd ever known. The kiss became more passionate, leading to more intimate caresses. When Hallie unbuttoned his shirt, he pulled back. "If I don't leave now, I won't be able to go at all."

"Stay," she said as she unbuttoned the last button and slid her fingers inside. "I want you, Jake."

He nuzzled her neck. "What about the kids and Pete?"

Hallie kissed his chin. "Everybody's sound asleep. We'll set the alarm, you can leave before they get up, and no one will ever know you were here." She found his lips. "Except for me."

"I like the way you think," he said as he picked her up and carried her upstairs.

Afterward, they lay entwined in dreamy fulfillment. Several minutes passed and Jake asked, "What are you thinking about?"

Hallie smiled. "I was thinking that we might have made a baby tonight. The timing's right."

He stiffened. "We should have used protection. I'm sorry, Hallie, I—"

Her gentle laugh interrupted him. "Don't be sorry. I'm not. I can't wait to have your baby."

"No," he said, forcing himself to roll away from her. "Three children are enough."

She sat up slowly. "There's always room for one more."

"No," he repeated.

She pulled the sheet up. "You don't want a child?"

"Three is plenty."

She rested her chin on her knees. "Don't you want to have a baby with me?"

He noticed the moisture in her eyes and took her hand in his. "I love you and I love your kids, Hallie. I want to share them with you, help you raise them and take care of them. That's enough for me."

"I'm glad you feel that way, Jake. I really am." She shook her head sadly. "But I was hoping for at least one more child."

"Honey, we have three beautiful, healthy kids. Let's not borrow trouble."

Her eyes narrowed. "I thought you were over feeling guilty about Corey."

"I'm trying to be practical. I don't want to risk

having another baby. There could be problems. I can't face that pain again.''

''There's little chance of what happened to Corey happening again. Isn't that what the doctors told you and Becky?''

''Yes. But there is a chance, and I don't want to take it.'' He paused. ''I'll be the very best father I can be to your kids, but I don't want any more, Hallie. Try to understand.''

''Listen to yourself,'' she said. ''You're accepting Mark, Andy and Katie as *my* children—not as yours.''

''That isn't true, and you know it. I love those kids and I want to be their father if they'll let me.''

''I want that, too. But I also want you to have a child of your own. I want to give you that gift.''

''You can't replace Corey.''

''Of course, I can't. I don't want to. But you can never be truly happy if you keep hanging on to your old fears, your old guilt. You have to let go of the past, Jake.''

He sat up and pulled on his clothes. He'd never considered the idea of having more children, although Hallie obviously had. He couldn't think with Hallie trying to reason with him. He had to be alone.

"I need to leave, Hallie. You've made me realize I have too many unresolved problems and I can't burden you with those. Maybe I didn't think this through. It may be too soon for me to deal with a ready-made family."

Hallie nodded, holding back her anger. Jake professed to love her, and yet he wouldn't let her give him unqualified love. "Of course, you're not ready, Jake. You're not willing to face the facts. Whenever things get too close for you, you run away."

"I can't talk about it right now. I have to think."

"What you have to do is admit your grief, Jake, and accept it. Then you can let it go."

He nodded sadly. "I need more time, Hallie."

"I know," she said softly.

He paused at the door. "You made me think I could live again. You gave meaning to everything I did. But maybe it's not that easy. Maybe I've lived in the shadows too long. I'm confused, Hallie. I don't know if things will ever work out for us."

"I realize that." She was amazed that her voice sounded so calm. Inside, she felt like screaming. How could she let the man she loved walk out of her life? How could she let him run away from the past when their only hope was for him to face it? But she couldn't do it for him. He had to do it himself.

He opened the door and didn't look at her when he said, "I'm sorry, Hallie."

"Me, too."

She fell down on her pillow and cried herself to sleep.

Chapter Nine

After Jake left Hallie that night, it was easy for him to succumb to the dark side of his nature and fall back into his old pattern. He slept all day and prowled around the cabin most of the night. He didn't go out, and stayed to himself. He didn't shave. He only ate when the gnawing hunger made it necessary. He couldn't work; the words had deserted him.

The night, which had once provided solitude and inspiration, mocked him now. It taunted him, reminding him of how empty and meaningless life was without Hallie. She was the light in his world, she was the comfort and succor he needed to feel whole and worthy. He needed her.

But he didn't call her. At times the desire to see her, to touch her, was so intense that it was a physical ache. Still, he didn't call. There was nothing to say that had not been said before.

He could offer no compromise. She wanted another child, he was dead-set against it. She thought a baby would help him overcome the pain of losing Corey. She didn't understand that he couldn't risk loving another child the way he'd loved his son.

She'd never known the heartache of bringing a child into the world, only to watch him suffer and die. She didn't realize that the emotional investment was too costly. The potential pain, too great.

He'd meant it when he'd said he could care for Mark and Andy and Katie. They were whole and strong. They were part of Hallie. He could give them love, but it was a different kind of love. Now they were lost to him, too.

Over the years Jake had buried the memory of Corey so deeply in his heart that he could barely recall the child's face. All he could remember were the machines, the tubes, the quiet desperation of the intensive care unit. During the second week of his self-imposed exile, it became very important for him to remember happier times.

He went into his bedroom, and for the first time since he'd left Chicago, he unlocked the chest where his photographs and videotapes were stored.

He found a framed portrait taken when his son was only a few months old. A toothless, glittering grin lit up Corey's small face. The photographer had been amazed at the ease with which he could elicit smiles from the child. Jake had explained that the boy had no reason to be unhappy. But that was before they'd discovered the leaky valve…before their world had crumbled.

Jake found the videotape of Corey's second birthday party and carried it into the living room. He switched on the TV and slid the tape into the VCR. Stepping backward, he sank onto the sofa, a reluctant witness to what had once been. As the flickering images of his former life rolled by, he was filled with ineffable sadness.

But in that sadness, the healing began.

During the third week, he often replayed the tape. It seemed incredible, but it was true: he'd been happy and fulfilled once. He'd had a family to love, work that challenged him. He'd been a part of something meaningful. The future had held only hope.

What did it hold now?

Nothing. The future meant nothing without Hallie. He needed her, he needed to belong again. He craved the feeling of attachment that came from loving others. At the core of his new awareness was a simple, primitive urge: he wanted to feel good again. He wanted to feel good about life and about himself.

Days passed and acceptance evolved out of his self-examination. Strength came from acceptance. Jake finally realized that he couldn't change the past. He couldn't have Corey back. He couldn't restore what was lost.

All he could do was try to start over. He could step out of the shadows and walk in the light again. The world would always be fraught with danger, heartbreak was forever waiting around every turn. But he couldn't let fear of the possibilities keep him from living his life to the fullest.

He had wanted his son to have the risky operation because it had afforded Corey a small chance for life. Now Jake had to find the courage to take a chance and reclaim his own life.

He unpacked other photographs, setting the framed ones in his office and other rooms of the house. Soon the mental images of Corey's last few days in the hospital grew dim, and Jake recalled more of the good times they'd shared.

The phone rang late one evening. "How's my favorite spook meister?" a voice clipped when he answered.

"He's seen better days, Suzy." Jake's voice carried a note of quiet resignation. "And worse."

"What's the matter, Jake? Talk to me."

Jake hadn't realized how much he needed to talk to someone until he began opening his heart to his old friend. When he got around to talking about Corey, Suzy seemed relieved that he had finally worked through the past. She told him that, and then asked if he was seeing anyone special.

"I was," he admitted. "But things didn't work out."

"And whose fault is that, Mr. Melancholy?"

"Mr. Melancholy? She once compared me to the Phantom of the Opera," he said with a laugh.

"I like her already. You're in love with her, aren't you?" His agent always had been perceptive. They often communicated through words left unspoken.

"Yes, I am," he answered.

"Then you'll just have to work things out, won't you?"

"It may not be that easy."

"Of course, it is. What's her name? What's she like? Tell me all about her."

He hadn't planned to talk about Hallie, but he needed to share her with someone who had loved him when he wasn't lovable. It was surprisingly easy to do.

"Hallie sounds like a lovely young woman, dear," Suzy said. "She's the one who's made the difference in your life, isn't she?"

"Yes."

Jake heard the frustration in his friend's voice. "Then you need to tell her that before it's too late."

"It's been a while. I don't know if she's still interested."

"Well, you'll never know unless you ask, Jake."

He'd never know unless he asked. Jake smiled as he hung up the phone. Leave it to Suzy Stein to cut to the heart of the matter. Was it too late already? Had he lost Hallie because he'd spent the past three weeks feeling sorry for himself?

He'd never know unless he asked.

It was quite late when he reached The Jacinta Inn. The moon was bright, but the house was dark, everyone was asleep. He didn't want to disturb Hallie, but he couldn't leave without talking to her. He decided to go around to the gazebo and wait for the dawn. When he got there, he found that it was already occupied.

"Hallie?" he said softly.

She started at the sound of his voice. She'd just been thinking about the first time they'd met and how ungraciously he'd treated her. She couldn't resist the temptation to repay him in kind. "What do you want, Jake?"

He stood in the entrance of the gazebo and looked at her. Her hair was loose and she was wearing a long, cotton gown. The thin material clung to her shapely body and glowed pale in the moonlight. She was so beautiful that his throat tightened and his pulse raced. How had he ever let old hurts stand between him and this woman he loved?

"I was hoping we could talk," he said at last. "If you're willing to listen."

For weeks Hallie had longed to hear those words. Just when she'd given up hope of ever seeing him again, and was getting used to the idea, he showed up to throw her life and her heart out of kilter again. She should be furious.

But she wasn't. She loved him too much for that. She longed to touch him, to assure herself that he was really there and she hadn't conjured him out of a wistful dream.

"What is there left to talk about at this late date?" she asked softly.

"I know I hurt you, Hallie," he began. He went to her and knelt on the floor beside her chair. She let him take her hands in his. "I'm sorry. I never wanted the shadows to touch you. I love you too much for that."

"I needed you these last few weeks, Jake. Where were you?"

His head dropped. It hurt him to know that he'd failed her. "I had to think things through."

"From now on, we're going to work things out together," she said firmly. "Your usual response to trouble is to retreat into yourself. I can't let you back into my life unless I can depend on you to be there for me."

"I'm tired of fighting life's battles alone. I want to be there for you, Hallie. These past weeks, I've finally made sense of my life. I know what really matters."

"Do you?" He squeezed her hands and she wanted to throw herself into his arms. She wanted to touch him, to brush away his fears as easily as she had once brushed the dark hair from his face.

He told her how he'd come to accept Corey's death. "You were right all along, Hallie. I had never worked through my grief. You helped me see that. I'm ready to go on, to start life anew, but I need you there. I've arranged an interview with *Publisher's Weekly* in which I plan to unmask Jonathan Dark at last."

"So you're finally willing to take the credit for what you do?"

"Or the blame, depending on what critic you read," he said with a wry smile. "But I can't do it without you. I love you, Hallie, more than I've ever loved anyone. Will you marry me and be with me forever?"

She considered his proposal. She was quiet for so long that he feared she would reject it. When she finally spoke, her voice was full of joy. "Yes, Jake. I'll marry you. I love you and I can't imagine my life without you. These past few weeks have been hell."

He pulled her into his arms and their lips met in a reaffirming kiss of renewal. "God, Hallie," he whispered into her hair, "I was afraid I'd lost you."

"We belong together, we give each other balance. Haven't you figured that out yet?"

"I'm beginning to."

"I've had time to think, too. It was selfish of me to insist that we have a baby, Jake. I want you to know that I'll be happy with you and the three we already have."

He held her face in his hands. "I've changed my mind about that, too. I can't think of anything I'd rather do than make a baby with you. That is, if you're willing."

Before she could respond, he kissed her, deep and hard. Her heart filled with love for the man who'd come so far to take her hand in his.

"As a matter of fact," he said with a sly grin, "we could start right now."

"You're pretty sure of yourself, Donahue." Her tone held a rebuke, but her hands were already working to free him from his clothing.

"You never know unless you ask."

*   *   *   *   *

SPRING

Spring is a difficult time for us as writers. Winter is much easier. When the days are gray and dreary, and blanketed by Oklahoma ice storms, we don't mind the self-imposed solitude so conducive to creativity. Cozied up in front of our computers, with the spark of our collective imaginations to keep us warm, we can lose ourselves in our work.

Then comes spring, heralded by the unabashed blooming of redbud trees, and with it come distractions. Suddenly, the world is brand-new and inviting, beckoning us away from winter industry. Unplanted gardens whisper our names, hammocks sway invitingly and walks in the park promise undiluted pleasure.

So, for us, spring is a season when we absolutely must have an engrossing project to keep our writing lives focused and productive. Otherwise, we succumb to earthly temptations, and our computers—and our imaginations—collect dust.

Out of the Dark was such a project. From the very beginning, we had fun with the story. Early in our career, we vowed that if writing ever became work we would give it up. Therefore, it must always provide more entertainment than conventional sources.

We began with a general theme of rebirth. Then we sat down together, and as often happens with collaborators, a kind of group think kicked in. We wanted to incorporate elements of the classic Beauty and the Beast story, but of course, our hero could not be too beastly.

So we invited Jake Donahue to join our little party and asked him to bring along an alter ego to indulge his darker side. We added a trio of curious children and an attractive widow ready to love again. We stirred it all up with a bit of mistaken identity, and the result is a make-believe story that commanded our attention and enabled us to close our windows on the very real allure of the new season.

We hope you will enjoy Jake and Hallie's story and that you will find it a satisfactory diversion this spring. Perhaps on a rainy day?

Pepper Adams

PEPPER ADAMS
DIXIE BROWNING
CAIT LONDON

YOU JUST CAN'T GET ENOUGH OF THEM!

Those fabulous authors, who brought you the dazzling Spring Fancy Collection. They're back and better than ever—bringing you...

THE BACHELOR CURE by Pepper Adams
Silhouette Romance, coming in April 1994
Molly Fox returned to her hometown just as handsome Clay Cusak was planning to leave. Could the lovely doctor prescribe a cure for Clay's wandering heart?

LUCY AND THE STONE by Dixie Browning
Silhouette Desire, coming in May 1994
Stone McLoud, Desire's *Man of the Month,* believed all the rumors about scandalous Lucy Dooley. And he'd be damned if he'd let her take advantage of him as she'd done with so many other unsuspecting men....

FUSION by Cait London
Silhouette Desire, coming in August 1994
When man-shy Taylor Hart inherited a home in Blarney Flats, Arkansas, she never expected to fall in love with the town, let alone a motherless little girl...and the child's impossible father—*Man of the Month* Quinn Donovan!

Look for these romantic, heartwarming stories, all coming your way...

Only from 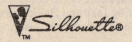 Silhouette®

IT'S OUR 1000TH SILHOUETTE ROMANCE, AND WE'RE CELEBRATING!

JOIN US FOR A SPECIAL COLLECTION OF LOVE STORIES BY AUTHORS YOU'VE LOVED FOR YEARS, AND NEW FAVORITES YOU'VE JUST DISCOVERED. JOIN THE CELEBRATION...

April
REGAN'S PRIDE by **Diana Palmer**
MARRY ME AGAIN by **Suzanne Carey**

May
THE BEST IS YET TO BE by **Tracy Sinclair**
CAUTION: BABY AHEAD by **Marie Ferrarella**

June
THE BACHELOR PRINCE by **Debbie Macomber**
A ROGUE'S HEART by **Laurie Paige**

July
IMPROMPTU BRIDE by **Annette Broadrick**
THE FORGOTTEN HUSBAND by **Elizabeth August**

SILHOUETTE ROMANCE...VIBRANT, FUN AND EMOTIONALLY RICH! TAKE ANOTHER LOOK AT US! AND AS PART OF THE CELEBRATION, READERS CAN RECEIVE A FREE GIFT!

**YOU'LL FALL IN LOVE ALL OVER
AGAIN WITH
SILHOUETTE ROMANCE!**

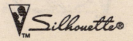

CEL1000

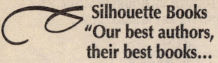

Silhouette Books
"Our best authors,
their best books...

DIANA PALMER
Soldier of Fortune in February

ELIZABETH LOWELL
Dark Fire in February

JOAN HOHL
California Copper in March

LINDA HOWARD
An Independent Wife in April

HEATHER GRAHAM POZZESSERE
Double Entendre in April

When it comes to passion,
we wrote the book.

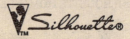

Don't miss these other titles by favorite author

PEPPER ADAMS!

Silhouette Romance®

#08724	CIMARRON KNIGHT*	$2.25	☐
#08753	CIMARRON REBEL*	$2.25	☐
#08842	THAT OLD BLACK MAGIC	$2.59	☐
#08862	ROOKIE DAD	$2.69	☐
#08897	WAKE UP LITTLE SUSIE	$2.69	☐
#08964	MAD ABOUT MAGGIE	$2.75	☐
#08983	LADY WILLPOWER	$2.75	☐
	*Cimarron Stories		

TOTAL AMOUNT	$
POSTAGE & HANDLING	$
($1.00 for one book, 50¢ for each additional)	
APPLICABLE TAXES**	$_____
TOTAL PAYABLE	$_____
(check or money order—please do not send cash)	

To order, complete this form and send it, along with a check or money order for the total above, payable to Silhouette Books, to: **In the U.S.:** 3010 Walden Avenue, P.O. Box 9077, Buffalo, NY 14269-9077; **In Canada:** P.O. Box 636, Fort Erie, Ontario, L2A 5X3.

Name:_____
Address:_____ City:_____
State/Prov.:_____ Zip/Postal Code:_____

**New York residents remit applicable sales taxes.
Canadian residents remit applicable GST and provincial taxes.

PABACK3

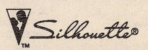

Fifty red-blooded, white-hot, true-blue hunks
from every State in the Union!

Look for MEN MADE IN AMERICA! Written by some of
our most popular authors, these stories feature fifty of
the strongest, sexiest men, each from a different state in
the union!

Two titles available every other month at your favorite
retail outlet.

In March, look for:

TANGLED LIES by Anne Stuart (Hawaii)
ROGUE'S VALLEY by Kathleen Creighton (Idaho)

In April, look for:

LOVE BY PROXY by Diana Palmer (Illinois)
POSSIBLES by Lass Small (Indiana)

You won't be able to resist MEN MADE IN AMERICA!

Also available by popular author

DIXIE BROWNING

Silhouette Desire®

#05637	JUST SAY YES	$2.75	☐
#05678	*NOT A MARRYING MAN	$2.79	☐
#05691	GUS AND THE NICE LADY	$2.79	☐
#05720	*BEST MAN FOR THE JOB	$2.89	☐
#05780	*HAZARDS OF THE HEART	$2.89	☐
	(Dixie Browning 50th Book)		
#05820	†KEEGAN'S HUNT	$2.99	☐
	†Outer Banks		
	*Man of the Month		

Silhouette Romance®

#08747	THE HOMING INSTINCT	$2.25	☐

Silhouette® Books

#20094	BAD BOYS	$5.50	☐
	(By Request series—a 3-in-1 volume containing complete novels by Dixie Browning, Ann Major and Ginna Gray)		
	(limited quantities available on certain titles)		

TOTAL AMOUNT	$
POSTAGE & HANDLING	$
($1.00 for one book, 50¢ for each additional)	
APPLICABLE TAXES**	$_____
TOTAL PAYABLE	$_____
(check or money order—please do not send cash)	

To order, complete this form and send it, along with a check or money order for the total above, payable to Silhouette Books, to: **In the U.S.:** 3010 Walden Avenue, P.O. Box 9077, Buffalo, NY 14269-9077; **In Canada:** P.O. Box 636, Fort Erie, Ontario, L2A 5X3.

Name: _____

Address: _____ City: _____

State/Prov.: _____ Zip/Postal Code: _____

**New York residents remit applicable sales taxes.
Canadian residents remit applicable GST and provincial taxes.

Silhouette®

DBBACK2